The Power of Love

APRIL M. SMITH

ISBN: 978-1500897123

This book is dedicated to my father, Edker Willis Smith, who left this world on June 4, 2013.

WE LOVE AND MISS YOU DAD!

ACKNOWLEDGMENTS

TO: Julie Norton. Carole Glasson, Kathy Reaves, Karen Hicks. You never stopped believing.

TO: The Cast of the 1970's TV show Emergency! They were my inspiration.

TO: Dawn Husted for the wonderful book cover.

http://dawnhusted.weebly.com/

FORWARD

"Have you asked yourself why I have never tried to kiss you?"

Carly shrugged her shoulders. "I thought you didn't want to."

Jimmy took her arms. "How could I not want to? You are a beautiful and exciting woman."

Carly couldn't look up at him, afraid he would see the need in her eyes to believe him.

Jimmy placed his finger under her chin forcing her head up. "I didn't kiss you, because I didn't think you wanted me to." Carly gave him a surprised look bringing a smile to his face. "Do you remember when you picked me up at the hospital?"

"Yes.' Carly replied lowly.

"I was teasing you about biting your lip." Carly nodded. "I cleaned the cut on your lip." She nodded again. "Then I leaned down kissing your lower lip like this." Jimmy captured her lip with his and slowly pulled away. "Do you remember what you said when I did?" Carly could only stare at his mouth, wanting to feel them again. Slowly she shook her head.

"You told me to stop and then went on about men assuming things or something like that anyway." Carly vaguely remembered saying something to that effect.

"Do you remember what I said?" Jimmy whispered close to her lips. Carly shook her head. "I told you it wouldn't happen again."

"I wasn't myself! I had just gotten off the phone with Michael and he had…"

"Had what, threatened you?"

"In a way, he scared me more than anything." Carly looked up at him with regret in her eyes. "I'm sorry for what I said…I never should have taken it out on you."

"I understand, I was just trying to do as you asked."

"If I asked you to do something now, would you do it?"

"What do you want to ask me?"

Los Angeles County, Ca. 1978

The rustling sound of the newspaper joined the murmuring of the other men of Station 15 as Jimmy scanned the sport section from his place on the sofa. His eyes caught an article for an upcoming race about the "The Making Smiles Foundation." The prize… One thousand dollars.

Jimmy gave a low whistle. "Maybe I should sign up."

"Sign up for what, Gates." Chip Keller asked from the kitchen table.

"Never mind, Chip." He replied without taking his eyes off the paper.

"Now Gates, I was only asking."

"I wasn't talking to you."

Chip shook his head. "It's a bad sign when you start talking to yourself, Gates."

"Shut up, Chip."

Chip shrugged his shoulders and gave the other men in the room a smile. The mischief in his eyes told the others the satisfaction he received from annoying Jimmy; it was one of his greatest pleasures.

"Squad 15, possible leg injury…Griffith Park."

Jimmy threw the paper aside and jumped to his feet meeting the other men at the door. He grabbed the rail on the back of the squad, slid around to the passenger side, climbed in the cab, slipped on his helmet and waited for the paper he knew Rick would hand him. Once in his hand, he jotted down the info and placed it in the glove compartment then leaned back against the seat.

Carly Gibson leaned against a tree watching as her ankle started turning an ugly shade of blue and purple. Frustration seeped through her, she had been in the lead and now - tears filled her eyes - she would not be able to finish the race. Closing her eyes, she sent up a silent plea of forgiveness. Her heart broke as she glanced back in the direction of the track. As hard as she tried she could not see a reason for her fall. The path seemed clear from obstruction, but something had tripped her, but what?

The sound of sirens could be heard in the distance as puffs of dirt made by the vehicle made it's way in her direction. A small glimmer of hope surged through her. *MAYBE IT'S NOT AS BAD AS I THINK. MAYBE I CAN STILL FINISH. I KNOW I CAN WHEN/IF I JUST GET BACK IN THE RACE.* Optimism always came easy for her throughout her life and this was one time she needed it most. The race meant too much to her to give up now. She inhaled a deep breath, squared her shoulders in determination, slowly released the breath and watched the squad come to a stop.

"I will finish this race, one way or another. I will." Carly declared as the paramedic on the passenger side stepped out. Her heart slammed against her chest, her pulse soared, her mouth went dry and she began to tremble – not from fear, but from her unexpected attraction to him.

Rick brought the squad to a stop along side the road and Jimmy opened the door, stepped out, hurried to the side compartment, sliding his body to the side to hold the door open to get the equipment out.

Carly shook her head. "No way Carly Gibson, you're not doing that again." The last thing she wanted was to find herself right back in the same place she was a year ago and something told her that the man walking toward her now could very well put her there. She planted her hands behind her on the tree she rested against and pushed herself up, keeping her weight on her left foot -she bit her bottom lip to keep from crying out. She swore to herself that she would never show weakness again and she meant to keep that promise.

Jimmy turned toward the woman who was now standing or should he say leaning against the tree behind her. He noticed that she kept her weight on her left foot as well as the hooded expression which descended across her beautiful face and he had to wonder why. As he approached her, her beauty struck him, with her dark hair pulled back and a few strands falling around her face. His footing stumbled when she pushed the strands away from her face with her hand.

"You all right?" Rick asked smiling.

Jimmy gave his partner a smirk making his steps more certain. He hurried those steps when she hopped, trying to keep standing, letting his gaze run over her as he did. She wore a pair of blue running shorts with a white tank top. The colors brought out the tan on her legs - which were long and shapely - her waist was trim and her breasts were…He cleared his throat and gave his head a mental shake.

Whetting her lips, Carly tried to dismiss the sudden surge of her heartbeat. The closer he came the more nervous she became, and she hopped back against the tree. One of his eyebrows rose and a slight smile played at his mouth. She stared into a face that processed the most beautiful pair of golden brown eyes – thick, run your fingers through it all the time because it's so luscious - black hair, and that smile that can light up a room! She could not help wondering what it would feel like to have those lips…She cleared her throat and gave herself a mental shake. GET A GRIP CARLY.

Jimmy reached the woman a moment before her good leg gave out and grabbed her around the waist then he eased her back to the ground while Rick set up the Bi-phone to contact Regional. "It's all right, I've got you."

BOY, DO YOU EVER. Carly thought.

He eased his arm from around her back while trying not to get lost in the bluest eyes he had ever seen. He forced himself to focus on her injured leg and made himself swallow. *Stop being ridiculous and do your job, man!* He let his hand run the length of her leg as he searched for the source of her injury. Her leg felt smooth and silky, almost familiar. Incredible would be more accurate if he were honest with himself. Disconcerted, he forced himself to remain focused on why he was there in the first place – a job he found difficult to do. His hands touched her ankle and she gave a low cry. "Sorry."

He has the sexist voice. "No, it's ok, really. I think I have just pulled something. It's much better than before."

Carly would have said anything to make him stop touching her the way he did, rather stop her reaction to his touch. He gave her a crooked grin and her heart went straight to her throat.

She had to get away from this man before he turned her heart to Jell-O. Glancing over to his partner, she scrutinized him. He had a nice smile, a safe smile. It didn't make her heart do crazy things in her chest; she wished that he were touching her ankle. If he were than she wouldn't notice the way his fingers felt against her skin or the gentle way he eased her shoe off her foot. She squeezed her eyes closed, trying to dismiss the unwanted feelings.

"Miss, are you all right?"

Carly's eyes flew opened at the sound of concern in the dark haired paramedic voice. She wanted to scream at him, *I would be if you would stop holding and touching my leg!* Instead she nodded her head.

Jimmy glanced back down at her ankle not liking the way it was swelled. "Looks like it could be a bad sprain, but I wouldn't rule out a fracture."

"I'll contact Regional and let them know we are bringing her in."

"No!"

Both paramedics stared at her in surprise. Jimmy leaned toward her, allowing her to get a whiff of his cologne.

He smells so good.

"Ma'am, you need to get an x-ray." Jimmy insisted.

Tears filled her eyes. "I need to finish the race."

He gave his head a slight shake. "I'm afraid that won't be happening."

"You don't understand, I have to finish - I just have too." Emotion almost choking off the last words.

The urge to pull this woman into his arms and soothe her felt natural. Somehow, he knew how she would feel in his arms – how her body would mold to his. The sensation rocked him to his core. Pushing out a long breath, he shoved the feelings away.

"I can see this means a lot to you, but you need to get to the hospital." His voice suffused with sympathy.

She lowered her head willing herself not to let him see how upset she was then an idea came to her and she lifted her head.

Seeing the expression in her eyes, he started shaking his head vehemently.

"I'm sorry Miss, but I'm on duty and I can't do what you are about to ask me." Tears had filled her eyes again and he felt his heart start to give in – *what is it about this woman compels me to fulfill her unspoken request.* He spotted Rick's amused expression and he tightened his resolve.

He can still remember shaking his head no so why was it he found himself doing the exact opposite. It surprised him that he could finish for her with only four miles left. What Jimmy didn't know was the director of "The Making Smiles Foundation" and Carly were close friends and being so he knew the importance of the race to her.

The fact they were already a good distance ahead of him by the time Jimmy found himself agreeing did not seem important. So, he let them pin Carly's number on the back of his shirt and he was off and running – literally. Still, he gave it all he had and he soon found himself within reach of the group. A smile crept onto his lips as he thought of how he must look, dressed in full uniform and shoes with a number pinned on his back.

I can hear Keller now. This money better be for something really important for me to put up with Keller's teasing. Even that thought did not sway him when he thought of the happiness on her face when he agreed. By the end of the race he was exhausted, sweaty and in first place. He could hardly believe he had caught up with them much less won.

He glanced out over the finish line and saw that Rick and the woman were waiting with broad smiles on their faces.

"Looks like I may have another patient on my hands. Need some 02 partner?" Rick asked with submerged laughter.

Jimmy gave him a smirk as he handed Carly her trophy and check for a thousand dollars. She took it happily then surprised them both when she grabbed his hand.

"Thank you. You have no idea how much this meant to me." She said emotionally.

At that moment Jimmy knew that the race meant more than just the money. Her eyes shinned with unshed tears and held a hint of sadness. *Why? What caused the pain I see in them?*

Something deep inside him stirred and it unnerved him. He removed his hand from hers and missed it immediately.

The moment she took his hand, she wished she hadn't and from his reaction she knew he felt the same.

"Thank you again Mr.…."

"Gates, Jimmy Gates. The man standing behind you is my partner Rick DeLaney." His voice distant and business like. *There that's better. Really? Than why do I feel I should wipe that sadness I see away?*

Jimmy, I like that. Carly tilted her head to the side. *It suits him.*

Carly smiled at Rick and received a smile in return. She liked Rick DeLaney, he was friendly, kind and somehow she knew he was very married. He was safe, the man standing in front of her however was far from safe. His dark eyes were to caring, his smile was too warm and his touch was to gentle. She had known his kind before, Jimmy Gates was a player and she needed to stay as far away from him as possible. "I'm ready to go to the hospital now."

"Me too - I think I need CPR."

Despite her need to stay untouched, she laughed as did his partner as Jimmy bent over placing his hands on his knees trying to regain his normal breathing. The light that filled her eyes made them sparkle and his heart flipped in his chest. *What is it about this woman?*

Wonderful, he has a great sense of humor too. Carly groaned to herself.

"I'll take her in Rick."

Surprised crossed both their faces and Carly stifled a groan. How was she going to survive the ride with him so close. *You really have to get a grip, girl. After today, you will probably never see him again.* The thought of that possibility made her stomach do a flip.

"Ok, Jimmy. I'll follow in the squad." Rick stated as he turned to gather the equipment. *Looks as if my "I'm never getting serious" partner is just about to do that very thing.* Hiding a smile he headed in the direction of the ambulance while his partner helped Carly to the gurney.

The ride to the hospital seemed to take forever yet flew by all at the same time or so it seemed to Carly. The fact that Jimmy found himself talking to the woman in front of him as if he had known her all his life almost had him jumping out of the ambulance before it even stopped. There was no way that he would ever let himself feel like that again. Jimmy followed her into the examination room then said a quick goodbye and hurried out the door.

Watching him leave left Carly feeling lost and relieved all at the same time.

Rick met Jimmy as he came out the door – well ran it seemed to him.

"What's your hurry? Is there a fire?"

"Very funny, besides I'm not in a hurry."

"Could have fooled me."

"If you must know that run made me hungry."

"What doesn't?"

Jimmy gave him a smirk as they headed for the squad and back to the station.

2

Rick backed the squad into the Apparatus Bay and turned off the engine. He faced Jimmy, laying his arm across the back of the seat. The silence coming from his partners side of the squad told him Carly Gibson had quite an effect on him.

"What to talk?"

"No, thanks." Jimmy opened his door and stepped out.

Getting out of the squad himself, he followed him into the kitchen, arriving just in time to see him pick up the paper, sit down then freeze. The next thing he knew Jimmy slung the paper and stood up.

"There's never anything in the papers these days." He stated as he passed Rick at the doorway.

Smiling, Rick walked over and picked up the paper. His smile widened. *A race for life.* The article was about the race that Jimmy had just won. *Yea, I think things could get interesting around here.* Setting the paper down he followed his partner out into the Apparatus Bay where he found him wiping down the squad.

Jimmy glanced up. "Not one word Rick, not one word."

Then he returned his attention to wiping the squad. Not that he really paid attention to what he was doing; his mind kept seeing the happiness that shined in Carly's eyes when he handed her the check. The blue in them sparkled with unshed tears. His heart did that flip again causing him to catch his breath.

Rick shrugged his shoulders. "I was just going to ask if you wanted help."

"Oh…well…sure." He tossed him a cloth then started to rub the same spot he had before.

Laughter glinted in Rick's blue eyes. "Ah Jimmy…if you keep rubbing that area like that, you will rub the paint off."

"Huh?"

He had to force the grin from his face. "The…spot…you…you are rubbing the paint off." He pointed toward the spot in questioned.

"What?"

Jimmy jerked his attention to the squad. "Ha, ha, very funny Rick."

Laughing out loud, Rick moved to the front of the squad and started wiping the headlight. "Jimmy?"

"Yea."

"She was pretty, wasn't she?"

He stopped cleaning for a moment, took a deep breath and slowly let it out. "Who?"

"Carly, of course. She's smart too and funny. We had the best conversation while we waited for you at the finish line."

"Is that so?" Irritation seeped into his voice.

Acting as if he didn't notice, he lowered his head a bit more and grinned. "Yea, do you know that she is an assistant to one of the largest contractor companies here in L.A?"

"Yea, she told me."

"Oh…she also runs in a lot of the kind of races like today."

"Yea, I know."

"Oh, did she tell you why this race meant so much to her?"

"No, but I'm sure you are going to tell me." There were no denying the irritation.

"Ahh…No, I was just wondering."

"Oh…No…No, she didn't." *Of course, I didn't really give her the chance. I almost broke my leg myself trying to get out of that ambulance.* He reached down and gave his ankle a slight rub.

"Hurt yourself there, Gates."

Jimmy glanced up with more irritation. *Why is it Chip is always around when he least wanted him to be.* He glanced up to see Chip standing at the back of the engine. "Keller, how long have you been standing there?"

Chip watched Jimmy straighten and smiled as he made his way toward him. He glanced over at Rick winking. "Long enough to know you hurt your ankle somehow."

Rick straightened. "Really, when did you do that?"

Chip grinned wider. "Must have been when he was running, huh Gates."

"Chip…"

"Squad 15…Boy shot…2244 Hillcrest Dr. 2…2…4…4 Hillcrest Dr. Time out 2: 45 pm."

Tossing his cloth at Chip, he ran around the side of the squad and jumped in. He grabbed his hat and slipped it on then took the paper Rick handed him once again then sat back against the seat. "I hate calls about kids."

"Yea, I know what you mean."

Carly watched as Dr. Barrett examined her ankle. "How bad is it?"

Kris waited a minute then set Carly's foot gently back on the bed. Crossing his arms, he walked up beside her. "I don't think it's broken, but we are going to take some X-rays just to be sure."

"So, it's only sprained?"

Uncrossing his arms he placed his hands on the bed next to her. "If I'm right and it's a very bad sprain then you will have to stay off it for at least a week."

"I see. I could use crutches, couldn't I?"

"You will be given some, but for the first couple of days I would like to keep you here."

Panic coursed through her. "Is that really necessary?"

He straightened and crossed his arms again. Despite the panic rising in her, Carly had to fight the smile that threatened to escape. *He must think that pose is threatening.*

"Miss Gibson, is something wrong? Is there some reason you don't want to stay?"

Yea, I hate hospitals. She shook her head. "I was just hoping to be able to go home and rest."

"That could be arranged, but you must promise me to stay off that ankle."

You must promise me…

The sudden loss of color in her face alarmed Dr. Barrett and he moved closer. "Miss Gibson, are you all right?"

Carly shifted her gaze to him, but didn't really see him. She stood at the side of a hospital bed. Alarms sounded throughout the room as people scurried around it. "You must promise me…" drifted up weakly to her from the bed.

The memory sent waves of despair through her and she was unable to control the onset of emotions which shook her entire body. She could feel herself biting her lower lip, but was powerless to stop herself. Once again she asked herself… why him? Why wasn't she the one? After all, it was her fault.

Taking her wrist between his fingers, he felt the rapid pace of her pulse. He wasn't sure what happened, but from the way she bit her lower lip, he knew something he said had triggered a painful memory.

"Miss Gibson, Can you hear me?" No response. He slightly turned his head and focused briefly on the nurse standing beside him. "Have Miss McCoy join me, right away."

The young dark-haired nurse bobbed her head. "Yes, doctor." Then she hurried from the room.

"Miss Gibson?"

The sound of people murmuring penetrated her muddled brain. She was no longer standing by the side of a hospital bed, but laying on one. Slowly the days' events and her reason for being there came back. Her cheeks flooded with color as fast as they had drained. Kris reached to steady her. "I'm going to admit you for a couple of days. I want to run some tests."

Embarrassment coursed through her when she realized she had reflected back to a day she wished she could forget. "That's not necessary. I'm fine." The emotion of the memory made her voice sound husky. The raised eyebrow on Dr. Barrett's face told her he didn't believe her. "Really I am. I guess today's events just caught up with me."

Kris crossed his arms again and narrowed his eyes. "That's the reason I'm going to admit you."

"Dr. Barrett, I'm fine. I can rest at home."

"That remains to be seen, so you just lie back and I will have a nurse come in to take you to your room once you are admitted."

When she opened her mouth to protest again he held up his hand. "Humor me, O.K. and let me do my job."

Sighing, Carly slowly nodded.

"That's a girl. We'll have you up and about in no time."

Keep a certain paramedic away from me and I will be right as rain. Why that thought entered her mind Carly didn't know, but what she did know was, she couldn't take the chance of letting him get close. She knew she was being unfair to Jimmy, but she could so easily fall for those brown eyes and that crooked grin. Even now her heart did a flip at the memory of them. Strengthening her resolve, she mentally squared her shoulders as if she were readying herself for a fight. In a way that's what she was doing. A fight to keep her heart safe. It was one she intended to win.

The door opened and she soon found herself alone in the room with the X-Ray attendant. It only took a few short minutes then she was transferred to a wheelchair and maneuvered out into the hall. Carly knew she didn't need to stay in the hospital, but they all seemed so concerned that she decided a couple of days couldn't hurt. Who knows maybe she could find out something about Jimmy that would tell her she was wrong.

Where did that thought come from? You just decide to forget about the man and here you are wanting to find a reason to be wrong. Do what you said you were going to do and forget the man.

"Nurse McCoy…"

"Yes."

"Do you know the paramedic that brought me in very well?" Carly groaned inwardly. *So much for forgetting about the man.*

"You mean, Jimmy? Yea, I guess so. He's been around here about six years. Why do you ask?"

"Oh, I was just wondering."

Daisy smiled. "Yup, that's our boy, no woman can resist him."

Carly tensed. *I was right about him.* Something deep inside started to ache.

"Now when I say that, I say it in a most loving manner." Daisy teased.

"I'm sure."

The coldness that Daisy heard come from Carly seemed so unnatural. "Miss Gibson, Jimmy is one of the kindest men I have ever met. He is also one of the most caring."

"I bet."

Daisy stopped the wheelchair and walked to stand in front of Carly. Her deep blue eyes flashing with protectiveness.

"Sure Jimmy has dated a lot. Why shouldn't he? He's handsome and devoted to the people he loves."

"I'm sorry, Miss McCoy, I didn't mean to upset you."

Daisy smiled an understanding smile. "Give him a chance. You will see what I mean."

Carly gasped. "Miss McCoy, I'm afraid I gave you the wrong idea."

"No, I think I have it straight."

"I'm not interested in Jimmy Gates."

"Yea and I guess that is why you are so defensive about it."

"I promise you, I am not interested in that man." She declared vehemently her own blue eyes flashing in return.

Daisy started pushing the chair again. "Yea, so you said."

Carly opened her mouth to protest, but stopped when she heard the sound of Jimmy's voice.

Funny how you know the sound of his voice already.

Oh, hush up. She reprimanded herself.

The sight of Jimmy standing on the side of the gurney pumping on a child's chest, halted any other argument she might of had with herself.

"Come on, come on breathe." He placed his mouth over the child's mouth and then started compressions again.

Carly clasped both hands over her mouth to cover the sobs that threatened to slip. She was once again back in that hospital room repeating those very same words. Tears fell unhindered as she prayed that Jimmy's pleading would have a different outcome than her's did.

"I'll be right back." Daisy stated as Rick ran by a few minutes later. It seemed like forever as Carly waited out in the hall. Her heart pounded in her chest as she waited to hear the outcome. A war played in her head with memories from the past and that young boy's struggle for life.

Finally the door opened and her breath caught in her throat. Hope clung within her until Jimmy, Daisy and Rick walked out the door. She knew the results before Daisy even spoke. Her eyes skimmed the corridor searching for the family of the young boy. It didn't take long to find them. They stood clinging together, the mother in her husband's arms while a young girl of twelve stood off to the side alone. Her heart went out to the young girl knowing exactly how she felt.

"You did all you could Jimmy." Daisy stated.

Carly squeezed her eyes closed. She couldn't watch the events unfolding in front of her. The pain that etched across Jimmy's face tore her heart in two.

"Yea, well it wasn't enough, was it?" He looked at the two of them for a second. "I'll be out in the squad."

Carly watched him as he stopped briefly to talk to the family. His hand reached out to cup the young girl's chin. After a few brief seconds he dropped his hand. His eyes caught Carly's just before he disappeared from view. She had a moment of Da ja vu and had to take a deep breath to release the feeling. The touch of someone's hand on her shoulder caused her to jump.

"Sorry, didn't mean to scare you. I just wanted to say hi and see how you're doing."

Carly glanced up at Rick's kind face. "Thank you, but I'm fine. My ankle isn't broken, but they want me to stay a couple of days, just to make sure I stay off it."

"Something tells me, that's a good idea." The heightened color in Carly's cheeks told him he had assumed correctly. Her gaze slid to where she last saw Jimmy. "Is he going to be alright?"

Rick glanced in the same direction. "He will be fine. He just needs some time to deal with the fact that we couldn't save the boy."

"I thought you weren't supposed to let things like this get to you."

"We're not, but you can't always stop it from happening, especially when it is a child."

"How old was he?"

"Ten, he and a friend were playing with his father's gun."

She covered the hand he rested on the arm of the chair with her own. "Will you let me know how Jimmy is later?"

Rick squeezed her hand. "Sure I will."

"I better get going."

"Rick?"

He stopped returning his attention to her.

"Tell him…tell him…"

"I'll tell him you asked about him." He replied with a smile.

"Thanks."

"Sure."

She wished she could help Jimmy in some way even if it was a shoulder to lean on. That thought sent another wave of Deja vu through her. Somehow she knew he would be alright, but still she sent up a silent prayer. *Please let Jimmy be all right.*

Daisy touched her shoulder. "Rick will watch out for him so you don't have to worry."

"I know I shouldn't, I don't even know him, but…"

Daisy squeezed her shoulder again. "There is just something about him." At Carly's nod, she smiled. "Like I said, that's our Jimmy. One moment you want to slug him, the next you want to hug him."

Maybe I was wrong about you, Gates.

Daisy leaned down next to her ear. "He really is so easy to love."

"I'm not interested in him."

"Whatever you say." Daisy stated as she pushed Carly to her room.

3

Ten...he was just ten years old! Jimmy slammed the door to the squad and headed for the locker room in need of a shower; he doubted that it would help wash away the fact that they had lost Daniel Parks. As he walked into the dorm, he ripped his shirt open, trying to get rid of the smell of blood; buttons flew across the room just as Chip and Max walked in.

"Whoa, there Gates." Chip declared.

Jimmy shot him a glance and slung his shirt in the direction of his bed, not caring that it landed the middle of the floor. Max started to speak when he felt a hand on his shoulder. and he glanced up to see Rick shake his head then walk over to pick up the discarded shirt. It was then that the two men saw the blood.

"The boy didn't make it?" Chip asked.

Rick shook his head again. "Jimmy is having a hard time dealing with the fact."

"Well, that explains his mood. I've never seen him so upset." Max replied.

"Yea, I know." Rick agreed.

The sound of the spraying water penetrated the room - the Klaxon sounded - Jimmy swore and ran out of the wash area zipping his slacks. He paused briefly when he saw Rick holding out a clean shirt for him.

"Thanks."

"Anytime Junior."

Both men ran for the squad while Jimmy tucked in his shirt. Once again, he found himself putting on his helmet and taking the paper from Rick. He was beginning to wonder if the day would ever end.

The engine and squad pulled to a stop as woman came running out of the house.

"Please, help my son."

Before the squad came to a full stop, Jimmy was jumping out.

"Where's your son?"

The woman coughed for a moment. "Upstairs. The flames…I can't get to him!"

"That's ok... Don't worry about your son I'll get him. How old is he?"

"Ten."

Jimmy froze for just a second. "Ok, you stay with my partner and I'll go get your son." Jimmy yelled to Rick as he grabbed his gear. "There is a ten year old boy trapped. I'm going in after him." He ran toward the house before Rick could reply.

"Jimmy wait!" He didn't like the idea of him going in after the boy alone, he needed to wait for back-up. The state he was in, he could take chances he normally wouldn't.

Max and Chip were already pulling their lines to fight the flames. Jimmy grabbed Chip's shoulder. "There's a boy trapped upstairs, I'm going to need someone to cover me."

Max nodded for Chip to go ahead and soon they were heading up the stairs. The flames were massive, but passable. Jimmy started searching rooms only to find each one empty. He was running out of hope that he would find the boy when suddenly he heard a low cry for help. Following the sound of the cry, he discovered the boy hovered in the back of a closet. Yelling through his mask, he reached in for him. "Take my hand." Coughing and gasping for air, the boy grabbed hold of Jimmy's hand. Jimmy shouted as he ripped his mask off to cover the boy's face. "Just breathe into the mask." The boy nodded his head as Jimmy lifted him over his shoulder. Coughing, Jimmy glanced around the room unable to distinguish which way he needed to go. Someone grabbed his arm and he focused on the voice.

"Jimmy, you alright?"

Rick?" He coughed again. "

"Yea, partner, it's me." Rick glanced at the boy over Jimmy's shoulder. "Need me to take him?"

"No, just led us out, O.K." Another wave of coughing consumed him.

"You've bet."

Not wasting another moment, Rick led him through the door and back down the stairs. The fire had been contained on the first floor, but the second was fast becoming an inferno. Barely able to see, Jimmy stumbled his way behind his friend, his chest felt like someone was sitting on it and every step he took became more difficult. The boy's weight seemed to be multiplying, but he refused to stop. *I'm not losing this one.*

Rick kept a close eye on both Jimmy and the young boy as he led them out of the house. When they were clear enough, Jimmy dropped to his knees and laid the boy on the ground. He wanted to check him over, but his continuous coughing prevented him.

The boy's mother ran to him cover him with kisses and hugs while Ricked tried to checked him over. Her sobs of thanks filtered out between each kiss. He found no signs of burns, but he had inhaled a lot of smoke. Picking up the Bi-phone, he contacted Regional. "Regional, this is County 15, do you read?"

"We read you loud and clear 15."

"Regional, we have a young boy, ten years old, victim of a house fire. No signs of burns, but he is suffering from smoke inhalation."

"Do you have the vitals 15?"

"Negative, Regional. Stand by."

"Standing by 15."

"I'll do it." Jimmy said between coughs.

"You sure."

"Yea."

Jimmy grabbed the BP cuff and placed it around the child's arm, checking his vitals.

"B/P 110/90, respiration 15, Pulse 60."

"Regional vitals are as follows. B/P 110/90. Respiration 15. Pulse 60."

"10-4 15, start IV D5W and transport."

"10-4 Regional. Regional we have another victim, male 28, weight approximately 160, also suffering from smoke inhalation."

"Rick, I'm fine."

"Gates, let Rick check you out." Captain Stone ordered.

"Cap, there's nothing wrong with me." Jimmy started coughing again.

"Ah, ha. Go ahead Rick."

Rick nodded. "Stand by Regional, vitals to follow." Smiling at his partner he stated. "Well, lets' just make sure O.K."

Jimmy started to object.

"Gates."

"Yes, Cap."

Jimmy shrugged out of his turncoat and let Rick take his vitals.

"Regional vitals are, B/P 140/100, Respiration 20, Pulse 90"

10-4 15, start IV D5W and Transport."

"10-4 Regional."

"Rick, I don't need…"

"Gates, you might as well just lie back and enjoy the ride."

Jimmy nodded, but he wasn't a happy camper. As they loaded him in the back of the ambulance the mother of the boy grabbed his hand. "I can't thank you enough for what you did. I truly hope you will be all right."

Jimmy sent her a crooked smile. "I'll be all right. I'm just glad we were able to rescue your boy."

Tears filled her eyes and gave a slight nod. She released his hand and they placed him in the ambulance. The last glance he had of the woman was of her running toward the front to climb in.

An hour later Jimmy was released from the hospital and on his way back to the station, but not before he inquired about Carly.

"She's doing fine, worried about you." Daisy stated.

"Me? Why me?"

"Well…for one thing she was here when you came in with the Parks boy and one of the student nurses said something in front of her about you being treated just now."

"Oh, so…"

"So…go see her."

"I don't know Daisy"

Daisy placed her hands on her hips and tilted her blonde head a little to the side. "If, I hadn't of seen it, I would never have believed it."

"Believe what?" Jimmy asked.

"Jimmy Gates, afraid to go talk to a woman."

Rick grinned loving the expression on his partner's face.

"I'm not afraid…I'm…well…it's just…"

At the expression on both Rick and Daisy's faces, he dropped his shoulders. "What room is she in?"

"205."

"I'll be back in a minute."

"Want some back up?" Rick teased.

"Very funny."

Both Daisy and Rick gave a low laugh as Jimmy headed for the elevator.

"He acts as if he is going to an execution." Daisy teased.

"Yea, his." This only caused them to laugh harder. "I'll be waiting out in the squad."

O.K, I'll let him know when he comes back."

"Thanks Daisy."

Jimmy paused outside of Carly's room, inhaled, then exhaled as he slowly opened the door. The last thing he expected was to find her crying and he quickly stepped to her bedside.

"Carly?"

Carly jerked up in surprise and wiped at her eyes. " I didn't know anyone was around."

"Is your ankle hurting?" Jimmy asked, sitting down on the side of the bed.

"My ankle?" Confused, she glanced down at her ankle realizing he thought it was the reason for her sudden onset of tears. "Oh…no…well…not really."

"Mind if I take a look at it."

Yea, I mind. "No, I guess it will be all right."

Jimmy stood up, moved to the end of the bed, and gently picked up her foot. When he heard her slight gasp, he glanced up. "Sorry, did I hurt you?"

"No…No…you didn't hurt me."

"If you say so." Jimmy stated as he gave her a small smile and set her foot back on the pillow she was using. He returned to sit beside her. "How long will you be here?"

"Just a couple of days, Dr. Barrett wanted to make sure I stay off my foot. I don't think he trusts me to behave myself if I were home."

"Should he?" Jimmy asked raising his right eyebrow.

"Of course. I would have been the perfect patient." She stated with mischief.

Jimmy's heart did a wild flutter and he had to force himself not to run of the room. Instead, he sent her a crooked grin unwittingly doing the same to her.

"Now, why do I find that hard to believe?"

"I don't know. Why you do?" She lowered her eyelids innocently for effect.

The playful banter between them put him at ease. He hadn't felt that comfortable since…" He shifted his position to his feet, putting a much needed distance between them.

The easiness Carly had felt between them seemed to have disappeared in a matter of seconds. Why she couldn't fathom, but she kept her thoughts *and* feelings to herself.

"I heard you were worried about me."

"I heard you were hurt."

They both spoke simultaneously.

"You first." Jimmy offered with a smile. He felt ridiculous being this nervous around this woman, but she made him feel things he never wanted to feel again. The *FOREVER* kind of things.

Carly shoved away the disappointment she felt by his standing to his feet. Why she missed his closeness she didn't know or understand and she *DIDN'T* want to know either. She was better off if they stayed as they were. He made her feel things…the *FOREVER* kind of things.

"I was just going to say…I heard you were injured."

"No, just inhaled a little too much smoke, that's all."

"Sounds serious enough to me."

"I guess it could have been, but I'm fine, see." He raised his arms as if to show her, giving her a crooked grin.

The beat of Carly's heart seemed to slam against her chest. *STOP SMILING AT ME THAT WAY! Please, stop or I will find myself falling…NO! That's something I will never do again.*

When she spoke her voice came out more stilted than she intended.

"I'm glad. I hope no one was hurt."

The smile dropped from Jimmy's face briefly. A guarded expression descended across her beautiful face. *What happened?*

"A young boy inhaled a lot of smoke, but he's going to be fine."

"I'm glad."

"Yea."

Silence filled the room. Jimmy shifted uncomfortably on his feet while Carly played with the edge of her covers.

"So." They said simultaneously.

A chuckle escaped from each of them.

He has the warmest smile.

She has the warmest eyes. One could almost believe…

Jimmy was about swallow his trepidation and ask if he could call when the door opened.

"Carly, I heard what happened. Are you alright?"

"Michael…"

The surprise on Carly's face told Jimmy she wasn't expecting him, but the man's next words made him glad he hadn't made the mistake of following his heart.

"Hi, I'm Carly's boyfriend."

Jimmy took the out reached hand. "I was just checking in on her to make sure she was doing alright."

I should correct him. Instead, Carly introduced them. "Jimmy Gates, Michael Hudson. Jimmy was the paramedic that tended me."

"Oh, well then I'm really glad to meet you. I want to thank you for taking such good care of my girl here."

"It was nothing, just doing my job." Jimmy glanced toward at Carly. "I better get going, Rick is probably wondering where I am."

"Jimmy?" He stopped at the door and faced her. "Thank you."

"Like I said, just doing my job." His voice sounded harder than he intended.

Carly watched him open the door and walk out and the tears started all over again. *Why are you crying? It's what you said you wanted.* Still she cried wishing that she could trust the way he made her feel. She wished she could trust him. Something inside her screamed. *You can!*

Jimmy slammed the squad door as he climbed in.

"I thought I was going to have to come after you. Have a nice chat?"

"Yea, all three of us."

"Excuse me?"

"Carly, myself and her boyfriend."

"Her boyfriend?"

"Her boyfriend. Let's go."

"Sure…sure." Rick wasn't sure what happened, but he did know one thing for sure…Jimmy Gates was a very unhappy man. Rick started the squad and headed back to the station with a smile on his face. Carly might have a boyfriend now, but something told him, he wouldn't be around long. Things weren't over for Carly and Jimmy…they were just beginning.

4

Boyfriend…*she has a Boyfriend.* Jimmy slung the paper he had been reading to the side and stood. He paced the length of his living room twice before returning to sit on the couch. *She should have told me.* The fact that she had no reason to tell him escaped him for the moment. *Maybe, I should go see her. Yea, that's what I'll do.* Grabbing his keys, he headed for the door. *What would you say?* He tossed his keys back on the table and headed for the couch then a few seconds later grabbed the keys again. This time when he reached the door he didn't think, he just left.

Carly sat in the wheelchair while her friend Karen Wingate stood beside her holding the crutches that she would need. Dr. Barrett stood in front of her giving a few last minute instructions, when he was finished he crossed his arms.

"I have your word that you will do as I ask, don't I?"

"You have my word." Carly felt as if she were a small child placed on restriction by one of her parents. Her face softened at the thought of her parents who lived back in Wyoming. They hadn't liked the idea of their only daughter moving to California by herself, but because they loved her and trusted her judgment, they soon came around to the idea – well – maybe came around wasn't exactly what they did – yet they had given her their blessings and told her to call if she ever needed anything.

Carly's thoughts turned to Jimmy Gates; how she needed to talk to her mom right now. She could just hear her now…*Carly, the reason you decided to move to L.A was because…*

"Carly, are you listening?" Karen asked, interrupting Carly's thoughts.

"Excuse me?" Carly had to give herself a mental shake before she could concentrate on what she needed to. "I'm sorry, I guess my mind wondered."

Karen shook her head. "You could say that again. Dr. Barrett was ready to readmit you."

Carly glanced up at Kris Barrett, his dark black hair with it's every strand in place, and his blue eyes sparkled as he smiled at her.

"I do apologize, Dr. Barrett. I don't normally…" Carly stopped in mid sentence at the sound of Jimmy's voice.

"Hi, Daisy, how's the most beautiful head nurse doing today?" Jimmy Gates came walking around the corner to see Carly sitting in a wheelchair. *Man, she's beautiful.* Jimmy cleared his throat and forced himself to look away. "Aaaa…what…Daisy."

"You asked me how I was doing – at least I assume you were talking about me since I am the only head nurse around."

"Huh?" Jimmy forced himself to pay attention to what Daisy had said. "Oh, yea, Of course I was talking about you Daisy. Why would you even ask?" As Jimmy finished his sentence, he let his eyes wonder in the direction of Carly.

"I wonder." Daisy mumbled. "Go talk to her instead of staring a hole through her." She stated as she gave him a shove.

"I will…I will, you don't have to shove." Jimmy gave her a wink and turned to do exactly what Daisy suggested.

"Carly… Carly?" Karen shook her head again. *There she goes again. Ever since Carly met this person- Jimmy Gates – Yea that was his name –she would space out on her.* "Carly, what are you looking at?" Karen turned her attention in the direction her was staring in. *Oh…I see...* Karen studied the man that had captured her friend's attention. Jimmy Gates stood six one, looked to be around a hundred and sixty pounds, with dark brown hair. *I like his smile. He looks has if he has a secret that he keeps just for himself.* Karen glanced briefly at her friend then back at Jimmy. She smiled when she saw Daisy give him a slight shove; the laughter from Dr. Barrett and Carly told her that they had seen it also.

Breathe, just breathe. Carly told herself as she watched Jimmy make his way over to her.

Jimmy's eyes crinkled at the corner when he saw the unsteady breath that Carly took. *So, I affect her the way she does me.* The knowledge pleased him. His smile widened as he stopped in front of her. "Hi Doc." Jimmy spoke out of curtsey; his eyes never left Carly's.

"Hello Jimmy." Barrett, smiled and gave them a slight wave goodbye. "I have rounds. I will talk to you later." He placed his hand on Carly's shoulder. "Stay off that ankle."

Carly glanced up at Dr. Barrett and nodded, then returned her attention to Jimmy. Her tongued darted out to wet her suddenly dry lips, causing Jimmy's breath to catch in his chest. *Is she deliberately trying to drive me crazy?* He decided against that thought, because if she were, that would mean she would be just like…

Carly grabbed his hand the moment she saw the glimpse of pain that appeared in his eyes. It was brief, barely a flash, but she knew at that moment that he had been hurt before and he was afraid to trust whatever was happening between them.

Jimmy wrapped his fingers around her hand clinging to the feel of it in his hand. Can *I trust this?* Carly gave his hand a squeeze. *Trust me, trust this.*

Karen watched the silent exchange between them. *Who knows, maybe after all that happened in Wyoming, her friend just might find what she deserved… happiness.*

Carly suddenly remembered that they weren't alone and pulled her hand from Jimmy's, missing it as soon as she did. Placing her hand on her cheek in embarrassment. "I don't know where my manners are. Karen, I would like you to meet Jimmy Gates. He is one of the paramedics that tended to me. Jimmy, Karen Wingate, my best friend and co-worker."

Karen and Jimmy shook hands. "Nice to meet you." They spoke simultaneously. She liked the way his smile reached his eyes, but she also noticed there was sadness about them also. The sadness she saw in them had to be because of the young boy that Carly had told her he lost the other day. Karen gave him a smile and made a decision.

"I was just about to take Carly home. How about joining us for dinner later tonight?"

Jimmy watched the surprise on Carly's face only to be replaced with a smile. "I'd love too; just tell me where and when."

Karen smiled at Carly then went to the nurse's desk and asked for a piece of paper.

"There's my girl."

Karen turned at the sound of Michael's voice giving a silent groan. She watched as Jimmy shook his hand. *Please, please don't leave her.*

"Anne, just the woman I came to see." Jimmy said as he made his way over to talk to her. He made sure that he was facing Carly as he talked.

It didn't escape Karen's notice and she smiled her thanks - not that Jimmy noticed – he was too busy watching Carly. *I'm glad you feel as I do about that man.* Making a decision, Karen wrote a quick note and handed it to Daisy. "Would you make sure Jimmy gets this?"

"Sure." Daisy replied.

"Thanks." Karen turned on her heel, her long sandy brown hair flipping around her shoulders and hurried back to stand next to her friend. "Hello Michael, what a surprise."

Michael gave Karen a dismissing nod. How he disliked Carly's friend. She always seemed to be around. It was irritating. "Hello Karen, I came to see if my favorite gal needed a ride home."

"That's O.K, I'm taking her home." Karen stated protectively.

Jimmy watched the display in front of him while still trying to act as if he had come to see Anne. He knew he was being unfair to her, but he didn't know how else to keep an eye on Carly. There was something about that guy.

Anne placed her hand on Jimmy's arm. "It's O.K Jimmy, I know you really came to see someone else."

"I'm sorry Anne. It' not fair that I…" Jimmy glanced up the moment that Karen placed her hand on the back of Carly's wheelchair.

Anne glanced in the direction that he stared in once again, this time when she looked the smile left her face. "Go, Jimmy."

He glazed at her. "I'm sorry Anne."

"Don't be Jimmy. I have a feeling that things aren't what they seem over there."

"So do I." He leaned over giving her a kiss on the cheek. He studied her young lovely face. Blue eyes shinned in an oval slender face framed with dark brown hair. "You're great you know."

"Yea, of course I do. That's why the best looking paramedic here is running off to help some other woman." Anne laughed at the embarrassment that crossed Jimmy's face.

The sound of Anne's laugh caused Carly to glance in their direction and her eyes locked with Jimmy's. He straightened, and Carly thought he looked like a cobra, all straight and tense, ready to strike.

"Carly, stop staring at that fireman and look at me." Michael demanded.

Jimmy caught a brief glimpse of fear come into Carly's eyes, that was soon replaced by something else.

"Don't ever talk to me like that again. Lets' go home, Karen." Fire snapped from her eyes as she spoke.

"Anything you say." Karen was more than happy to comply. Stepping behind Carly's chair, she started to push her toward the doors.

Michael blocked her. "I'm not through. I thought you and I could go out to eat tonight."

When Michael reached out and touched her face, it was all Carly could do not to flinch away or to look over at Jimmy. "I'd love that Michael, but I'm really not feeling up to going out tonight."

"Then I'll come to your place." Michael insisted.

What part of no, doesn't this man understand? "Not tonight. I just want to go home and rest. You don't really get a lot of rest in the hospital, you know. Can we make it another time?"

Michael hesitated so long that Carly wondered if he would fight her on this. "Sure, you go home and rest. I'll walk out with you if that's O.K."

Rather than fight him on the subject - it was easier for her just to agree.

Jimmy watched as the three walked out of the hospital and was about to follow, saying a quick goodbye to Anne when Daisy stopped him. "Karen asked me to make sure you got this."

He took the note, opened it with precision. "Jimmy, Here is the address to our apartment. 320 Westwood, apartment 110, Greenwood Apartments. I think I should also let you know that despite the way things look with Michael and Carly, they are far from being close. Karen"

Jimmy folded the note, placed it in his pocket and walked out the doors. The moment he stepped through the doors, he heard Michael once again trying to convince Carly to go out with him. "Is there a problem here?" Three pair of eyes focused on him in surprise, but he could have sworn he'd seen relief in both Carly's and Karen's eyes. It wasn't lost on Michael either.

Michael straightened. "No problem here."

Jimmy walked around to stand beside of Karen. Carly had already gotten in the car. Her hand rested on the seal of the window and he reached behind Karen placing his hand over hers. He gave it a squeeze almost causing Carly to sigh in relief. *How can his touch make me feel so safe?*

Jimmy turned just enough so it would seem he was looking at Karen, but also allowed him to see Carly as well. Karen's body blocked Michaels' view. He reached up and touched Karen's face. "We still on for tonight?"

Karen suddenly became aware of how Carly must feel whenever he touched her or gazed into her eyes, Gates had a way about him that was for sure. "I'm not sure, I really don't want to leave Carly home by herself."

"Then we can eat in. How about Chinese?"

"Well, if it's O.K with Carly?" Jimmy glanced at Carly for appearances sake.

"Sure, I will probably be fast asleep anyway. This medicine Dr. Barrett has me on puts me out like a light."

"You sure, I wouldn't want to be the one to keep you up." Jimmy gave her a wink causing Carly to turn a bright red.

"Gates…is that your name?" Michael asked with irritation.

Jimmy faced Michael with a slow and deliberate motion. "Yes."

"I had planned on going over tonight also, but Carly seemed so tired I decided against it. Maybe you should too."

Jimmy shrugged as if it made no difference to him. "Like I said, it's whatever the ladies feel like doing." He left the rest to Carly and Karen.

Karen turned to face her friend, making Carly have to move her hand from under Jimmy's. *I miss it.*

"Would you mind if Jimmy came over tonight?" Karen asked trying to sound normal. She was shaking so badly that she thought Michael would notice.

"No, I know it has been awhile since the two of you have seen each other, besides like I said, I will probably be fast asleep once my head hits my pillow." It had been hard for Carly to sound so indifferent and she hated the thought of Jimmy seeing anyone, but her. *It is just a rouse, remember that.*

Jimmy wrapped his arm around Karen's waist and pulled her against him. "I'll see you tonight then." He whispered against her lips just before he gave her a slight kiss. "You better get Carly home before she falls asleep."

Karen nodded and walked around to the driver's side door. When she was in Jimmy leaned in and whispered against Carly's cheek. "I'll see you later." Carly gave him a small smile and then Jimmy said loud enough for Michael to hear. "I'll be over around seven."

Karen gave him a wave then backed the car out and headed toward the house. If she wasn't careful, she could find herself falling for her friend's guy.

"What's that smile about?" Carly couldn't keep the jealousy out of her voice.

"Carly, you know all that was done for Michael's sake."

"Yea, I know. He didn't have to kiss you."

"It was a peck that's all."

"I know…still…"

Karen reached over taking her hand. "You do know that fireman is crazy over you, right?"

"He is?" Carly blushed at the sound of excitement in her voice.

"You know he is. There is no mistake about who he is coming to see tonight." She gave Carly a reassuring smile and a jab in the arm with her elbow. "Who knows, maybe tonight you will get a kiss of your own."

Carly bowed her head so Karen couldn't read her expression. *You had better believe I will, even if I have to tie him down.* Carly laughed aloud at her own thought. *Now that would be funny!*

"What's so funny?"

"Nothing." At Karen's disbelieving look, she laughed again. "Honestly."

Karen raised an eyebrow sending Carly into another fit of the giggles.

"I think those pills are working too well."

Carly knew the laughter was because Jimmy would be coming to see her that night and she suddenly felt like a young school girl, scared, excited and nervous all at once. There was one thing she was sure of; before the night was over she would know how those lips she had been dreaming of really felt.

Jimmy watched as the car pulled away, he gave Michael a nod goodbye and headed for his car. He had seen the surprise and hurt that crossed Carly's face when he had given Karen that slight kiss and wanted to reassure her that it was just to keep things calm. Tonight the only lips he wanted to feel were the lips he had been dreaming about for the past two days. He touched the paper in his pocket as he pulled into his parking area at his apartment never realizing that he had been followed.

At seven pm Jimmy brought his Land Rover to a stop in front of Carly's apartment building. He pulled out the paper with the address on it and smiled. The address had sounded familiar so he had stopped by the station on the way to get the food. He could still see the Captain's face on B shrift when he burst out laughing. The address was one of many calls that

Rick and he had over the years. They had been working together less then a year and had a call to a woman not able to breathe; sometimes he could still feel that girdle hitting him across the face. His smile widened at the memory as he opened the door and got out. He reached in, grabbed the food and wondered as he shut the door whatever happened to that woman.

Carly sat in her room brushing her hair for what seemed like the hundredth time. She had changed clothes so many times she had lost count. The sound of someone knocking caused her to jump and she placed her hand over her heart, trying to calm her breathing. "Come In."

Karen opened the door and stopped in her tracks. Her mouth dropped open as she stared at the room in front of her. Clothes were thrown on the bed, floor, and chairs. Her gaze worked its way around the room finally coming to a rest on Carly. "I can assume that this is one room of the apartment that Jimmy won't be visiting tonight."

"Karen!" Carly shouted and jumped to her feet forgetting about her ankle.

Jimmy raised his hand to knock on the door when he heard the scream.

"Carly, is everything alright." He called through the door.

A moment or two later Karen opened the door. "Everything is fine, Carly just forgot to stay off her foot."

"Is she ok?"

"Sure, she will be out in a few minutes.

"Think she may need some help?"

Karen's eyes sparkled with mischief. *Nah, I can't do that to her.* "No, I'm sure she'll get the hang of the crutches soon."

"Yea, those crutches can be tricky."

"Sounds like you had some experience with them." Karen stated as she took the food out of Jimmy's arms and lead him to the counter dividing the kitchen from the living room.

"A few times, I suppose." He replied as he came to a stop a few steps behind. Memories of that day came back in a rush and he felt a blush creep up his neck. The good thing was Karen wouldn't know why.

She turned back to face him as his crooked grin appeared. *I know I've seen him somewhere, but where?' It was driving her crazy that she couldn't remember.* "I guess you have had your fair share of injuries being a firefighter." The memory tugged at the recesses of her mind.

"My share, I guess."

"I am amazed that anyone would do what you do." She remarked as she now led him to the living room, motioning for him to have a seat on the sofa.

"Why's that?"

Why is he answering me in short clip answers? "I guess because it's such a dangerous job." She said with a shrug.

She looks familiar. "I suppose it can be"

Carly hobbled out of the bedroom just as he finished speaking. Jimmy stood up and walked to stand beside her. He leaned in next to her ear and whispered. Carly smiled and shifted her wait on the crutches, his smile sent her heart into a fast pace.

"Is that better?"

"Much."

Karen sat back watching the exchange between them. Carly wore a pair of blue slacks with an off the shoulder tan top. Her hair she wore down, parted on the side. Jimmy wore a pair of brown slacks, a tan button up shirt and a pair of Swede shoes. With both having dark hair they looked like the perfect pair. "I'll go get everything ready for dinner, while you two talk." Karen stated as she stood up.

"Need any help." Carly asked.

"No, you need to get off your feet…excuse me, I meant foot."

"Ha, Ha."

Karen laughed as she went to set the table and Jimmy helped Carly to the couch. When he had made sure, she was settled, with a pillow under her ankle, he sat down beside her and placed his arm on the couch behind her.

Carly stared at her ankle for a moment wondering how to start the conversation, though just having him sitting beside her was nice too.

The silence was almost Karen's undoing. *What are they teenagers?* She shook her head. Maybe she could get the conversation started and they would take it from there. "Jimmy was just telling me about some of his rescues."

I was? Jimmy thought as he raised an eyebrow.

"I bet you have had some interesting ones." Carly stated.

"Yea, I guess so." Jimmy remembered the girdle incident. "In fact, there was this one time…"

"Go on." Carly encouraged when he hesitated as she shifted on the couch.

Jimmy placed his index finger against the side of his nose. "It's was nothing."

"I doubt that somehow. Please, I would like to hear about your job."

"Well, it's…a little embarrassing."

"I won't laugh." Jimmy gave her skeptical look. "Cross my heart." To emphasize her promise, she crossed her chest with her finger.

What is it about her that makes me want do as she asks? "Well, Rick and I…"

"Rick?" Karen asked from the dining room.

"Jimmy's partner, he's really nice." Karen raised an eyebrow. "He's also very married." Carly finished.

"Oh."

Jimmy laughed then turned his attention back to Carly. "We had a call for a woman having trouble breathing. In fact, we responded to this very apartment."

The sound of breaking glass brought Jimmy to his feet. "You alright?"

"Yes, I just dropped a glass." *It can't be him.*

Jimmy hurried to check on her anyway and helped clean up the glass. It was when he stooped down in front of Karen that he realized where he had seen her before. Slowly he rose to his feet. "It's you."

Karen blushed. "Guess I have changed a bit."

"Yea, you could say that…not that there was anything wrong with you before…it's just…that…"

"It's ok Jimmy. I get that reaction a lot. I lost the weight after the girdle thing."

"What girdle thing?" Carly asked from the couch. She wasn't quite sure she liked the fact that they had something in common that she didn't know about. *Stop that Carly Gibson, Karen is your best friend and she would never do what…* Carly shoved the memory and feeling away.

Jimmy rejoined Carly on the sofa and picked up her hand. The uncertainty and pain he saw briefly cross her face made him want to reassure her. "That's what was embarrassing. We had to cut…"

"Jimmy had to cut, his partner didn't look to keen on the idea."

"No, I don't think he was."

Both of you stop! The urge to scream was over whelming, but Carly restrained herself. "So you had to cut it?"

"Yea, and when I did it slapped me right across the face."

Carly covered her mouth with her hand.

"It's O.K, go ahead and laugh. It was a few years ago anyway."

"No…No…I promised…I wouldn't."

Jimmy squirmed for a moment, but never removed his arm from behind her, if anything, he moved closer and his hand ended up on her shoulder. Carly hid her face on his shoulder trying control the laughter. When she raised her head she found herself staring into his very dark and sexy brown eyes. All laughter ceased and her lips went dry.

Jimmy found himself mesmerized by her laugh and how easy and natural it felt having her in his arms. He wanted to stay where he was and he wanted to run from whatever was happening all at the same time. He watched as she licked her lips and felt his heart give a jerk. He gave himself a mental shake. *Keep it light Jimmy, keep it light.*

Carly saw the minute he drew away and wanted to reach out to grab the moment back, but knew she couldn't. Why did she always do that? It was a fault she intended to correct. There was no way, she would ever feel that pain again. *He's a player, remember that. You saw how easy it was for him to turn his attention. Keep it light, Keep it light.* Moving away, but not too far away, she glanced over at Karen. "Is dinner set?"

"Almost. Why don't you both go out on the balcony?"

"Why?" Carly and Jimmy asked simultaneously.

Karen gave them an innocent smile. "I just thought it would be nice to eat out there tonight. It's a warm spring night."

Jimmy and Carly looked at each other. A few seconds later Jimmy shrugged. "I'm game if you are."

"Sure, why not."

I'll help Carly outside and then come back in to help you." Jimmy informed Karen.

Never looking up Karen stated. "Oh, that's O.K. I can get it. You two spend some time getting to know each other." There she had said it; she was tired of watching them dance around each other and if she had to push a little so be it. When neither moved, she put her hands on her hips. "Go!" She stated as she pointed toward the door to the balcony.

"O.K, O.K, you don't have to shout." Jimmy teased. He turned to help Carly up and hand her the crutches. Karen stood watching the slow progress they were making and wanted to scream at the man to pick her up. She remained quiet though and turned her attention to gathering up the dishes on the table. After several trips and Jimmy's offers of help and her refusing, they were able to sit down and eat.

To Jimmy's surprise and pleasure, he was able to relax and just enjoy his evening. All thoughts of the past forgotten as the conversation turned to easy topics. Carly and Karen talked about their work and then pumped Jimmy for recounts of some of the rescues he and Rick had been on.

Carly found herself drawn to the sound of his voice. She knew the comfort it could give first hand, now she was finding the humor and at times serious sides.

Glancing down at her watch Karen decided it was time that Carly and Jimmy had some alone time. Gathering up the dishes, she made her excuses and left them to themselves.

When all was quiet in the apartment, Jimmy and Carly studied each other.

"I had a good time." They said at one.

Jimmy grinned. "I'm glad we did this."

"Me too."

Unsure as to what he should do now, Jimmy hesitated. Everything had been so easy before, it was something he never had to think about, until he met Carly. There was something special about her and it was that which worried him.

Ahh…Carly…I'm not sure how to say this without sounding…"

"Like a jerk?"

"I guess." It amazed him how easily she had begun to know what he would say. It also unnerved him.

"Why don't you just say what you want to say?"

"I don't want you to get the wrong idea."

"I see."

Carly lowered her head, wanting to run and hide.

"No, I don't think you do. I'd like to see you again."

Carly's head jerked up. "Oh? I thought…"

"Yea, I know what you thought. Like I said I want to see you again, but…"

"But what?"

"I'm not interested…ready…for anything serious."

Carly wanted to cry with relief. "Believe this or not, but I feel the same way."

"Really?"

"Yes, really. I moved to Los Angeles a year ago because of a relationship that didn't work out. It's not something I am willing to go through anytime soon again."

"I can understand that."

"Can you?"

"Well, don't look so surprised; I can feel too you know."

"I'm sorry…I didn't mean."

The pain he had inflected by his words showed clearly on her face. It was the last thing he wanted to do. He took her hand in his and ran his thumb across the top.

"No, I'm sorry; I shouldn't have said that. Forgive me." He stood and walked to the railing looking out over the city, trying to distance himself from the pain he saw reflected in her blue eyes.

"This city is beautiful at night." The lights from the city spread out in front of him like a line of twinkling stars. As far as you could see there were lines of reds, greens and whites from the cars and street lights, shinning in the dark. The sound of a siren caught his attention and he strained to see if it was a rescue vehicle or a fire engine.

"Yes, it is. Sometimes when I can't sleep, I come out here and just watch the lights from the streets and listen to the sound of the cars that pass below."

"Really?"

"Yes. I know that sounds silly…"

"No, I do the same thing sometimes. Especially after I've had a hard shift, it's relaxing."

"One day I would like a house of my own away from the city, but for now, I'll take the quiet night." The sound of another siren rang through the air. "Though sometimes it's not always peaceful." She interjected with a smile.

"When I'm at the station and we get a call in the middle of the night, it's sometimes hard to fall back to sleep when we get back."

"What do you do to relax?"

"Maybe go into the Day room and read, go stand outside and listen to the night sounds of the city or lie in my bed and think about something relaxing."

"Like what?"

"Riding, skiing, or rock climbing."

"O.K, I can see how riding could be relaxing, but skiing and rock climbing?"

Jimmy's voice grew with excitement, he turned to face her and sat with one leg braced on the balcony ledge. "Oh, yea, the feeling of knowing it is you and the cliff. It somehow makes you see that everything else is trivial except at that moment and when you are out on the water and you feel it under your feet…it's freedom somehow."

"I've never done them, except horse back riding." Carly was finding it hard to concentrate on anything, but the site of his leg resting on the ledge.

"Well, maybe after your ankle is better we can go out on the water sometime."

She jerked her eyes to his and forced herself to concentrate on his last words. "I think I'd like that…only…"

"What?"

"Do you think we can skip the skiing part and just do the sailing?"

Jimmy laughed sending tiny shivers through her. "Sure, for the first time or two anyway."

"Oh thanks a lot."

"You're welcome."

They sat in silence for a moment and then Jimmy glanced at his watch. "I'd better get heading home. I have to work tomorrow and that means getting up early."

"I understand; I had a great time tonight and I want to thank you for your help with Michael today."

"I was glad to help." Jimmy sat for a moment longer then stood. "I'd better be going." Why he felt it difficult to leave he didn't want to dwell on.

"I guess so. You will need all your rest for work tomorrow."

Yea, like I will be resting with wondering what it would have been like to kiss you goodnight. Jimmy thought.

Carly stood and reached for her crutches just as Jimmy did. Their hands met and they stared at each other. Carly wasn't sure, but she thought he muttered, 'Oh what the hell.' Just before, he wrapped his arm around her and pulled her against him. His tongue darted out to wet his lips just before he bent down to kiss her. The moment their lips met, Carly knew there was no way that she could be causal with Jimmy. As his kiss deepened, she kept telling herself. *You have to.*

Jimmy broke the kiss and stared into her eyes. How could he keep things causal with her? *You have to.* He kept repeating that to himself as he stepped back away from her.

"Thanks again for a great evening."

"It was my pleasure."

"I'll call you." He whispered.

"I hope so." Carly whispered back.

Why they whispered neither knew. Carly walked Jimmy to the door, said another goodnight and slowly closed the door behind him. She leaned against the door closing her eyes.

Karen opened her door at the sound of the front door closing. She saw Carly leaning against it with tears running down her face. "What happened?"

"Nothing…everything."

"Carly?"

Carly opened her eyes and stared at Karen for a moment. "I just met the man, I think I'm going to marry and it scares the life out of me."

"Why?"

Carly pushed herself away from the door. "Because he doesn't want anything serious and because what he does for a living scares the life out of me!"

Carly made her way into her room where she threw herself across her bed and cried. It made no sense to her, why after such a wonderful night, but something told her that Jimmy Gates would break her heart whether he meant to or not.

5

Having given up long ago of pushing the wild strands of hair behind her ear, Carly raised her face to accept the tiny sprinkles of water that hit her like a gentle rain and her eyes drifted shut as she became one with the movement of the boat. A satisfied sigh eased passed her lips and she opened her eyes. The brilliance of the sun glistened across the water as the blue of the sky enhanced the green of the trees and housetops along the shoreline and she leaned closer against the rail. She marveled at the difference time had made.

Had it really only been two weeks since she had met Jimmy? She allowed herself to glance up in his direction as he stood at the wheel. *How can it be such a short time when I feel as if I have known him all my life?*

Another sigh eased passed her lips as a warm glow began deep inside her with the thought. Two weeks ago she nursed a sprained ankle and now she stood on the deck of the boat on her first date with the man she could easily see herself spending the rest of her life with.

Jimmy stood at the helm watching Carly as she stood by the rail. When she leaned forward, he started to yell for her to be careful, but then she stepped back and turned to look up at him, flashing him a smile. His heart did an unfamiliar flip and he suddenly knew he could easily spend the rest of his life that woman. He waited for the feeling of desperation to flee, but it never came, that alone made him uneasy. Yet, he found himself calling for Chip to take over the wheel.

"Chip…Chip!"

Chip poked his head up out of the cabin.

"Yea?"

"I need you to take over for awhile."

"Ahhh…Gates."

"Chip!"

"Sure."

Chip glanced back down the steps of the cabin and sighed.   "Karen, darling, I've been called to duty. Think I could eat that sandwich up here?"

"I'll bring it right up."

"Thanks Hon..."

Jimmy shook his head when he stepped back to let him take the wheel. "I should of had Jillian and Rick come with us."

Chip grinned. "Yea, but then you wouldn't have had as much fun."

Jimmy shook his head again. "Chip, sometimes…"

Karen stepped up on deck. "Here you go Chip."

"Thanks." As he took the sandwich, he placed his other arm around Karen giving her a hug. "Keep taking care of me like this and I just might ask you to marry me."

"Keep saying things like that to me and I just might accept."

When Chip almost choked on his bite, Jimmy slapped him on his back. "I think you might have met your match, pal." Jimmy gave Karen a wink then made his way over to Carly.

Chip and Karen watched with interest at the scene in front of them and when Jimmy placed his arm around Carly's waist, they smiled at each other.

"If Gates isn't careful he won't be single much longer." Chip teased.

"That's what I'm hoping."

"Are you saying that Carly is trying to trap Jimmy?" Suspicion filling his expression as he spoke.

"Of course not! Carly wouldn't do anything like that. What I meant was…from what I have seen when those two are together…"

"Yes." Chip's interest peaking.

"Well, they have something special going."

"What do you mean?"

"Watch them; have you ever seen Jimmy act that way with any other woman?"

Chip started to tell her that he acted the same with every woman, but when he glanced at them again, he knew she was right. He watched as Jimmy brushed Carly's hair away from her face with his hand letting it linger on the side of her face, even from where he stood he could see the smile on his friend's face. Something was different in the way Jimmy looked at Carly. "Nah, Gates married…never gonna happen."

Karen sent him a smile. "We'll see."

He raised his eyebrow. "I have a feeling that you will try and narrow the possibility."

"Me? Why Chip Keller I am shocked that you would even say such a thing."

"Ah, ha…right."

The sound of Karen's laughter drew Jimmy and Carly's attention.

"It looks like they are getting along pretty well." Carly stated.

"Yea."

"Is that a problem?" Carly asked, wondering why he seemed disapproving?

"No, of course not."

"Then why do you look concerned."

"Do I, didn't mean to."

Carly glanced back over in Karen and Chip's direction then back at Jimmy as he stared at their friends.

Jimmy blinked against the sun as he watched Karen's dark hair flip around her face from the wind, when he blinked again her hair was no longer black, but red as the setting sun and he knew that if he looked into her eyes he would see a pair of emerald green eyes looking back at him. The vision revived an emotion in him he thought was long buried.

"Jimmy, are you alright?"

It took him a moment to focus on the woman standing in front of him. "I'm sorry…what did you say?"

"I asked if you were o.k."

"Sure…why would you ask?" He answered with a crooked grin.

Carly gave a slight shrug of her shoulders. "I don't know…I guess you looked a little upset."

"Did I?"

Jimmy had no doubt that he had been, but he was sorry that he had let his feelings show. He hugged Carly to him, giving her a light kiss on the top of her head. "I'm fine."

Carly knew something had happened when he heard Karen laugh, but decided it was best left alone. *When he's ready to talk, he will…I hope.*

"Come on; let's go below for awhile away from prying eyes." He gave a slight nod toward Chip and Karen.

Carly smiled with understanding. They were both watching them as if they had nothing better to do. *Karen, when we get home…*

"Jimmy!"

Jimmy let his eyes follow in the direction Chip was pointing in then sprinted into action at the sight before him. A boat no more then twenty feet from them was on fire and someone was waving wildly to flag them down.

"Chip!"

"I'm already calling it in."

"Good, now speed this boat up!"

"Doing that as well."

Jimmy nodded and caught Carly as she stumbled when the boat jerked into high gear. He gave her a reassuring smile and then turned his attention back to the scene in front of him. "Damn!" Jimmy muttered as he released his hold on Carly and ran for the side of the boat. The person he had seen waving their arms was a woman…a woman with hair as red as the setting sun. His heart caught in his throat as he watched the boat explode, tossing her into the ocean. Jerking off his jacket, he climbed onto the railing and dove into the water.

"Jimmy!" Carly screamed and ran toward him just as he dove into the water. Her breath caught in her chest and she covered her mouth to keep back her screams. Her heart beat wildly against her chest until she saw him come up out of the water. Relief flooded through her when his head broke through the water, but she never took her eyes off him. She watched him swim toward whoever had been thrown in the water and pulled the person up against him. It wasn't until Chip and Karen appeared beside her that she realized the boat had stopped. Chip stepped onto the running board and when Jimmy neared the back of the boat , he reached for the woman.

Carly thought he would pull himself out, but instead he flipped and headed back toward the burning boat. She wanted to call out, but knew it would be pointless, so she made herself focus on the woman they had pulled from the water. She found herself studing the woman, her hair was a rich color of red, probably natural if the freckles the woman wore were any indication. She had an attractive heart shaped face with a dainty nose and mouth. It was a face that would make any woman jealous. Her wet clothes fit like a shapely glove making Carly feel suddenly inadequate and she ran her hands over her own curves. Why she felt threatened by the woman she couldn't fathom, bit she did. Dismissing her strange feelings, Carly concentrated on helping chip with the CPR. While she did the compressions; Chip gave the woman mouth to mouth.

When Jimmy was sure that Chip had her safe on the deck and was starting CPR, he headed back toward the burning boat. He was within just a few feet of it when it exploded again sending debris flying into the air and he flinched as pieces of the boat fell on him. He stared in horror, knowing that if anyone else was on that boat they were dead. Once again, he swam back toward the boat and to the woman who had haunted his dreams. Jimmy pulled himself over the railing and ran to where Chip was working. "I'll take over."

Carly moved away allowing Jimmy in. She watched as he counted to five then pushed on the woman's chest, pointed at Chip and let him breathe into her mouth, then he would start counting again as he pushed. "Come on, Come on…Breathe." Jimmy pleaded.

Carly gazed at him in surprise; the sound of his voice told her this was personal to him. That threatening feeling returned and she started biting her lower lip. *She's beautiful and she means something to Jimmy.* The sound of the woman coughing brought Carly back to the situation in front of her. Her fears and thoughts of what this woman could or did mean to Jimmy pushed away.

"Sandy? Can you hear me?" Jimmy said as he leaned toward her.

Carly watched as she opened her eyes. *Green. Just as I thought they would be. Not just green, but a beautiful emerald green.*

"Jimmy?"

"Yea, sweetheart, it's me." Tenderly wiping her hair from her face as he spoke.

The tender way he touched the woman made Carly feel as if she had stepped back in time. She was once again standing in the apartment she shared with her boyfriend watching as he told another woman how much he loved her. He had touched that woman as Jimmy was touching the one in front of her now. Tears she thought had long dried up started to fall.

"Jimmy?" Carly choked out seeing the wood sticking out of his side for the first time. How could she have not seen he was hurt? She knew how, because she had been too wrapped up in her own thoughts.

Jimmy jerked to face her only to stop from the pain that ripped through his side. Chip was on his feet and jumping over Sandy's legs to get to him.

"Jimmy, don't move…

"Don't worry I won't. How bad is it, Chip?"

"You have a piece of wood sticking out of your side."

"How big?"

"It looks to be about half the boat, if you ask me."

"Chip, that's not funny!" Carly yelled.

Jimmy tried to give her a reassuring smile a her, but it hurt to turn. "Carly, it's ok…it feels like half the boat if you want to know the truth."

"Gates that isn't funny. Why are you joking, when you are hurt?"

"Why not?"

Carly couldn't answer him, she was shaking with fear and anger toward him for putting himself in danger, anger at the woman for being the cause of the danger, but mostly she was afraid of losing him to the woman that he had just saved.

Carly glanced down at the woman and saw the fear showing on her face. *What did he say her name was…Sandy? Yea that was it. She looks as scared for him as I am…* Suddenly, the anger she felt for the woman left and was replaced with empathy. Their eyes connected and in that one look, Carly knew why she had walked away - there was no doubt in her mind as to why Jimmy was so tentative to the woman in front of her - they were once lovers. She closed her eyes, only to open them and once again stare into Sandy's. The concern she saw in them told her Sandy still cared for Jimmy. She could see the slight hint of tears. *You left him because of his job.* It wasn't a question.

Sandy recognized the silent question which seeped into the other woman's eyes and Carly found herself relating to her. In one quick move, she moved to kneel beside her. "Are you hurting anywhere?"

"Just my head, but Jimmy always told me I was hard headed so I should be alright."

The slight scoff/laugh Jimmy gave made Carly glance up, but it was the approval in his eyes that made her heart skip a beat. It was a look of pride as well as a question in them and she held out her hand to him, in answer to that question. Jimmy took her hand and gave it a squeeze then returned his attention to Sandy.

Carly sat back on her heels as she watched the man in front of her. She knew that his job was dangerous – she had even gotten a taste that day of how dangerous – yet, even though she was scared of what could happen to him, she couldn't walk away. Something must have showed in her face, because Sandy touched her arm. Glancing down, Sandy mouthed…"wait until he is fighting for his life." A chill ran down her spine and she quickly focused on Jimmy who was running his hands over Sandy's legs. Chip was standing behind Jimmy making sure that he didn't make any sudden moves.

It seemed like forever, but the helicopter finally arrived with the Paramedic's from Station 15's B- Shift. When Sandy and Jimmy were loaded into the chopper, Carly, Karen and Chip turned the boat to shore.

Karen wrapped her arm around her friend's shoulder. "Jimmy will be fine."

"This time, but what about the next?"

Karen shifted her gaze over at Chip behind the wheel. "I guess we will just have to take it one day at a time."

"I guess we will." Carly said smiling at her friend, having seen the exchange between the other two.

6

Silverware clanked, ice fell into glasses, which was soon followed by the sound of pouring liquid, and low whispers of people's conversations filled the air all around Carly as she waited in the hospital cafeteria, but all she heard was the sound of her heart beating as she waited for news about Jimmy.

"What is taking so long? Why doesn't someone come and tell us something?" Carly asked then jumped up and walked away from the table.

"Carly, Jimmy is going to be fine." Chip replied from behind her.

"Is he? What about the next time." Carly snapped as she spun around to face him. "You can't think like that."

"Why not?" Her eyes radiating fear and anger, she flung her arm out to emphasize her statement. "Jimmy is in there with a piece of wood in his side because of this job you all love so much. He wasn't even on duty, and he still has to jump in when someone is in trouble."

"Would you want him any other way?" Chip asked reasonably.

Carly's eyes brimmed with tears as she nervously chewed her lower lip - a habit she had since she was a child. "I want him alive." She whispered.

Chip slipped his arm around her shoulders and started to reply when Carly spotted Dr. Barrett. She rushed to him barely stopping before she stumbled into him.

"Jimmy…is he alright?" Anxiety coursed through her making it difficult to breathe while she waited for Dr. Barrett's answer.

"He's going to be fine. The wood didn't penetrate anything vital, but the injury did require stitches."

When he finally answered, Carly felt as if she would almost pass out from lack of air.

Kris grabbed her arms to steady her.

"Will he have to stay in the hospital long?" Carly asked apprehensively.

"I'd like him to stay the night and then he should be able to go home tomorrow."

"When will he be able to go back to work, Doc?" Chip asked.

"Maybe a week or two…That reminds me, has anyone called Rick?"

"Yes, I did right after we got to the hospital, he should be here any minute." Chip replied.

As if on cue, Rick walked into the cafeteria along with Jillian. "How's Jimmy?"

Though he showed the essence of being calm, his voice held a note of concern.

"Hi Rick, He's going to be fine. I was just telling everyone that he will have to stay over night and can go home in the morning." Dr Barrett answered.

"What about work?" Rick asked.

"In a week or two."

"Can we see him?"

"Sure, but he has been given something for the pain so don't stay to long."

"Sure."

Once Dr. Barrett left Rick glanced toward Carly. "How are you?"

"I'm O.K."

He arched an eyebrow. "You sure, you look a little shaken up."

Carly bristled. "Why shouldn't I be? I just watched Jimmy jump off a moving boat and then get close enough to another one to have been killed when it exploded."

Rick understood why she felt as she did, goodness knows he had heard it more than once from his wife, but he always came back to the same answer - *it was his job*. The gentle touch of Jillian's hand on his arm had him shift his gaze in her direction.

"Let me talk to her." She mouthed.

He nodded his head and walked over to stand near Chip and Karen. After Jillian had taken Carly's arm and walked away he turned his attention to Chip. He was introduced to Karen and wondered where he knew her from. When he realized where he had seen her before, he laughed and they started talking about the call.

Chip's ears seemed too literally perked up when he heard about the girdle. "Oh, you wait Gates. I will have some fun with this."

"Now Chip, you better not say anything to Jimmy." Rick stated.

"Rick, you know me."

"Yea, Chip I know you. That's why I'm warning you."

Chip grinned leaving both Rick and Karen to believe that he wasn't going to keep the secret.

 Low bits of laughter drifted across the space to where Carly and Jillian sat.

"I understand how you feel…"

I wish people would stop saying that to me. They don't know how I feel, just how they would feel.

"Rick and I talk about things, but we usually try and take it a day at a time…"

How can she live with this fear?

"We live in the moment as they say. We cherish the time we have together because we know that in a flash it could be gone – not – just because of Rick's job - but…" Sadness entered Jillian's eyes. "Rick and I lost a baby a few months after we were married."

She sat up straighter suddenly able to focus on someone else's pain rather than her own. "I'm so sorry."

Karen gave her a small smile and shook the pain of the memory away . She cleared her throat before continuing, "We hadn't planned the pregnancy, but we were happy about it. It wasn't long after we found out; I was in a car wreck and I miscarried."

"I don't know what to say." Carly whispered.

"There's nothing to say. The point I'm making is, because of that we try not to take our life together for granted. Oh, we have our disagreements and there are days that I want to strangle him, but in truth, my life wouldn't be worth much without him."

"So you don't mind what he does?"

"I'm proud of what he does. Do I worry about him? Of course, it's part of loving him. His job is who he is and I wouldn't change anything about him…Well…maybe one or two things…" Carly laughed as Jillian continued. "But, I love him for what he believes he needs to do."

"I see; I know I shouldn't worry about Jimmy…I mean…we aren't married…this was our first date." She let her words slowly fade away.

"Don't you see, it's because you do care that makes you special. The last woman he was serious about nearly destroyed him."

Carly straightened despite herself. "How?"

Glancing around, she made sure Rick wouldn't hear what she was about to say next. She leaned in closer to Carly and placed her hand over hers. "I really should let Jimmy tell you, but knowing him he won't say a word." Carly leaned closer so she could hear Jillian as she lowered her voice. "Her name was Sandy Mason…"

"Sandy?"

"Yes, has Jimmy told you about her?" Jillian asked in surprise.

"No…I…just can't see him with someone named Sandy."

"To tell you the truth, either could I…still she seemed to really care about him. Whenever they weren't working; she's a nurse here at Regional."

"Oh…"

"Well, she was until a few months after she and Jimmy broke up. I'm getting ahead of myself…now where was I?"

"Ahh…Sandy really seemed to care about Jimmy."

"Oh, yea, that's right. They did everything together; they had a lot of the same taste in things, food, music, books. Then Jimmy was hurt in a burning house and we thought we were going to lose him…" Jillian's voice broke at the memory.

Carly grabbed her hand. "He made it though." She said in reassurance though the thought of his life in danger again sent chills through her.

Jillian nodded her head and cleared the lump in her throat. "Yes, he did…but…"

"But…"

"Sandy decided that she couldn't handle being married to a firefighter. She made him choose between her and his job."

"She did?" Carly understood that need and felt a connection to the woman.

"Yes. Jimmy chose his job. Now, that's not to say he didn't love her because he did and he was devastated when she broke the engagement off."

Karen's voiced turned husky and she cleared her throat once again. "It was weeks before he would come around, all he did was work. Rick tried talking to him, but he shut himself off. Slowly, we started seeing the old Jimmy come back, though it took awhile."

"I see…what do you think would happen if they ever ran into each other again?" A sinking feeling set in the pit of her stomach as she waited for Jillian's answer.

"Well, I don't know…I think it would be a shock to him, he might even start to pull away again." Jillian smiled. "Unless the right woman was there to make sure it didn't matter." She nudged Carly with her shoulder.

"Well, maybe that right woman hasn't come along yet."

"Maybe she has and she and he just doesn't know it yet."

"Maybe."

Yes, it's me sweetheart. The memory of those words replayed in Carly's mind. She couldn't help thinking that Sandy had showed up a little too soon. Her thoughts were interrupted by the sound of Rick's voice.

"Anyone over there want to go see a certain paramedic?"

Jillian gave her husband a smile, gave Carly's hand a squeeze and pulled her to her feet. "Come on…let's go see our favorite guy."

Carly raised her eyebrow and Jillian corrected herself.

"Ok, your favorite and my second favorite."

For the first since they left the boat, Carly laughed.

Jimmy tossed his head back and forth, as he slept.

"I'm sorry Jimmy I just can't live this way. You have to make a decision…me or the job."

"Sandy, I can't make that decision. I love you, but my job is who I am."

"If you love me, then you will do as I ask and find some other kind of work."

He walked to the door of their bedroom, turning to face her.

"If you love me at all you would not ask me to choose."

"There shouldn't be a choice. You should want me under any circumstances."

"Shouldn't that go for you as well?"

"Don't put this on me. You are the one that has a job that could hurt you or worse...I don't want to go to your funeral!"

Jimmy walked to her and pulled her into his arms and buried his face in the back of her head. The scent of honey filled his senses and he tightened his arms around her. "I know my job is hard on you, but who would I be if I didn't have it?"

"You would be alive!" Sandy cried as she pushed him away. She had to have space between them, because when he held her like that her love for him vanquished her fears and reason. She wouldn't let that happen this time – she couldn't.

"No, you make a decision, here and now...me or the job." Her voice shook from the emotions raging inside her. She knew she was taking a chance, but it was a chance she had to take.

Jimmy walked to the bedroom door and stopped, lowering his head as he spoke. "I'll see if I can stay with Rick and Jillian tonight. I'll be back tomorrow to get my things." He started to leave then paused. "I would appreciate it if you weren't here when I came to get them." He then walked out the front door letting it gently close behind him.

"I can't…If you love me…" Jimmy murmured in his unconscious state.

"I do love you Jimmy, that's why I came back." Sandy answered. "I tried to live without you, but it seems you are etched into my very being. Nothing is the same without you in my life. "

Reasoning told her that her chance with Jimmy had long passed, but her heart couldn't accept that fact. Her mind flashed back to the woman on the boat. She saw the way she watched him, her eyes revealed more than Sandy thought she had intended. Even with that she knew if she had some time with Jimmy that they could get back what they had. There was just one problem with that reasoning, she had seen the way Jimmy had returned the woman's expression. He had gazed at her like that once upon a time.

Sandy tenderly brushed his hair back with the tips of her fingers. "I can't be too late. There has to be something I can do to get you back." The sound of the door opening sprung her into action and she leaned in and placed her lips on Jimmy's and heard the small gasp behind her.

She didn't have to be told who the gasp came from and she slowly stood, still holding Jimmy's hand. Surprise crossed her features when she realized not only was the woman from the boat there, but so were the people she once was so close to. A flash of regret sprung up, but was quickly squelched when she watched her competition flee from the doorway.

Turning away from the eyes that were trained on her, Sandy gave a small smile. *That should take care of her. Poor Jimmy, you don't even know what just happened.* She leaned in giving him another kiss then turned to face the three-left staring. "I should be getting back to my own bed. I just wanted to make sure Jimmy was O.K."

She eased back down into her wheelchair and then pushed herself toward the door. Her whole body shook, but on the outside she remained calm. If the anger on Rick's expression as he stepped back to hold the door open was any indication, she could kiss any support from him goodbye. A sense of loss filled her, because they had all been so close, but she wanted Jimmy back and nothing and no-one would stop her. She straightened her shoulders and rolled past them with her head held high. "Rick, Jillian, Chip, it's good to see you again. We'll have to get together soon to catch up, maybe after Jimmy is back on his feet."

No one answered her, whether it was from surprise or anger she couldn't tell. It wasn't that they didn't like Sandy-at least not the Sandy they used to know – but they had seen how hard it was for Jimmy after she broke things off…they weren't ready to see him go through that again. Once she left, the three walked over to see Jimmy sleeping. The Sandy that just left was not the Sandy they once knew.

"Someone needs to find Carly." Jillian stated.

"As soon as possible." Rick confirmed.

"Maybe I can catch her." Jillian said, already heading for the door.

Why am I so upset? *It's not as if we meant anything to each other.* Carly got as far as the elevator before Karen caught up with her.

"Carly wait!" Karen called out.

She turned to face her friend losing the battle to keep the tears back. "I can't do this again, Karen."

Karen pulled her into her arms just as Jillian arrived.

"Carly, don't leave." Jillian pleaded.

"I can't stay…I'm sorry…I hope things work out for Jimmy and Sandy this time." The elevator doors opened and Carly attempted to step into it when Jillian took her arm. "It wasn't what it looked like."

"I know you are only trying to help, but I can't do this again. It's best if I just walk away now."

"Jimmy wasn't even awake."

Disbelief spread across her expression to be quickly followed by resentment. "I don't know why Jimmy put you up to this or even why you would agree to it, but I am not a simpleton nor am I blind. I know what I saw." This time when she hit the elevator button she did it with force.

Again Jillian grabbed her arm and spun her with more force than she intended. Anger seeped into her eyes as well as her voice. "Jimmy didn't put me up to anything and I would never cause someone pain like I saw in your eyes."

Not willing to be swayed, after all she let herself be fooled once before by someone she thought she could trust. "I guess, I wouldn't know that since we really don't know each other." Carly tried to turn away again when the elevator doors opened again, but Jillian had a strong grip on her arm.

"No, we don't know each other, but I got the impression that you really cared about Jimmy, maybe I was wrong." She released Carly's arm, crossed her own and gave her a "Tell me I'm wrong" stare. "Am I wrong?"

A strong urge to lie to her consumed Carly, but she knew she couldn't. "You're not wrong."

A sigh eased from Jillian. "Good. Can we sit down?" She gave her a nod and the three women moved to sit in the waiting room chairs. Once they were settled, Jillian spoke.

"Sandy kissed him, not the other way around.

Carly gave her a skeptical look. "That wasn't how it looked to me. He was returning that kiss."

"In his sleep."

"Jillian, I may look naive, but I promise you I'm not…" Carly felt herself getting angry. *Why did people always think that of her?* She started to stand, but the touch of Karen's hand on her arm stopped her.

"Carly, please…Come back to the room and see for yourself." Jillian stated.

"You have to be kidding, right? I'm not going anywhere near that room or Jimmy Gates again. I should have listened to my instincts the first time I met him. Jimmy Gates is a player and I want to stay as far away from him as I can get."

The anger in Carly's voice surprised Jillian only to be replaced with her own anger and she sat back against the chair. She waved her hand toward the elevator. "Then that is what you should do if that is how you feel." Jillian climbed to her feet and headed back down the hall, stopped, and faced Carly again.

"You are wrong about Jimmy; he is a kind and caring man who I would trust not only my life with but that of my children and my husband, which I do everyday that they are working together. As dedicated as Jimmy is to his work, he is to his friends and the people he loves. You don't deserve him if you can't see the kind of man he is. So go ahead, walk away and hurt the one man that every woman dreams of meeting."

Jillian turned on her heel and stormed away leaving Carly surprised and flabbergasted by her outburst. She glanced at Karen and received a shrug of the shoulders. "I'm all out of advice. This is something only you can decide. Me on the other hand, would give the man the benefit of the doubt."

"How can you say that? You saw what I did."

"Yes, I did, but I also know that you are looking for any reason to run and hide."

"I am not."

"Yes, you are. You judge every man by your ex-boyfriend and how he treated you."

"No I don't." It came out between a shout and whisper. She wasn't sure how she managed that, but it's how it sounded.

"Oh yes, you do. You run from anyone that makes you feel; and honey you are so ready to run and get as far away from Jimmy Gates as you can get."

"That's not true. I…I…" Carly couldn't deny what her friend said.

"It scares you how fast you have come to care about him and so you want to hide away."

"I wanted to give him a chance, but I knew…" She let her words fade away.

"What…that he would break your heart like Mathew did or scare you the way Michael does?"

"Jimmy would never hurt me, I know that."

"Yet, you are afraid that he will break your heart. You said that the first night he was over, remember?"

"I remember." Carly slumped her shoulders and leaned back in the chair.

Karen leaned toward her. "What do you want to do?"

Carly glanced down the hall toward Jimmy's room. "I want to believe what Jillian said…"

"But…"

Carly straightened in the chair making a decision. *Jillian is right, I don't deserve him…but I will.* She stood, took a deep breath and walked back down the hall to stand in front of Jimmy's room. She knew once she opened that door and walked through that she was taking a huge step; one she wasn't sure she was ready to make, but one she wanted to make.

Jillian glanced up when the door of Jimmy's room opened and smiled when she saw Carly step into the room. She stood and walked over to her taking her hand. "I'm glad you came back."

"You sure you want me back?"

"Of course, I meant what I said to you, I was just hoping you would change your mind."

Carly watched Jimmy sleep for a moment then walked over to sit beside him. Rick stepped back out of the way then motioned for everyone to follow him outside. Carly sat beside Jimmy's bed holding his hand as she watched him sleep. She wasn't sure how long she sat like that; she only knew that the man lying in that bed was starting to mean way to much to her, way to soon.

"Hi."

She jerked her eyes up from staring at his hand in hers. "Hello, how are you feeling?"

"Great." He said with a smile.

"Really?" She asked tilting her head and crossing her arms – missing his hand as soon as she let go.

Jimmy gave her a crooked grin.

"Oh, no you don't Gates."

"What?"

"You're Trying to use that grin of yours to persuade me."

"My grin could do that?" He asked innocently.

Carly shook her head and moved away from him. "Gates, you are impossible."

Jimmy missed her hand in his. "So I have been told."

She gave him a half smile and walked back over to take his out stretched hand, loving the feel of it. "What am I going to do with you?"

Jimmy raised one eyebrow and sent her another grin. "I don't know, but it would be fun to find out."

Carly gasped in surprise as he tugged on her hand. She sat down on the side of the bed being careful not to touch his injured side. The smile she gave him sent his heart racing. He reached up with his other hand to touch her face. "I'm sorry our day turned out like it did."

She gave a slight shrug. "That's ok; it was a good day for the most part."

"Well, being here wasn't exactly in my plans for the night."

Her lips curled into a small smile. "Exactly, what were your plans fireman Gates?" Carly asked as she leaned lower.

Jimmy stared at her mouth remembering the kiss they had shared that night at her apartment. "I guess we will never know."

"Excuse me?" Carly straightened. "What did you expect to happen?" The spark in Carly's eyes made them turn even bluer.

I need to make her mad more often. Man, she is one beautiful woman. "Now, don't go getting your feathers ruffled. I just meant I wasn't sure what you would want to do."

"Oh."

Was that disappointment he heard in her voice?

Why do I sound disappointed? Because you are. Carly stood and walked to stare out the window. She studied the steady flow of people walking in and out of the hospital.

"Carly, is there something wrong?"

"Who's Sandy?"

Carly was as surprised by her question as Jimmy was, but now that she had asked it, she found she really wanted him to tell her. The fact she already knew was something he didn't have to know.

"Why would you ask me that question?"

The pain in his voice made her turn to face him. She remained where she was and answered him. "The woman on the boat."

"What about her?" Jimmy's voice turned cold and unfeeling.

"You called her sweetheart after she said your name." She glanced down at her hands. "Was that because you knew her?"

"I knew her once a long time ago." His voice lowered to almost a whisper; taking on a distant sound.

"I see."

Jimmy glanced back up at her. "How did you know who she was?" He knew the answer to that without having to ask, but he wanted to hear her lie to him. After all that would be what she did. Seemed he never could find someone that would be honest…

"Jillian told me." She watched him nod his head. "After I saw you kissing her."

"What?" He sat up and grabbed his side and waited for the pain to subside. He felt Carly's hand on his shoulder and slowly opened his eyes.

"I never kissed her."

"Yes, I'm afraid you did."

"I don't remember kissing her on the boat."

"It wasn't on the boat…it was here in this room."

As hard a she tried, Carly couldn't keep the hurt out of her voice.

"Carly, I swear I don't remember."

"I doubt that you would…you were asleep."

Jimmy gave her a questioning look, but when she nodded her head, he shook his. "Why would I do that?"

"Well, I would have to guess that she kissed you and you responded to her kiss."

"In my sleep?"

"It's possible…if you still cared for her, it could happen. You probably remember how it felt to kiss her and you…"

"I don't remember anything of the sort." His voice came out curt.

Carly shook her head as the truth of what she said hit her. "I think you do."

"You're wrong."

"Am I? I don't think so. As much as I want to be, I really don't think I am."

"You are…things between Sandy and I ended a long time ago."

"Maybe, but I know from my own experience that sometimes even when we try our best to forget, our hearts won't let us."

"What are you saying exactly?"

Carly took a shaky breath and slowly let it out. The last thing she wanted to do was walk away from him, but if he needed to find out exactly how he felt about Sandy – well – she had to give him that chance. "I'm saying…maybe you should try and work things out with Sandy."

"There's nothing to work out. She made her decision and we both have had to learn to live with it."

"Have you Jimmy - learned to live with her decision?"

"Yes, I had no choice."

"My point exactly. If it had been up to you…would you have let her walk out of your life?"

Jimmy moved his hand from out of under hers. "This is pointless."

"What is?"

"This discussion…things are over with Sandy and I don't want to relive them."

"I see…very well…I won't push…I…well, I just wanted you to be sure of how and what you are really feeling."

"What I am feeling now is aggravated at this whole conversation. Sandy is out of my life and I thought we…"

"Yes?" Despite herself, Carly found herself hoping and as she did, she waited for him to finish as she bit her lower lip.

Jimmy watched her bite her lower lip and gave a silent sigh. *Man, she had away of making him forget everything just by a simple act as she was doing now.* He reached out his hand and took hers. "Carly, I don't know where this thing between us will go or even if it will go anywhere, but the one thing I do know is that I want to keep seeing you."

"You do?"

Jimmy smiled at her child like voice. "Yes, if you do that is?"

"Yes." It was a simple, but straight to the point answer.

"Good. As I said before, I am not interested or ready to be serious, but I think we could have a good time."

Carly nodded her head. "I know you are right…"

"But?"

"No, buts…just I want to make sure that pursuing our friendship is what you want…not what you feel you are obligated to do."

"It's what I want Carly. I enjoy being around you. I…can be myself and I haven't been able to do that since…"

"Sandy."

He stared into hers eyes. "Yes."

Carly nodded and squeezed his hand. "I feel the same. Ever since Mathew and I broke up I have always felt…" She wasn't sure exactly how to say what she meant, but she needn't have worried because Jimmy finished her sentence for her.

"On Guard?"

"Yes!" She sighed in relief.

Jimmy nodded his head. "Yea, it always feels as if you are preparing for the worst and worried that you will care to much too soon or that the other person would."

"Exactly!"

Jimmy smiled that smile of his sending her heart into her throat yet again. "That didn't happen with you...something told me that it was safe to…"

"Let go?" She suggested.

"Yes." He whispered.

"It's scary, you know…to suddenly find yourself comfortable with someone again."

"I know, but I'm willing if you are?"

Carly smiled back at him then held out her hand. "Friends?"

"Friends." Jimmy said as he shook her hand. The door silently closed without them even knowing someone had been there.

7

Drafts of the upcoming project spread across Carly's desk; she let her hand slide across the papers to find her next set of statistics then jotted down a few notes. Her eyes drifted to the clock on her wall and she jumped to her feet. "I'm going to be late." Quickly, she rolled the documents and slid them back into the container and slipped them in the bin where they could be easily retrieved when she returned. The phone rang as she headed for the door and for one brief moment she considered not answering it. *It could be Jimmy.* Taking a deep cleansing breath, she picked up the receiver.

"Hello."

"Hi, beautiful."

Carly slumped against the desk. *When will I learn to listen to my instincts?* "Michael, I was just on my way out."

"Great! Meet me for lunch."

"I'm sorry Michael, I can't."

"Why not, do you have other plans?"

Relieved she didn't have to make up an excuse for once, she stated. "As a matter of fact, I do."

"With whom?"

Carly stood to her feet; irritation seeping through her body and into her voice. "A friend needs me to bring him home from the hospital."

"Him? Who is this guy? Is it that fireman?"

Carly bit her lower lip regretting her slip. "He's a friend, Michael, that's all."

"I don't like it."

Fed up, Carly tightened her resolve. "I'm sorry, but I really don't care if you don't." She bit her lip harder knowing that being so out spoken with Michael would only cause problems, but enough was enough.

"Carly, we are…"

"Michael…I don't know how many times I have to tell you that we are nothing. I consider you a friend, but that's all. I wish that you would accept that." Irritation replaced her nervousness.

"Never!"

Carly let out an exhausted sigh. "You leave me no choice. Please don't call here or at my home any more."

"You don't mean that!"

"I'm afraid I do, Michael. Goodbye." She hung up the phone and took an unsteady breath then she picked her briefcase up once more and headed for the door. This time when the phone rang she opened the door and walked out.

Release papers in hand, Jimmy waited patiently for his ride home. His gaze slid around the room at the familiar setting and he gave a low laugh. A small, crooked smile eased onto his face; if he thought of this surrounding as familiar then he had been in that room one too many times.

That smile was the view that greeted Carly when she opened the hospital room door. Her heart gave a flip the minute she saw him and she wondered again how a slight smile could affect her as it did. When he turned that smile on her and it widened, her heart took flight and she had to take several deep breaths to calm it down.

"Right on time."

The sound of his voice jerked her out of her thoughts and back to her present problem with Michael. Remembering their conversation from earlier brought back the tension she felt when she left her office and she gnawed on the inside of her lower lip.

"What's wrong?" The sudden weariness that appeared in her eyes alerting him. He moved to retrieve a tissue from the bedside table and winced in slight pain. He came to his feet slowly being all too aware of the stitches in his side, but stood anyway and moved to stand in front of her.

His sudden appearance in front of her made her take an uneasy step back and her defenses rose. *When had he moved?*

"What?"

"I asked you what was wrong."

"Nothing." She was unsure if it was kindness on his part or him trying to demand answers, so she flashed him what she hoped was a convincing smile to cover her irritation. "Why would you think something was wrong?"

"Oh…I don't know…maybe because you have bitten your lower lip so much that you have made it bleed."

Carly touched her tongue to her lip then jumped when Jimmy touched her chin. He raised an eyebrow at the flash of irritation he saw in her eyes, but continued to place the tissue against her lip. "There all better." As if to prove his point, he leaned down and kissed her injured lip.

"Don't!" *I wish he would stop doing that when I'm not expecting him to.*

Jimmy stared at her in surprise. "I guess I assumed that we…"

Annoyance snapped in her eyes. "Why do men always assume that just because a woman is nice to them that we are wanting more!"

To say he was surprised by Carly's reaction would be an understatement, but he also knew something had happened to cause such a reaction.

"I'm sorry, it won't happen again." It wouldn't either, not until she asked him, would he even attempt to kiss her again. If he had learned one thing from his experience with Sandy, it was to know when and not to risk his heart. He attempted to step away when she reached out and grabbed his arm.

"Jimmy…I'm sorry. I didn't mean that or to snap either." Tears brimmed at the edges of her eyes and her hand shook on his arm. He covered it with his own, but he meant what he said, he wouldn't make a move to kiss her until she asked.

"Forget it."

She blinked back the tears. "I am sorry… It's not you."

Jimmy nodded his head in acceptance and patted her hand once again. "I understand." He gave the room one more glance. "You ready to go?"

"Wanting to get out of here, huh? Carly gave him her best teasing smile.

Loving that she even tried to tease him considering the way her hand still shook, he gave it another pat. He returned her smile. "Ready, willing and able."

Carly noticed that his smile didn't reach his eyes, instead there was weariness in his expression and knew she was responsible.

Opening the door to his apartment, Jimmy stepped back to allow Carly to enter first then he stepped in and closed the door with a sold thud. It wasn't exactly a slam, but it was loud enough to make Carly jump and she spun around to face him.

He crossed his arms and arched his eyebrow.

"Are you going to tell me, what is bothering you?"

Swallowing the lie, she shrugged. "There's nothing to tell."

His stern expression told her he didn't believe her and she quickly glanced around the apartment to give herself time to think. The living room consisted of one steel framed brown leather recliner placed strategically next to a steel framed sofa, also made of brown leather. A glass, steel framed coffee table sat in front of both pieces of furniture with auto and fire magazines spread neatly across the top and a patchwork, fringed, area rug with brown, tan and burgundy, covered the dark hardwood floor of the living room while the window behind the sofa allowed the flow of sunshine to fill the room making it feel light and airy. A breakfast bar separated the two rooms from the kitchen and a hallway to the left of the living room led to what she assumed the bathroom and bedroom. A blush crept into her cheeks with the last thought.

"Carly?"

She jumped guiltily at the sound of Jimmy's voice. "I'm sorry, what did you ask me?" The lift of his eyebrow told her she wasn't fooling him.

"I asked if you were going to tell me what is bothering you."

"I told you, there's nothing to tell."

"Then why are you so jumpy?"

"I'm not."

Deciding that she needed to change the subject, she glanced around the apartment again. *There.* Carly walked to a picture on the wall of a man and a woman with a small child standing in front of a moderate, but nice ranch style home. "Is this your parents?"

"Yes." His voice low behind her made her jump and she realized he had once again moved without her hearing him. He touched her shoulder and a loving smile eased across his face. "My father is a Waupun Indian and my mother is white."

"Really? You look like your father."

"So I have been told." The smile dropped and he moved away, making her wonder what had just happened.

"Did I say something wrong?"

Jimmy shook his head as he eased down to sit on the couch, holding his side the whole time.

She rushed to sit beside him. "Are you hurting?"

"A little."

"Do you need to take anything?"

The concern he saw in her expression erased the memory that had come out of nowhere. Even though it had been years since he lost both of his parents, the pain of that loss could blindside him.

"No, it's not that bad."

"Maybe you should rest."

"That's ok, I have laid around enough."

"You will continue to lay around too."

Jimmy's eyebrow raised at her tone bringing a smile to her face. "What's so funny?"

"Seems I make you do that a lot."

"What?"

Carly laughed as she pointed at his eyebrow. "That - raising your eyebrow."

"Am I?"

Laughter bubbled up in her throat, making it impossible for Carly to speak so she nodded instead.

"Then maybe I should do it all the time if it will keep that laughter in your eyes." Jimmy teased, giving her a wink as well. The mischief she saw in his eyes made her heart skip a beat and she almost let herself believe things could work out for them, but the quick flash of

Michael's call that morning brought her quickly back to reality. The smile left and her eyes misted over and regret made the blue of her eyes darken. "I guess I better go."

"Whoa, wait a minute." Jimmy reached out to her with his left arm causing him to twist, a move he soon regretted and he sucked in his breath then let it out slowly.

"You really need to stop moving like that."

"I wouldn't have to if you would tell me what the hell is wrong." The look on Carly's face made him regret the harshness. "Look, I'm sorry, I should never have…"

"It's ok, really."

"No, I didn't mean to snap like that."

Carly gave him a smile. "Guess I owed you one from earlier." He smiled the way she hoped. "Jimmy, stretch out and try and rest, please."

He hated how she always seemed to change the subject on him and any other time he would have kept at her until she told him what was wrong, but in truth…he really didn't feel up to arguing so he nodded and did as she asked.

Carly stood so that he could put his feet up on the couch and reached for the pillow that was at the other end. *Funny, I didn't notice that before.* She placed the pillow under his head. *I wonder, how many nights he spent sleeping here?* She patted his shoulder. "You rest and I will make some coffee." Jimmy nodded his head and closed his eyes.

She made her way into the kitchen and realized she didn't know where he kept anything. "Jimmy, where do you keep your coffee?" Not hearing an answer, she walked back into the living room, finding him asleep. She stooped down next to him letting her eyes trace his features. His eyelashes lay long and dark against his cheekbones – which were high, an indication of his heritage – as well as his nose which looked to lean to the left slightly, making her wonder if at some point it had been broken. His mouth was slightly parted with a hint of a crooked smile. *I wonder what you are dreaming about?*

Carly cleared her throat and stood, reprimanding herself as she did. *Why are you staring at his mouth? That kind of thinking will only get you in trouble.* She walked back in the kitchen and as quietly as she could hunted for the coffee. Finding it cabinet beside the refrigerator, she placed the coffee in the filter and filled the back of the coffee maker with water then flipped the switch to on. Once she had it made, she checked on Jimmy again then glanced around the room.

What do I do now? My drafts, I can work on them while he is sleeping. She quietly took her keys from her purse then picked up his keys. Why she felt the need to lock the door behind her as she left the apartment she had know idea. It took her only a few minutes to get to her car; she reached in getting her case and then moved so she could shut and lock the doors. When she turned around, she ran into a solid breathing wall.

"Jimmy, I was only gone for a moment…" Her voice trailed off and fear raced through her. "Michael!"

"Surprised to see me?"

Carly pushed her fears deep down inside, squared her shoulders and stood her ground. "As a matter of fact, I am. What are you doing here?"

"I came to get you. We need to talk."

"We have nothing to talk about." She made to move around him only to have him grab her arm and pull her up against him.

"That is where you are wrong." He sneered the words at her, making the blue of his eyes snap.

The only other time she had seen someone that angry had almost cost her her life. Swallowing the lump in her throat, she shoved him back. "It's you that's wrong, Michael. I told you on the phone I didn't want…"

He grabbed her again jerking her against him again and twisting her arm behind her back. "I know what you said and I won't accept it."

"You have no choice."

The smile he gave her sent chills through her. "Again you are wrong, you don't have a choice. Lets' go."

"I'm not going anywhere with you!" Carly struggled to get away from him.

"You just keep making the mistake that you have a choice." Michael grabbed the back of her hair jerking her head back, bringing tears to her eyes. "Guess I will just have to convince you." He jerked her closer – if that was possible – covering her lips with his. The harder she struggled the more brutal he became.

"Let her go."

Michael jerked his head up to see Jimmy standing not two feet from him.

"You going to make me?"

"If I have to, yes." He glanced at Carly, stating calmly. "Go to the apartment." Carly was all too willing to do as he said, but when she went to move Michael tightened his grip on her arm. "I won't tell you again. Let her go."

Michael stared at Jimmy for a moment wanting to tear him apart, but there was a crowd starting to form and the last thing he needed was the police involved. When Michael released her arm, Carly almost cried with relief. She quickly picked up her briefcase and ran to stand next to Jimmy.

Jimmy nodded toward the apartment building. "Go on into the apartment."

"Aren't you coming?" Carly hated how her voice shook.

"I'll be there in a minute."

"Jimmy…"

"I will be there in a minute." The hardness in his tone left nothing to debate. Carly spun on her heels feeling like a child sent to her room. *Oh, you wait Gates, you just wait.*

Jimmy watched as Carly went through the door then he made a step closer to Michael. "I don't want to see you near her again, is that clear?" His voice deepened to a low growl.

"You going to stop me fireman Gates?"

"If I have to." Jimmy wasn't a violent man, but he knew that this guy wouldn't take anything serious, but a threat. "Are we clear?"

Michael's eyes narrowed. "Oh, we're clear alright."

"Good." Jimmy turned and walked slowly back toward his apartment with Michael watching him.

"Fireman, this is not over…you can count on that."

At the sound of the door opening Carly spun to face Jimmy, she had never been so angry in her life. "Don't ever treat me like a child again!"

"Maybe I wouldn't have to if you didn't act like one."

"Excuse me?"

"You heard me. Why on earth would you put yourself in that position?" His fear for her made his voice sound harder than he intended. And that fear and anger hook him to his core. *How could she put herself in harms way?*

"How was I to know that Michael would be there? I just went to get my drafts to work on."

She had a point there, but the fear he felt when he saw the way she was being brutalized still pounded through his veins and he wasn't ready to admit that to her. "Maybe you didn't know, but you knew something was wrong."

"How would I know that? I'm not psychic!"

"You have been jittery and jumpy ever since you picked me up at the hospital, so don't try and tell me that you didn't think he would show up somewhere." His voice sharp and low.

Carly dropped to the couch covering her face. He was right and she knew it, but she didn't want him feeling sorry or protective about her, she wanted him to want her, to love her, but she was too afraid to let him in.

Jimmy watched her shoulders begin to shake and he let out a slow breath knowing his anger stemmed from fear. He walked to stand beside her then slowly sat down. "Carly...I'm sorry...it's just when I saw him hurting you...I..."

"It's ok, Jimmy. You are right...I did know something could happen, but..."

"What?
"I started to feel...safe...so I let my guard down."

Jimmy touched Carly's arm causing her to flinch. "Let me see your arm."

"It's ok."

"Carly." His voice was calm, but insistent so she moved her hand and let him examine her arm. There was an ugly bruise already forming on her upper arm.

"Damn, him."

"Jimmy, it's not that bad, really."

"I'll be right back."

"Where are you going?"

"Just sit right there, ok."

When Carly nodded, he walked down the hall of his apartment, coming back a few minutes later with a wet cloth. She was surprised when he tilted her head back slightly and pressed the cloth to her lips causing her to flinch.

"Sorry." Jimmy felt the anger start to return at the swelling of her mouth. "I swear, if he ever comes near you again."

"Jimmy, promise me you will stay away from him."

He stared into her eyes. "I will as long as he stays away from you."

Carly lowered her eyes knowing the chances of that happening were slim.

"Why didn't you tell me?"

"I didn't want to bother you with my problems."

"I might have been able to help." He replied in a soothing voice.

Carly gave him a weak smile. "How, by coming to my rescue as you did now?"

"By making sure you were never alone." He stood and walked to the kitchen counter. You know that you can't go back to your apartment."

"I don't see why not."

"Are you willing to risk him coming after you when you are there alone?"

"Karen would be there."

"True, but she wouldn't be able to stop him if he decided to fulfill his threat, now would she."

"No, I guess not."

"Do you have someone else you can stay with? Someone he doesn't know about."

"No."

Jimmy pushed away from the counter. "Then I guess you will just have to stay here."

Carly came to her feet in a flash. "I will do no such thing. "

"Why not? You can have my bedroom and I will sleep on the couch." He raised his eyebrow. "Unless you wouldn't mind sharing."

"What kind of woman do you think I am! I can't believe that after what just happened you would..." Carly stopped her rant when she saw him starting to smile. "That wasn't funny Gates."

"You don't think so?"

"No."

"Then why do I see that sparkle in your eyes."

"I don't know what you are talking about."

"Really?"

"Yes."

Jimmy made his way over to her, making her step back a little. The back of her knees hit the couch and she fell to a sitting position. Jimmy smiled. *Maybe she isn't as indifferent to me as she wanted me to think?* "Something wrong?" He asked.

"No…no…of course not."

"Uh Huh…sure there isn't." He reached beside her causing her to slink away. "You don't have to be afraid of me."

"I'm not." She whispered.

"Could have surprised me." He said, picking up the phone.

She gave him a questioning expression which he ignored and dialed the number he wanted then waited for someone to answer.

"Hello."

"Rick, I'm glad your home."

"Jimmy, how are you feeling?"

"Pretty good. Rick, I need to ask a favor. Could you meet Carly and me somewhere?"

"Sure. What's up?"

"I'll explain when I see you. Ahhh… could you bring Jillian with you?"

"Sure, I'll see if we can get the neighbor to watch the kids."

"Thanks Rick."

"Where do you want to meet?"

Carly sat listening to Jimmy make arrangements for her. She knew that he was only trying to help, but it felt as if he didn't trust her to take care of herself.

 "I appreciate what you are trying to do, but I can't let you take over." She told him the moment he hung up the phone.

Jimmy stared at her in surprise. "Take over? I'm not trying…is that what you think I am trying to do?" Carly dropped her eyes from his. It wasn't until he sat down next to her that she made herself glance up.

"Carly, the only thing I am trying to do is find you a safe place to stay until you can find another apartment."

"Why would I want another apartment?"

"I don't know…maybe because some sick-o knows where you live." Jimmy stood up exasperated. "I don't know how to help you – you challenge me at every turn."

Carly stood facing him. "Maybe that's because you keep making decisions for me and not including me in those decisions."

"Well, I thought you would be happy for the help."

"Maybe I would be, if that was what it was."

"Of, course it is. Why else would I do anything?"

"To control me!"

"Control you!" Jimmy placed his hands on his hips, turned away and turned back. "Is that what you think…that I am trying to control you?"

"Why wouldn't you…you're a man, aren't you and that's what men like to do…Control…"

"Lady, I don't care what you do, but I refuse to let your stubbornness make you a target."

"That's my decision to make!"

Jimmy threw up his hands. "Fine! I give up…if that's how you feel, go I won't stop you."

Good, I will!"

Carly grabbed her purse and almost ran for the door. She threw it open, ran for the elevator, pushed the button then watched as it opened and closed. When she felt Jimmy's hands on her shoulders, she turned into his chest crying. "I don't know where to go?"

"Come on."

Jimmy guided her back inside his apartment and closed the door. He walked her to the couch and sat down with her while she continued to sob into his shirt. His hand ran up and down the back of her head in a soothing motion.

"Let it out…you have had a frightening experience and you deserve the right to cry."

His words just made her cry harder as she clung to him. After awhile, her tears subsided and she lifted her head in embarrassment. "I'm sorry."

"Don't be." Jimmy glanced at his watch. "I'll tell you what, you stay here and I'll go meet Rick and Jillian."

"No…you are right. I need some place to go."

"You sure, I mean I don't want you to think I am being controlling or anything like that."

Carly lifted her eyes intending to tell him what she thought when she saw the crooked grin he gave her. "Not funny, Gates."

"Really? Hummm…I thought it was." She gave him a slap across his arm and he laugh. "Why don't you go freshen up and then we will leave to met Rick and Jillian."

Carly nodded and did as he suggested. Twenty minutes later, they were sitting across from Rick and Jillian talking about what to do next.

8

Tiny squeals of delight filtered through the air as Jimmy swung Rick's daughter Jenny up off the ground and then into circles, his son Christopher jumped excitedly near by yelling, "Me next! Me next, Uncle Jimmy!"

Visions of Jimmy playing the exact way with their own children rushed through Carly's mind as she watched from Rick and Jillian's back deck and her heart pounded against her chest knowing that she had fallen head over heels in love with the man after only two short months.

"He's great with the kids, isn't he?" Jillian stated as she walked up to stand beside Carly.

Carly glanced in her friend's direction and gave her a smile. She had started to think of her as a sister. Jillian DeLaney with her brown hair and eyes, stood five feet five – the same height as herself – had a heart as big as the out doors, but could become - Carly had discovered - a she bear if she thought someone she loved was being wronged. Rick and Jillian were a lot alike in that way.

When she contemplated what kind of marriage she wanted, she knew she wanted a marriage like theirs. Carly let her gaze ease back to Jimmy who was now throwing ball with Chris. The hand on her back told her she hadn't answered Jillian's question.

"I'm Sorry, Jillian I guess I was lost in my own thoughts."

"That's ok…I used to do the same thing whenever I watched Rick with kids before we were married." Jillian gave a small laugh. "In fact, I use to imagine him playing with our kids and here he is years later doing that very thing."

A slow steady blush eased up Carly's neck into her cheeks. Jillian placed her arm around Carly. "Who knows maybe Jimmy will be playing with his own kids…it's just the matter of finding the right woman."

"I'm not that woman." Carly stated squaring her shoulders before she turned and walked into the house.

Surprised by Carly's reaction, it took Jillian a moment to follow her into the kitchen. "How do you know? Have you even given him a chance?" The slight drop of Carly's shoulders told her, her suspicions were correct. "I didn't think so. What I want to know is why not?" Silence filled the air and Jillian pointed toward the back deck doors. "That man has been over here more in the last month than he has the entire six years he has been Rick's partner."

"He hasn't even tried to kiss me since that first night he came to my apartment." Carly exclaimed in her defense.

"Excuse me?" Surprise clearly filled her voice as well as her expression. "Are you saying all those dates that you have been on he…never once…"

Carly shook her head. "I don't blame him; he's just not over Sandy."

"Has he told you that?"

"No…"

"Then don't start finding things that aren't there." Jillian walked to the door of the kitchen as she tapped her finger against her chin. "You and Jimmy have plans today, don't you?"

"Yes, he says he has somewhere special he wants to take me."

Jillian spun around with a huge smile on her face. "There you go!"

Carly jumped at Jillian's sudden exclamation. "What?"

"He wants to take you somewhere special. Doesn't that tell you anything?"

Despite the way her heart did a flip in her chest, Carly felt skeptical. "Do you think tonight he might at least kiss me?" A wave of embarrassment rushed over her at her words. *I sound like a teenager.* The next thing she knew, she was enveloped in a bear hug as her friend whispered, "Lets' hope so", in her ear. *At least I'm not the only one who hopes he does.*

Jimmy came through the kitchen door a few minutes later, gave Carly a quick smile and headed for Rick and Jillian's bathroom. "Just let me wash up and we can go."

"Now?" Carly wasn't sure if it was surprise or irritation she heard in her voice.

"Yea, something wrong?"

"I need to change."

Jimmy let his gaze slide over her; she wore tan shorts, a blue striped sleeveless blouse, and white tennis shoes and his heart did a flip and pounded against his chest, making it hard for him to speak. "You look fine. You might want to pull your hair back though." He gave her another smile, tweaked her nose then headed for the bathroom, leaving Carly standing with her mouth open. Slowly, she glanced at Jillian and saw the same surprise on her face.

Rick smiled and leaned to give his wife a kiss on the cheek. "You might want to close your mouth before you catch a fly." He laughed when she shot him a shut up look and placed her hands on her hips.

"You know where he is taking her don't you?" Jillian asked suspiciously.

"Of course I do, but I'm not telling." Rick glanced in Carly's direction. "You better hurry, Jimmy is anxious to get there."

Carly gave a slight shrug then made her way through the house trying not to hurry, but her heart raced in her chest with anticipation and her feet seemed to be keeping pace. She entered the room she shared with Jennifer, hurried to the dresser and picked up her brush. Her hand shook with excitement as she ran the brush through her hair and swept it back into a ponytail. A few strands fell along each side of her face, but not enough that it would warrant her taking the time to bush her hair. As she refreshed her make-up, she thought about the last month. She and Jimmy had been seeing each other every chance they got. One date particular, they had gone to the fair - thinking about that day still made her smile, they laughed so much her sides hurt for two days.

Her smile widened with the memory; he had recounted the rescues he and Rick had done on that very same Ferris Wheel. "Who knows maybe we will get caught up here." He had leaned in as if he was going to kiss her and her had heart stopped for a moment in anticipation when all of a sudden he moved away. Her heart skipped again with the memory of that moment and once again she wondered why he pulled away. There had been other times as well, like when they went water skiing and horseback riding, but he always changed his mind. It was a mystery to her, one she didn't know if she would ever discover the answer to.

"Hey, you ready?"

Carly jumped at the sound of his voice.

"You alright?" Jimmy asked in concern.

"I'm fine, guess I was day dreaming." Carly gave him a smile.

"Are you sure that's all?"

"I'm sure."

"Alright then, if you're ready we better get going. We don't want to be late."

"Where are we going?"

Jimmy gave her that crooked grin of his. "You'll see. Come on lets' go."

He grabbed her hand and led her out of the house. As they passed Rick and Jillian in the living room Jimmy stated, "Don't wait up."

Rick smiled. "We won't. Have fun you two."

Jillian shook her head. "Why do I suddenly feel old enough to be his mother?" Rick opened his mouth, but Jillian stopped him. "Don't you dare Rick DeLaney, don't you dare."

Rick laughed pulling her into his arms. "I was just going to say, you don't look old enough to be our kids mother."

"Sure you were, so why don't I believe you?"

"I don't know." Rick gave her a passionate kiss wiping all thoughts out of Jillian's mind except how much she loved the man she was married to.

"Jimmy, give me a hint."

"Sorry you will just have to wait."

Carly slumped in the corner of her seat.

"Sulking won't work."

"Jimmy, please give me a hint."

"Well…" He thought for a minute and smiled. "Ok…lets' just say that where we are going, you will really have a rocky time."

"That doesn't make sense."

"Guess you will just have to wait then."

Carly crossed her arms and mumbled under her breath.

Jimmy laughed and she stuck her tongue out at him which only made him laugh harder. Twenty minutes later Jimmy pulled off the road into a parking lot and she started to ask where they were when she saw Karen waving at her. She opened the car door and got out and hurried over to her friend.

Chip and Karen had started seeing each other after the boating day and Jimmy wondered if maybe things were getting serious between them.

Jimmy stepped out of the car as Chip met him. "Hi Chip."

"Jimmy." They listened to the girls as they talked raising an eyebrow.

"Are we sure about this?" Chip asked.

"Oh, they'll calm down once we get inside. Did you tell Karen?"

"No…Did you tell Carly."

"No and it's driving her crazy." The men laughed bringing the women's attention their way..

Carly crossed her arms and stared at Jimmy. "Do you know what they have planned?"

"No, Chip wouldn't tell me anything. I was hoping you knew."

"Jimmy would only say that I would have a rocky time."

"That doesn't even make sense."

"That's what I said."

"You two ready?" Jimmy asked as him and Chip moved to stand next to their dates. .

"Sure." The two women replied a bit reluctantly.

"Well, let's go." Jimmy held out his arm for Carly to take and she glanced at Karen as she placed her hand in the crook of Jimmy's arm.

"I thought you trusted me?" Jimmy asked.

"I do, but you are being so mysterious."

"That's what makes this all so fun. Lets' go before we are late."

Chip followed Jimmy's example and patted Karen's hand. "Don't worry, you will love this!"

"I'm sure I will."

"Trust me." Something told Karen she wasn't going to like what they had planned.

Jimmy held the door open for Carly and Karen to precede him then followed with Chip right behind.

"Keller, you are on my heels, back up." Jimmy whispered.

"I want to see their reaction too, Gates."

Jimmy smiled knowing the women weren't going to be too happy about the plans he made.

Carly stepped through the door. "No way, Gates!" Realizing exactly what he had in mind.

"Try it."

"You are not getting me to climb that!"

Jimmy looked at huge man-made cliff she was pointing at.

"Carly, didn't you love the water skiing we did?"

"Yes, but…"

"and the horseback riding?

"Yes, but…"

"You said you didn't want to try them either, but once you did, you were fine. You loved it."

"This is different."

"Why?"

"It just is."

"That's not an answer."

Carly stuck her chin out. "It's all of an answer you are going to get."

"Then you haven't given me a reason that you can't try this, besides you will be tied off."

"I will?"

"Yes, so you will be perfectly safe, I promise."

Carly stared at him for a moment. "Promise?'

"Cross my heart hope to…"

"Don't…please don't say that."

"Ok, I will be right beside you."

Carly took a deep breath. "Very well, lets' do this."

Jimmy hugged her to him and kissed her head. As soon as he realized what he did, he stepped back.

'Why does he do that?' Carly wondered.

Karen noticed the change in Jimmy too and looked at Chip for a clue. Chip's only response was a shake of the head.

Jimmy took Carly's hand and led her to the line that led to the cliff. It seemed like she had waited forever and it only made her get more nervous by the moment.

"Tell him you are afraid of heights?" Karen whispered beside her.

"No…this means too much to him…I can't."

Jimmy heard them whispering and glanced at them. "Everything alright?"

Carly gave him a smile she didn't feel. "Everything's fine."

"Next!"

Carly jumped at the sound of the man's voice. *You can do this. Just keep telling yourself you can do this.* They fit her into a harness then watched as Jimmy was too - somehow, it made her feel better. They walked to the cliff and she looked up. She squeezed her eyes closed briefly, took a deep breath, placed one hand one the bulge in the stone and then another. She concentrated on getting through each step, not hearing or seeing anyone including Jimmy. The next thing she heard was, "You d id it!" Carly looked around her seeing Jimmy smiling at her and realized that she had climbed to the top. She looked down, closing her eyes briefly again after seeing how far she was from the floor.

"Carly, are you alright?"

She forced the lump out of her throat. "I'm fine, but I'd really like to go down now."

"Sure, follow me."

Carly watched the way Jimmy worked his way down, taking deep breaths with every step she followed him down. *You can do this. You can do this.* Finally, she found herself on the ground then her legs gave out from the fear she had been holding back. The color drain from her face and Jimmy reached out to catch her just as she collapsed. He unhooked her from the rope and carried her to a chair near by. "Chip get me some water."

"On my way." Chip stated as Karen watched the tender way Jimmy stroked Carly's hair back away from her face.

"Carly, open your eyes." When there wasn't any response, he glanced up at Karen. "Why didn't she tell me she was afraid of heights?"

"She didn't want to disappoint you."

"She could never disappoint me." Jimmy responded lowly. Chip returned with the water and handed it to Jimmy along with a cloth. "Thanks Chip."

"Is she going to be alright?" Chip asked.

"She'll be fine." Jimmy wet the cloth and wiped her forehead with it. "Carly, open your eyes sweetheart." He sighed when he saw her eyes starting to flutter. "That's a girl."

"What happened?" Carly asked as she slowly forced her eyes open.

"You fainted. Why didn't you tell me you were afraid of heights?"

"I saw how important it was to you." She replied, embarrassed by the commotion she caused.

"Don't ever do things just because I want you to, I asked you if there was a reason you didn't want to try this. You should have told me then." Jimmy replied as he cupped his hands against her cheeks.

"I know…but…"

"No, buts, the next time you know something I don't, you better tell me. Understood?"

"Understood."

"Can you stand?"

"I think so."

"Well, lean on me when you do."

Carly nodded her head and did as she was instructed. His cologne filled her senses and did crazy things to her heart. She glanced up at him as she stood seeing something flash in his eyes. She wet her suddenly dry lips and watched as he leaned toward her only to have him once again pull back. *What do I have to do, draw you a map?*

Deciding that Rock Climbing was out for the rest of the day they headed for the nearest restaurant, then went for a walk on the beach. All in all, it turned out to be a very good day with only one exception, Jimmy still hadn't kissed Carly by the time they returned to Rick's house. After saying a quick goodnight, Jimmy went straight home, and go into a cold shower.

Michael stood back watching the scene in front of him and held his breath as he watched Carly climb the man- made cliff. *Why are you doing that? You know you are afraid of heights. If she falls Gates, you will pay.* He did notice that Gates kept an eye on her so he couldn't even be jealous when he reached out his hand to support her. *She doesn't look good. Hold on Carly, you're almost to the bottom.*

Her progress to reach the ground felt interminably long to Michael and once Carly was on the ground he sighed with relief, though it was short lived. The color drained from her face and she crumbled toward the floor. Michael took an instinctive step in her direction, only to see Jimmy catch her.

A small crowd started to form around them so he inched his way closer. Mixed feelings coursed through him at the way Jimmy tended to her, he was grateful, yet at the same time, he wanted to tear the man apart. The flutter of her eyes told him it was time to step back, the last thing he wanted now was to be spotted after a month of searching to find out where she was staying.

He ran his hand through his blonde hair sighing once again when she stood up. The concern subsided and the anger returned when he saw the way Carly looked at Jimmy. Michael's eyebrow rose slightly when Jimmy stepped back and his expression hardened, he thought Jimmy would have kissed her. *Why didn't you, Gates?*

A surge of hope raced through his veins. Maybe things weren't as great between them as he thought. Somehow, the thought made Michael feel better. Being extra careful not to be spotted - with his height of six foot - three, he wondered if that was possible - he followed them out the door. It occurred to him that being in relatively good shape - he worked out three times a week - he could easily take that paramedic apart. A slow smile eased onto his face when he contemplated the idea.

Lost in his own thoughts, Michael realized he almost missed them leaving and he hurried to his car, berating himself for his lack of attention. *I can't lose them…I have to know where she is staying.* Yet, losing them was exactly what happened. *Where did you turn off, Gates?* Michael wondered as he pulled off to the side of the road. *How did I lose you?*

He slammed the palm of his hand against the steering wheel. Stomping on the gas pedal he spun his car around, sending sand flying up into the air. The squeal on the pavement could be heard miles down the road. "I'll find you Carly and when I do you will wish I hadn't!"

Jimmy woke early the next morning, the events of the day before flooding through his mind. Splashing water on his face, he tried washing the memory away. Water dripped from the tip of his nose and chin as he stared into the mirror. "That was a little too close, Gates."

He reached for the towel hanging near by and dried his face, then picked up the shaving cream, filled his palm with the foam and applied the lather to his chin and neck. All the while Carly's beautiful face danced in his mind. He gave himself a mental shake and began to shave. Still the image persisted and his heart raced and a knot seemed to form in his stomach. When she opened her eyes he had never been more relieved and the desire to kiss Carly had been almost overwhelming.

"Ouch." Jimmy dabbed the towel against the small nick on his chin. "That's what you get for letting your mind wander." He scolded himself.

The rest of the morning was spent finishing getting dressed for work and forgetting how much the desire to kiss Carly consumed him. The only way he could distract himself from that thought was to focus on the other event of the day. Michael. When Jimmy left, he had made a point of getting as far ahead of the man as he could and taking a route he normally wouldn't take, leaving Chip to wonder what he was doing. What had him stumped was how did Michael know to be there? What Jimmy couldn't know, is rock climbing was a sport Michael loved and did on a regular weekend basis; blind luck had him there on the same day.

Rick stood in front of his locker, putting on his uniform shirt as his partner walked through the doors. "Morning."

"Yea."

"What's up with you this morning?" Rick asked as he stopped buttoning his shirt.

"What? Oh Nothing." Jimmy replied absentmindedly.

Before Rick could say anything else, Chip walked into the locker room. "What was up with you yesterday, Gates?"

"What happened yesterday?" Rick asked.

"Oh, Gates here - jerking his thumb in Jimmy's direction - decided that he would give us a tour of the city."

"Chip, it wasn't that bad."

"Oh no?"

"No."

"What happened yesterday?" Rick repeated.

"Nothing." Jimmy said as he dismissed Chip's statement.

"Nothing, huh?"

"That's what I said Chip, so drop it."

Rick turned to Chip, placed his hands on his hips under his unbuttoned shirt. "What happened yesterday?"

"Gates…"

"I'll tell him." Jimmy stated irritably.

"Good, then maybe I will finally know why I got a tour of the city along with Karen and Carly."

"Shut up, Chip."

"Is someone going to tell me what happened yesterday?"

"I'm telling you…just give me a moment."

"Get comfortable Rick, this may take more than a moment." Chip commented.

Rick smiled shaking his head.

"Do you want to know or not?" Jimmy asked irritably.

"Yes!" Rick and Chip replied at once.

"If you must know I was trying to lose someone."

"Yea, I know- *ME!*" Chip said as he poked himself in the chest.

Rick smiled again, but the smile soon left.

"It was Michael I was trying to lose."

Rick straightened. "Michael? He was at the cliff climbing center?"

"Yes. I noticed him when I carried Carly to a chair after she fainted."

"Carly fainted?"

"Yes…it turns out she is afraid of heights."

"She climbed anyway?"

"Yes."

"Why?" Rick asked.

Jimmy stared at his shoes feeling guilty and embarrassed.

Chip swooped in answering Rick's question. "She didn't want to disappoint him." Pointing a thumb in Jimmy's direction.

"Ahh…really?"

"Yes. You know Rick, I do believe Jimmy boy has found himself a future wife."

"I have not!"

Surprise covered both of their faces.

Jimmy waved them off. "Forget it."

Rick decided it was best to let that part of the conversation drop and hoped Chip would too. "How do you think Michael knew where you were?"

"I don't know, I stayed up half the night trying to figure that out. Rick, what if he knows Carly is staying with you and Jillian?"

"Lets' hope not."

"We can't take the chance. I would hate myself if something happened to your family because I asked you to help Carly out."

"We are happy to help."

"I know and we appreciate all that you have done."

"But…"

"I think it would best if Carly found another place to stay."

"Where?"

"I don't know!" Jimmy yelled as he threw up his arms.

"I do."

Rick and Jimmy glanced at Chip.

"Where's that?" Jimmy asked.

"With you."

"Not funny, Chip." Jimmy stated as he turned to get his uniform out of the locker.

"I wasn't joking."

"Chip, the reason she is at Rick's is because she wouldn't stay with me."

"Well, I couldn't blame her there."

"Oh, shut up Chip."

Jimmy started dressing as Chip continued. "I'm serious, under the circumstances that you offered."

"What circumstances is that Chip?"

"Well, you aren't married and that might have made her feel uncomfortable."

"Yea…what would be the difference this time?"

"You could marry her."

Rick dropped his head and groan. *Chip I am going to kill you.*

"Ha Ha…very funny."

Chip shrugged his shoulders. "Well, it would be one way to keep her safe."

"Chip, I am not getting married just to keep her safe."

"Ok, Ok…it was just an idea."

"A lousy one." Jimmy grumbled as he finished getting dressed.

"I was only trying to help."

The sound of the Klaxons stopped any retort Jimmy might have made..

"Saved by the bell." Chip mumbled.

Jimmy gave Chip a *We'll finish this later* glance then ran for the squad.

"Station 15… Station 116…House fire…2021 Klaxon Avenue.

 The crew of Station 15 pulled to a stop in front of the burning house. The second fully involved as they jumped out of the vehicles.

"Chip, you and Lambert take the front of the house. Gates, DeLaney, you both take the side of the house." Captain Stone yelled.

"Right, Cap!" They replied in unison.

Just as Jimmy and Rick were reaching the side of the house, glass shattered from above their heads spraying them with tiny pieces of glass. They glanced up as a woman stuck her head out the window.

"Help me, please help me."

A brief moment of shock washed over them as they wondered how anyone could still be alive in that. The next moment they were running for the squad and grabbing their air masks.

"Cap, we have a woman trapped on the second floor. We're going in to get her." Jimmy yelled over the noise of the fire and the equipment.

'What?" Captain Stone yelled in surprise as he looked up at the house. Seeing the woman almost ready to jump, he ran toward the house.

Ma'am, wait! The paramedic's are on their way up to help you."

"Hurry! Please hurry! I can't get out!"

"They are coming, I promise. Is there anyone else in there with you?"

"My grandfather was in another room. I don't know if he got out!"

"Ok, ma'am, hold on."

Jimmy and Rick ran toward the house with a ladder and Mike joined them to hold the ladder.

Rick went up first to help the woman out the window. As he helped her climb out the window, he realized she was pregnant. Looking over his shoulder, he yelled back to Jimmy. "She's pregnant Jimmy."

Jimmy shook his head in disbelief. *What else could happen now?*

Rick started to move with her down the steps when he heard a sound from inside the room. Evidently, the woman heard it also because she jerked her head up to look at the window. "My grandfather…"

Rick steadied her on the ladder as he moved to let her pass him. "Don't worry, ma'am. I'll get him."

Jimmy watched Rick as he headed back up the ladder. "Rick, it's too late!"

"I have to try!" Rick called back.

Jimmy's heart went to his throat as he watched his partner climb through the window into the burning house. "Please God, watch over him." Having no choice but to let him go Jimmy helped his victim down the ladder then over to the squad. He sat her down on the ground where he placed oxygen over her nose and mouth and took her vitals. He was listening to the baby's heartbeat when he heard a yell from behind. He looked up to see Rick lowering someone out the window.

"Grandfather." The woman sobbed.

Jimmy ran toward the ladder as Rick leaned out the window to slide the victim onto Captain Stone's shoulder, a few seconds before Jimmy reached his destination an explosion occurred. The force of the blast sent the ladder, Captain Stone and the woman's grandfather falling to the ground and Rick back into the burning room. Jimmy checked Captain Stone, and the victim over making sure they weren't seriously injured, while Max and Chip fought the blaze that now seemed to be everywhere then Mike helped Jimmy get the Captain and the grandfather to the squad. It was then Jimmy realized that Rick was still in the burning house. Leaving Mike to help the others, he ran back for the house throwing the ladder against it.

"Jimmy, it's too late! Rick couldn't have survived that explosion!" Chip yelled.

"I'm not leaving him! He wouldn't leave me!" Jimmy yelled as he ran up the ladder without his gear - having removed it when they brought the woman out. He climbed through what was left of the window, his eyes and throat immediately consumed with smoke, making speaking almost impossible. "Rick…" He yelled coughing. "Rick answer me."

"Jimmy…"

Jimmy ran to the other side of the room where the voice rose from. He stooped down beside his friend, coughing. "Come on partner, lets' get you out of here." Rick couldn't speak and he wasn't sure he could move; he hurt everywhere. Jimmy pulled him to his feet, and laid him over his shoulder. The groan that slipped from Rick's body told Jimmy how much pain his friend was in.

"Sorry, Rick." Jimmy whispered as he made his way back to the window. Mike was there to take Rick from him. Once Rick and Mike were safely on the ground, Jimmy climbed out the window. He had almost made it to the ground when there was another explosion. It sent him flying through the air and he landed soundly on his back. It was a moment or two before he could move. When he was able to climb to his feet, he looked back up at the room they emerged from, it was totally inflamed. He spun around and ran to help the victims. While the crew of engine 116 helped fight the fire, Max, Chip and Mike helped Jimmy with the four people on the ground.

Once all vitals were taken, Jimmy called Regional and treatment started for all involved. The worst of the four being the grandfather and Rick, both whom had suffered severe smoke inhalation, burns and head trauma. The ride to the hospital was a long one for Jimmy. His attention seldom left Rick's condition unless he was spoken to.

Captain Stone sat beside the young woman on the seat of the ambulance while Rick and the grandfather were stretched out on gurneys. He watched Jimmy as he kept track of Rick's vitals, yet never slacked on his duties toward the other person either. *That's what makes him a good paramedic.*

"Will my grandfather be alright?" The woman asked lowly.

Jimmy gave her a small smile before answering. "We are doing all we can for him. His vitals are good and holding steady so that's a good sign. Try not and worry, ok." When she gave him a small smile and nodded, he spoke again. "How are you feeling, any contractions at all?"

"No, I feel fine."

"Good." He gave her another smile then looked back at Rick.

"Will he be alright?" She asked.

Jimmy's shoulder slumped a little. He took a deep breath and slowly let it out before answering her. "I hope so." Seeing her tears, he touched her shoulder. "You sure you're not in any pain?"

She shook her head. "I'm fine. It's just…I don't know how to thank you all for what you did. Especially him…if he hadn't gone back in after my grandfather…he wouldn't be hurt now."

He reached out and took her hand. "Rick did what he is trained to do and because it's the kind of man he is."

"He must be a very special man then."

A slight smile eased across his lips. "He is."

The woman gave his hand a slight squeeze, surprising him. When he glanced away, he saw Captain Stone watching him and wondered if maybe he had let his professionalism slip.

"Rick will be alright. He's strong and has a lot to live for."

"I know Cap."

The rest of the way was in silence. It seemed to take forever, but in reality, it was a matter of ten minutes. After Captain Stone stepped out, he helped the young woman out, the grandfather next, then Rick.

They were each taken to separate exam rooms, Jimmy followed Rick and helped them put him on the table. He suddenly became overwhelmed with the thought of the times Rick had done the very same thing for him. He stepped back feeling helpless and useless. The fear he had forced back started making its way to the front and had to blink several times and take deep breaths to be able to breathe at all. He wiped his hands on his slacks wondering why they were suddenly damp.

Dr. Barrett and Daisy worked on Rick, putting in an airway then hooking up another IV. Jimmy licked his dry lips wondering when he was going to wake up from this bad dream when the sound of the monitor went off. He watched in horror as Rick's heart flat lined and Barrett was yelling for the crash cart! With each zap they gave to Rick's chest Jimmy jumped. He clenched and unclenched his hands, rubbed them on his pants then clenched and unclenched them again.

Jimmy wanted to run from the room, yet he knew he had to stay for Rick, knowing if the positions were reversed that Rick wouldn't leave him. *I'm here Rick, I'm here.* The sound of the monitor beeping again shooting a wave of relief through him. "Doc…will…he be alright?"

Dr. Barrett pivoted to answer the low spoken question. "His vitals are weak and he has had a severe head injury. The next forty-eight hours will be critical."

Jimmy felt as if his legs were suddenly made of jelly and he stumbled back against the cabinet that was behind him. " Are you saying he could die?"

"I'm saying the next forty-eight hours are critical. If he makes it through, then his chances will increase."

"Increase…which means he could still die after that."

"I wish I could give you something more hopeful, but…"

"I understand." Jimmy gasped out. "I better call Jillian."

He opened the door and found himself staring into the faces of the rest of station, including Captain Stone.

"How is he?" Chip asked.

Jimmy waited a moment before answering and then repeated what Dr. Barrett told him.

"Don't worry Jimmy, Rick will pull through." Captain Stone stated.

"Yea, I know. Look, I need to call Jillian. I'll be back in a few."

"Sure." Cap answered.

They watched Jimmy walk away with a slight slouch to his shoulders. It was going to be a long forty-eight hours for Station 15.

Jimmy sat at Rick's bedside with his elbows propped on the side of the bed and his fingers entwined. His chin rested on his hands as he stared at his friend who was breathing with the help of a machine. He squeezed his eyes shut willing Rick to open his eyes. The touch of a hand on his shoulder brought Jimmy to his feet and he turned on his heel to see Jillian standing behind him. The tears in her eyes brought them to Jimmy's as he pulled her into his arms. "I'm so sorry, Jillian."

She ran her hand up and down his back in a comforting manner. "I know, me too."

Jimmy pulled away. "I got to him has fast as I could."

Jillian's eyes rounded in surprise. "I'm not blaming you."

"I blame me."

"Why?"

"I should be there."

" Rick wouldn't want you to blame yourself. You got to him and brought him out. That is the important thing." She stared at her husband lying still and took a shaky breath. "He will be alright; he has to be."

Jimmy hugged her once again then sidestepped to let her sit beside him. She picked up Rick's hand bringing it to her lips. "Don't you leave us Rick DeLaney. We need you, do you hear me?" The slight squeeze on her hand told her he did. "That's right, my love. You fight your way back to me." She kissed his hand then placed it back on the bed never letting go.

"Jillian, do the kids know?"

"Yes, they are outside with Carly. I wanted a chance to spend some time with Rick before I brought them in."

"Have they been prepared for what they will see?"

"I did my best to explain it to them. I think Chris understands a little better then Jen." Jillian stared at the tube running down her husband's throat, the wires from the heart monitor attached to his chest and the Iv's in his arms. "How do you explain something like this?"

Jimmy placed his hand on her shoulder feeling the slight shaking of her shoulders.

"I can't lose him Jimmy, I just can't. He's everything to me." Jillian choked out.

"I know Jo, I know."

Jillian turned a tear stained face up at him. "Do you Jimmy? Do you understand how it feels to truly love someone? Do you know what it feels like to know that everyday when the person you love goes to work, you wonder if he will be coming home that night and being afraid of the day that you receive a phone call that makes those fears reality?"

Jimmy wanted to respond, but found his throat blocked with the lump in it. He could answer yes to all those questions. He loved Rick like a brother and he remembered how he felt when he lost his friend Daniel a few years back. He had seen what it did to Daniel's wife and now he was watching things happen all over again.

He thought of Sandy, the reason she had left him was because of the reasons Jillian had stated and there was Carly. Though he wouldn't admit it to himself, he was falling for her and that scared him. He looked at Rick lying in the bed with tubes running everywhere and knew he could never do that to someone else. It was better if he never married or had a family.

"I'll go check on the kids, let me know when you are ready for them to come in." Jimmy stated lowly.

As he turned to leave, Jillian grabbed his hand to stop him. She stood and wrapped her arms around his waist. "I'm sorry, I shouldn't have said that to you. I know how you feel about Rick and I know how worried you are right now."

Jimmy hesitated a moment before he hugged her to him. "It's alright, you are right, I don't know how a wife feels, but I have seen first hand what this job does to them." He kissed the top of her head. "I'll go check on the kids."

Jillian watched him leave. *Please don't push Carly away because of this.* She sank into the chair and watched Rick, his breathing was slow but steady, she could only hope that he would wake soon and smile at her with that smile she so loved. "Please come back to us. Please."

When the door closed behind him Jimmy leaned his head against it.

"Jimmy?"

He straightened and looked into Carly's beautiful blue eyes then reached out and pulled her to him.

Carly wrapped her arms tightly around him. The tears she had been holding back fell against his shirt. When he came out of the room he had looked so tired and worried. He still wore his uniform and she could smell the smoke that covered them. His eyes for the brief moment she had seen them were red-rimmed and sad. As he held her against him, she could hear the wheezing in his chest and pulled away so she could look at him; her heart broke at the sadness that filled his eyes. "Have you had anyone check you out?"

"What?"

"Have you been checked out by a doctor?"

"I'm not the one on a ventilator, Carly." He snapped.

He walked away from her going to watch the kids as they sat holding each other's hand. Something inside of him started hurting again as he slowly made his way over to the children. He pushed the pain he was feeling further down inside him. What Jimmy Gates couldn't realize at that moment was that he had found his hurt zone. A place he would shove all the pain he was feeling. As he approached the children, they saw him and jumped up to run into his arms, crying against his shoulder. Jimmy felt very close to doing the same.

Carly watched the three of them as he walked them back to the chairs. He sat down beside Chris and put Jennifer on his lap. Slowly Carly walked over to sit beside him while he tried to answer their questions. She could see the affect the questions were having on him, but he never conveyed it to the children. Instead, he was their strength and in that moment Carly knew that in loving the man beside her she had found her knight in shinning armor. She never wanted to let him go.

Jillian sat beside her husband's side, talking to him quietly, hoping the sound of her voice would bring him back to her. She was losing him, she could feel it and she wasn't ready for that to happen.

"Rick DeLaney, don't you dare give up! I will never forgive you if you do." Tears sprung to her eyes and she laid her head on his arm. "Please, Please I'm begging you...come back to me. You have to; I don't know how I would make it without you."

Jillian let her tears fall because she knew once the children came in she would have to be strong for them. Slowly she raised her head. "I love you." She kissed his cheek, stood and walked to the door.

The sight of the door opening brought Jimmy to his feet, still holding Jennifer in his arms as Jillian walked toward them.

"Chris, Jennifer, do you want to visit with your dad now?"

Chris came to his feet. "I do, I want to tell dad about our hero day."

Jillian smiled then look at Jennifer. "Jen, you ready?"

Jennifer tightened her arms around Jimmy's neck. "Can Uncle Jimmy come too?"

Jimmy started to tell her that it would be best if it was just her, Chris and mom to visit first when Jillian spoke up.

"Of course uncle Jimmy can come. He's family after all and daddy needs all his family, doesn't he?" Jillian wore an expression which told Jimmy she wouldn't hear of any arguments.

Jostling Jennifer in his arms, he gave her a hug. "Of course, I will come with you." Jennifer hugged his neck feeling better because she was scared of seeing her daddy with tubes in him. Jillian waited until Jimmy and Jennifer had walked toward the door before reaching out and taking Chris's hand. They started to walk away when she stopped. "Carly, you're family too."

Carly shook her head seeing the way Jimmy had stopped and straightened. "No, I had better stay here." Jillian took Carly's hand with her free one. "Nonsense, besides I really could use another friend in there." How could Carly refuse…she couldn't so she agreed and allowed herself to be pulled along.

Jimmy's back tensed knowing what Jillian was doing. Yes, she needed support and he wouldn't deny her that, but he also knew she was trying to prove a point to him. They all walked into Rick's room in silence. Upon seeing her father, Jennifer shoved her face into Jimmy's neck and started crying. Chris teared up, but didn't let them fall. Instead he straightened, walked over to his father and started talking about his hero day at school. "So Dad you have to get better. You have to be there, because you are my hero. You and Uncle Jimmy both are, but because you are my dad, you are even more so."

Jennifer cried harder, Carly couldn't hold back the tears at the sound of pride coming from Chris and Jillian held Rick's hand as she leaned down to whisper against his ear. "I told you, you were needed, but I forgot to tell you how much you are loved. Come back to us sweetheart, please come back."

Jennifer straightened in Jimmy's arm. "Put me down Uncle Jimmy. I want to talk to daddy too." Jimmy set Jennifer on her feet and watched as she walked slowly to stand by her father's bed.

"Daddy, it's me, Jenny. I don't have a hero day at school, but I don't have to, because you are my hero everyday."

Chris stuck his tongue out at his sister. Carly stifled a sob by hiding her face in Jimmy's chest. Jimmy sucked in his breath and Jillian just cried. After a few minutes Jimmy took the kids back out into the hall while Jillian stayed behind. Carly suggested she take the children home and Jimmy nodded his head in agreement. Before Carly left, she kissed him on the cheek and told him to call if there was any change. He said he would, but stood ridged when she left.

A wall was up now that he didn't intend to let down, not again. The consequences would be too great if he did. He turned to face Rick's room then fell into a nearby chair, letting the events of the day catch up as he cried silently and alone in the hall.

9

Stepping into the elevator at Regional Hospital, Sandy pushed the button which would take her to the ICU floor. Memories of her time as a nurse there coursed through her and she had to fight back the overwhelming feelings. A lot of the memories were of her and Jimmy talking over a cup a coffee on her break or a quick kiss as they passed. They were simple memories, but they still filled her heart with love when she thought about them. The moment she heard about an injured paramedic from station 15, she feared it could be Jimmy and that fear affirmed her decision to walk away from their relationship. Yet, the moment she learned the injured man was Rick, everything changed and her feelings for Jimmy rushed back and she knew where she would find him.

The elevator doors opened and there at the end of the hall was Jimmy, sitting with his head in his hands. She would recognize that man's form anywhere, after all she knew every inch of it. She made her way toward him and her heart skipped a beat; once in front of him, she laid her hand on his shoulder. "Jimmy?"

Jimmy jerked his head, coming to his feet at the same time, straightening to his full six foot one inch height. "Sandy, I…what are you doing here?" His thoughts ran rampant as he gazed into those green eyes he knew so well - ones that haunted him for months - he thought he could never forget them. *What is she doing here?*

"I thought you could use a friend."

Jimmy's eyebrow arched up. *It's as if she read my mind.* Why it surprised him he didn't know, she had always seemed to know what he was thinking or feeling, it was one of the things he both loved and hated about her. Still, that was a long time ago – *not so long ago –* and after what Rick told him about how she acted after he had been hurt, he couldn't help but wonder why after all this time, she suddenly decided to come back into his life. "I'm ok."

Sandy gave him that half smile she used to do. "Jimmy, don't try and use that line on me. I know you remember and I know when you are lying."

Trouble was she did know him, a fact he wished wasn't true. "Sandy…I appreciate your concern, but I really can't think about anything right now except Rick."

"Then don't think, just sit and let me be here with you."

Jimmy started to tell her that he didn't think it was such a good idea when the door to Rick's room opened. He made his way toward Jillian as she stepped out. "Jo, is everything alright?" Jillian glanced up, then fell into his arms sobbing. *Please God, no!* His heart thumped against his chest. "Jo what happened? Is it Rick?"

"Rick is holding his own." She cried into his shoulder. Jimmy sent up a silent prayer as she continued. "I just needed to get away for a moment. It's…so…hard…watching…him…like…that."

Jimmy hugged her tighter knowing that she needed to lean on someone. "It's ok Jo, let it out." Jillian cried the tears that she had been holding back since she heard the news. "I can't lose him Jimmy, I just can't."

"I know…I wish…I wish it was me in there instead."

"Don't say that Gates! Don't you ever say that again." Sandy yelled. Both Jimmy and Jillian could only stare at her. "I'm sorry Jillian for what has happened to Rick, I truly am…he doesn't deserve this and neither do you." Sandy stared at Jimmy with tears in her eyes. "Do you understand now why I asked you to decide? I didn't want to be where Jillian is now! Can't you see that?"

"I know why you left Sandy and I understand more than you think, but this isn't the time to talk about what happened to us. This isn't about you and me. It's about Rick and that's all."

Sandy took a shaky breath. "You know I thought I could do this. I thought I could put how I felt about you behind me, but I know now I can't. I love you Gates and I always will."

Jimmy stood in shock as Jillian studied the woman standing in front of her. Something wasn't right; she couldn't put her finger on it, but she knew something was off with Sandy's performance. Jillian shook her head. *I don't have time to think about this. Rick needs my strength.*

Jimmy, would you go sit with Rick while I go find Dr. Barrett?"

"I can find him for you."

"No, I want to ask him something about Rick's treatment and I'd rather not do it in his room."

"Sure, I'll go sit by him."

"Thank you." Jillian kissed him on his cheek. "I know he'd appreciate you being there."

"I wouldn't be anywhere else."

"I know." She patted his arm and then turned to walk away.

"Jillian, may I see Rick?" Sandy asked.

Jillian hesitated before answering. There once was a time when she would have gladly said yes, but now she didn't trust her because of the hurt she had caused Jimmy. She had a very bad feeling about Sandy's sudden reappearance. Still, how could she tell her no? "Sure, but don't stay long, ok."

"I won't."

Jillian nodded her head then glanced at Jimmy, he gave her his crooked grin and she knew he would make sure her wishes were carried out while she was gone.

Sandy watched Jillian walk away then followed Jimmy into Rick's room. When she saw Rick, her knees buckled and Jimmy reached out to and steady her. She hid her face in his chest letting the memories of days gone by fill her head. Wrapping her arms around Jimmy, she stepped closer. *He...looks so pale.*

"Yea, I know."

"I'm so sorry Jimmy, really I am." Sandy whispered against his neck before giving it a slight kiss.

Whether it was instinct or need to feel close to someone Jimmy pulled her tighter against him. The familiarity washed over him and he was transported back to another time. "I don't know what I will do if he dies."

"You can't think about that. You have to focus on him surviving."

"If I can't?"

"You can...I know you Jimmy, remember; I know you will find a way to help him."

"I may not be able to this time."

"Yes, you can and I will be here to help you whenever you need someone to believe in you." She kissed his neck again sending old feelings through him. He looked down into her oval shaped face with her red hair falling down around her shoulders and saw a woman with dark black hair and the most beautiful blue eyes. "I need you."

"I'm right here Jimmy. All you have to do is reach out."

Jimmy stared into her blue eyes. *Do I dare…what if she walks away like…*Carly wouldn't do that. She is everything he was looking for and he needed her strength now more then ever. "Carly…" He whispered just before he bent his head to kiss her.

There was a gasp behind him and he turned to see who it was, coming face to face with the woman he had thought he was kissing. He looked from her to Sandy realizing his mistake.

The pain in Carly's eyes cut him to the core and he reached out trying to explain, but Carly spun on her heels and left never giving him the chance. He started to go after her, when Sandy grabbed his arm. "Let her go. I'm the only one you need."

Jimmy pulled away from her in disgust. "I think you should leave Sandy."

"Why? I thought you needed me?"

"I misspoke. Please do as I ask and go."

"If that is what you want, but I will be around if you need to talk…or anything else."

Jimmy gave her a disbelieving look then went to sit by Rick. When the sound of the door closed behind him, he sighed in relief. He touched Rick's shoulder. "Hey partner, I really could use some of your advice, right now. So I need you to wake up, ok." When Rick neither moved nor opened his eyes Jimmy closed his eyes and said another silent prayer.

Carly ran from Rick's room as if it was on fire. Tears fell down her face uncontrollably. Her heart was breaking. How could this happen again? She wondered. *You are a fool Carly Gibson. You knew this would happen, yet you let yourself fall for the man. When will you ever learn?*

The doors to the elevator opened just as she reached it and Jillian stepped off with her kids in tow. One look at Carly told Jillian that things didn't go as she hoped. She hadn't lied to Jimmy when she said that she wanted to ask Dr. Barrett a question, but when she saw Carly with the children she decided to take advantage of the situation. Plus, it gave her time to find out how her children were dealing with their father's condition.

Jillian asked the kids to go sit in the chairs by Rick's room and waited for them to do as she asked then she turned her attention to Carly. "What happened?"

"It's not important. I'll take the children home now." Carly stated as she wiped the tears from her eyes.

Jillian grabbed Carly's arm. "What happened? Is It Rick?" Jillian knew it wasn't about Rick, the tears she saw Carly crying were tears of a broken heart.

"No…Rick is fine."

"Thank goodness." She placed her hands on her hips. "Then what is it?"

"Nothing, really. I better get the kids home."

"The kids are fine. Now tell me what is wrong." Just then the door to Rick's room opened and Sandy walked out. "Oh, I see."

Carly dropped her head. "Jillian, please…just let me take the kids home."

Jillian watched the way Sandy walked toward them. She was acting as if she had just claimed a prize. Sandy let the tip of her tongue run over her lips as she came to a stop beside them. "Just like I remember." She stated giving Carly a meaningful glance. Then she pushed the button to the elevator, stepping on when the doors opened.

Jillian saw the tears start again and put her hands on her hips. "What did that woman do?"

Carly shook her head. "Nothing."

"She kissed him didn't she?"

"I would say it was a mutual thing."

"I don't believe him!"

Jillian grabbed Carly's arm. "Come with me."

"No…Jillian…I can't."

"Yes, you can and will. Now come on!"

Jillian pulled Carly down the hall, stopping just outside Rick's door. "Chris, Jennifer I would appreciate you both staying right there, alright."

"We will." The children stated as one.

"Thank You. Carly and Jimmy will be out in a few minutes to take you home."

The children nodded and then looked at each other. "Mom's mad, Carly and Jimmy are in big trouble." Chris told his sister.

Carly saw the nod Jennifer gave her brother and groaned. *I didn't do anything.* Carly thought to herself as Jillian opened the door and pushed her through.

Jillian found Jimmy sitting by Rick's bed with his hand on Rick's shoulder. "Jimmy?"

He turned to face her, surprised to see Carly as well. "Everything alright?"

Jillian pushed Carly toward Jimmy. "I don't have time for this and I don't have the strength to worry about what is going on between you both. I need to concentrate on my husband. So I would appreciate it if you both would leave."

"Jo…"

"I'm sorry, but I don't want to hear it. Please, just take the kids home and work things out."

"We'll leave if that's what you want."

"It is."

Jimmy nodded his head, walked past Jillian stopping at the door. "I'll call later and check up on Rick, if that's alright?"

"That will be fine. Now please, take my kids home."

Jimmy nodded again and opened the door. He waited for Carly to precede him then followed her out. When the door closed behind him, he spoke. "I'll take you back in my car."

"Thank you, but I have Jillian's car."

"You can leave that here. Jillian may need it for some reason."

Carly agreed then walked over to the children. "Uncle Jimmy is going to take us home, you two ready?"

"Yes." They both chimed in together.

Carly held out her hands for them to take and the four of them left the ICU floor looking very much like a family. Jimmy picked up Jen and laid his hand on Chris's shoulder.

"Let's go home."

The drive back to Rick and Jillian's was done in silence. *The chill in the air could be cut with a knife.* Jimmy thought. By the time they pulled into Rick's driveway a half hour later the kids had fallen asleep, so Jimmy helped Carly carry them into the house. Once Jimmy made sure they were settled he headed for the front door. "I'll call to see if you need anything later."

"I'm sure we will be fine."

Jimmy nodded his head then walked out the door to the car.

Carly watched him leave and felt tears start again when she saw him stumble. She threw the door open and ran to him, putting her arms around his waist to support him. "Jimmy, come back into the house and rest."

He waved her off. "I'll be alright."

"Jimmy, please."

"I said I'll be alright!"

Carly stepped back, turned and made to head back toward the house, the grip on her arm stopped her.

"I'm sorry Carly, I didn't mean to snap. It's just…"

Fighting back the anger building up from the recent events Carly forced herself to give him an understanding smile. "It's alright." She turned to leave again, but he didn't let go of her arm. Carly glanced from his hand to his face and he slowly released her arm.

"You sure you are alright?" Carly asked, despite the anger and hurt she felt.

Jimmy nodded. "Yes. I wanted…to explain about earlier."

"You don't have anything to explain." She stated and stiffened her resolve.

"I thought I was…

Carly cut him off. "I really should get back to the children."

Deciding against trying again, Jimmy let the subject drop. Maybe it was better this way. If Carly thought he still had feelings for Sandy then he could spare her what Jillian was going through.

"I'll call you later."

Carly nodded and turned away, stopped and faced him once again. "Jimmy, try and get some rest."

He gave her that crooked grin she had come to love and reached up and touched her check. "I'll try."

Carly smiled in return then walked back into the house and walked to the watched living room window. His movements to slow as he stepped back into his jeep and her concern increased. When he leaned his head back against the headrest and pressed his palm against his chest she took a step toward the door. Enough was enough and she was going to make that man listen to her and come in and rest. The sound of his jeep engine brought her to a halt and she swung around to stare out the window and watched as he back out of the driveway.

The next couple of hours she spent trying to keep busy with one project or another, but all thoughts turned to Jimmy and her worry increased. Carly gave her head a quick shake and set the bowl of batter she had been mixing down with a loud thump. Why did she care? After all, didn't he kiss another woman? She waited for the anger and hurt to resurface, but the only thing she felt was her concern…and love for the man. There had to be a reason why he kissed Sandy. Yet, is there ever a good reason for him to kiss that woman?

"Carly Gibson, you have to be crazy. Are you really going to give that man a way out?"

She grabbed the bowl and began stirring vehemently which sent cake batter flying across the counter. Letting out a low groan she sat the bowl down and grabbed a cloth. As she wiped the counter the thought crept back into her head…*Maybe there is a good reason.* Wiping harder she shook her head and spoke out loud.

"No, there is no good reason."

Are you sure?

"Yes."

You sure?

Was she sure? She should be, shouldn't she? The problem was Carly didn't think she was sure. A nagging feeling that something more was going on. Doubt started to make it's way through her certainty. Maybe, she should let him explain? Slowing her swipes, Carly straightened. Should she trust her heart? It betrayed her once before, how could she trust it now? *Because, Jimmy is nothing like him and he may need you.* On that last thought Carly quickly dumped the contents of the bowl, cleaned and put everything away then hurried next door to make arrangements for the children.

Jimmy headed straight to the shower, stripped out of his clothes, turned the water on and stepped in letting the water wash away the smell of the smoke; wishing that it could wash away the guilt as well. Twenty minutes later he stepped out and dried himself off. He walked into his bedroom wishing the tightness in his chest would ease off. He could still taste the smoke from the house fire and his lungs were starting to hurt. He had been so worried about Rick that he didn't care about himself. After slipping on a pair of jeans he made his way back into the living room, stretched out on the sofa, adjusted the pillow under his head and closed his eyes.

The sound of someone knocking woke him and he sat up rubbing his hands over his face. At another knock he stood and walked to the door. Swinging the door open with the intent of telling the person to go away, he found Carly on the other side, tapping her foot impatiently.

"Carly, is everything alright?"

"That's what I came to find out."

"Excuse me?"

Carly crossed her arms in front of her. "Are you going to make me stand out here in the hall while we talk?"

"Oh, sorry." Jimmy stepped back allowing her in and the whiff of her perfume caught his senses as she passed. He squeezed his eyes closed for a moment, pushing the rush of feelings away.

The pillow on the couch with the indention in it caught Carly's attention the moment she stepped into the room. "I'm sorry, I woke you."

Jimmy glanced at her in surprise then saw the pillow. *She's observant.* "It's ok, I need to get back to the hospital anyway."

The slight wheeze coming from him was easy to hear. "Good, then you can get checked out while you are there."

"I'm ok."

"No your not, I can hear the wheezing every time you breathe."

"It'll pass."

"Jimmy…"

"Carly, I'm fine. I have inhaled more smoke than this before."

"I still wish…"

"I'm fine."

Carly's shoulders slumped in surrender.

"Thanks for caring though. It's nice to know someone does." He stated touching her chin.

"I'm sure Sandy cares." Carly hadn't intended to say anything at all, it just slipped out. "I'm sorry, what happens between you two is none of my business." Jimmy's hand dropped from her chin and he took a few steps away.

Carly watched the muscles in his back flex from the tension in his shoulders. Her mouth suddenly went dry at the thought of what it would feel like to touch his back. Again a flash of Jimmy kissing Sandy brought her back to her senses. She wasn't there to fantasize, she was there to make sure he was alright. Something must have showed in her expression because his next words caused her to catch her breath.

"I thought it was you." Jimmy stated lowly.

Carly jerked her eyes up surprised to find his back was still to her. "What?"

Slowly pivoting to face her, he repeated. "I thought it was you."

Carly shook her head. *What kind of idiot does he think I am?*

"As crazy as it sounds, it's the truth."

"Jimmy, you haven't even tried to kiss me before, so why would you kiss another woman thinking it's me?"

"You were who I wanted it to be."

"You know, I may look like a fool, but I'm not."

Anger replaced her concern and Carly took a step toward the door. Jimmy step in front of her stopping her departure.

"Have you asked yourself why I have never tried to kiss you?"

Carly shrugged her shoulders. "I thought you didn't want to." The words barely audible because her heart pounded quickly in her chest.

"How could I not want to? You are a beautiful and exciting woman." He placed his hands on her arms; feeling the slight tremble.

Carly couldn't look up at him, afraid he would see the need in her eyes to believe him. It was bad enough that she could hear the pounding of her heart much less have him hear. Placing one finger under her chin, he forced her head up. "I didn't kiss you, because I didn't think you wanted me to." A surprised look crossed her face, bringing a smile to his. "Do you remember when you picked me up at the hospital?"

"Yes.' Carly replied lowly.

"I was teasing you about biting your lip." Carly nodded. "I cleaned the cut on your lip." Again she nodded. "Then I leaned down kissing your lower lip like this." Jimmy captured her lip bottom lip and slowly pulled away. Carly absently licked her lips and forced herself to breathe evenly.

"Do you remember what you said when I did?" She could only stare at his mouth, wanting to feel them again. A brief nod was his reply. "You told me to stop and then went on about men assuming things or something like that anyway."

Carly vaguely remembered saying something to that effect.

"Do you remember what I said?" Jimmy whispered close to her lips. This time a shake of her head was his answer. "I told you it wouldn't happen again."

Really, he was going to use that against her, maybe he wasn't so different. "I wasn't myself! I had just gotten off the phone with Michael and he had…"

"Had what, threatened you?"

"In a way, he scared me more than anything." There was a mixture of understanding and anger seeping into his eyes. She could tell by the darkening of the his brown eyes. "I'm sorry for what I said…I never should have taken it out on you."

"I understand, I was just trying to do as you asked."

A teasing smile formed across her lips as she leaned closer to him and whispered against his ear. "If I asked you to do something now, would you do it?"

Jimmy's pulse quicken and his heart felt like it wanted to out of his chest from the pounding. He licked his lips quickly and in a husky voice asked, "What do you want to ask me?"

Letting her voice sound as sultry as she could answered with a quick nip on his ear then said, "Will you kiss me, for Pete's sake?"

Jimmy smiled. Two could play this game. He tugged her up against him, letting his form meld to hers.

"All you had to do was ask."

The allure of his half smile and the feel of his bare chest against her blouse weakened her defenses and the anger she felt when she arrived eased away. Her eyes clung to his mouth and she longed to feel them against hers. She didn't have long to wait. He leaned in and his mouth covered hers in a slow enticing kiss. She leaned into him letting her hands trace the muscles in his back. *I was right, he feels so good against my hands.* Carly let out a small groan of pleasure as his kiss deepened and a moment later was left wondering why he had stopped. "Carly, if we don't stop now then…"

With breath held, Carly shifted cutting off his words. "Who said I wanted you to stop." She whispered against his mouth.

Jimmy groaned capturing her lips once again, this time it was a more passionate kiss leaving her breathless and needing to be closer to him. When Carly moved closer – something Jimmy didn't think she could do - he swung her off her feet and carried her into his bedroom. He laid her on the bed then waited to see if she was sure it was what she wanted. Carly tugged on his arm until he was once again kissing her. Slowly, she let her hands run over his back bringing a groan of pleasure from him. They made love that afternoon with passion, desperation, and a needing to feel loved, and connected. While they were together the world felt right for a moment.

10

Carly lay wrapped in Jimmy's arms letting her fingers trace his chest and stomach. The tips of her finger touched the scar on his stomach and she raised her head. It wasn't the first time she had noticed it while they were making love. She had kissed it tenderly hoping somehow that it replaced the memory of that moment.

Jimmy watched Carly as she traced the path of the scar.

"How did you get this scar?" Carly asked without looking up or stopping the movement of her finger.

Jimmy could barley concentrate. *She is going to drive me crazy if she doesn't stop.*

"I was hit by a car."

Carly sat up straighter giving Jimmy a good view of her breasts. "When?"

"A year ago."

"This is going to sound like a stupid question, but…how bad was it?"

"I lost my spleen, broke my right leg and had a concussion."

Shifting so their bodies met Carly asked in a whisper, "What happened?"

Jimmy took a deep breath trying to remember to breathe, having to lick his lips before he could answer.

"It was about midnight when the station got this call. It turned out to be nothing, so Rick and I headed back for the squad. When I walked around to my side, a car sped up the road. The next thing I knew I was flying up hitting the windshield and then laying on the road."

Carly's hair fell down around them framing their faces like a curtain. "You could have died." The thought of never being able to be with Jimmy as she was filled her with sadness. She placed her head on his chest listening to the sound of his heartbeat. Turning her face into his chest, she repeatedly kissed it.

"Carly…do you know what you are doing to me?" He rasped out.

She raised her head just long enough to answer. "I'm making love to you."

Jimmy groaned as she began her sweet torture all over again. When he couldn't take it any longer, he rolled her over so she was under him and started an assault of his own, one that left Carly crying out in ecstasy.

Carly woke wrapped in Jimmy's arms and she let the memory of the past couple hours fill her. Finally forcing herself to move from his embrace she slid out of bed. An overwhelming desire to crawl back in beside his sleeping form surged through her body, but she had been away from the children too long. She released a soft sigh, gave him a tender kiss on his forehead, quietly dressed, walked into the living room, made sure the front door locked behind her and headed for the car.

Michael sat outside Jimmy Gates's apartment building waiting for Carly to emerge. It had been over two hours since he'd seen her go in and he didn't have any doubts as to what was happening inside. The thought struck him that she would never come out of the building when she appeared. Her hair was askew and falling down around her shoulders and her cheeks...her cheeks were flushed. His hands gripped the steering wheel wishing it was Gates's throat. "You will pay for this Gates. I swear you will." He stated.

When Carly started backing out of the parking space, he ducked down in the seat. Once she was past, he straightened and put the car in reverse. *I will find out where you are staying this time.* He watched her every turn and soon found himself in front of a nice ranch style house. The lawn was immaculate and there were rose bushes along front of the house.

Nice place, too bad you won't be able to enjoy it much longer. Michael opened the door, ready to sneak up behind her when two young children came out of the house next door.

"Carly!"

Carly smiled at Chris and Jennifer as they ran to greet her. "Hi you two, I'm sorry I have been gone so long."

"That's ok. Mom said you were talking to Uncle Jimmy." Chris stated.

Carly blushed knowing that wasn't exactly what they had been doing.

"Your mom called?"

"Yes, just now. She called to tell us Daddy's awake!" Chris said excitedly.

"She wants you to take us back to the hospital." Jennifer finished.

"I wanted to tell her." Chris yelled.

"You told her about Daddy being awake. I can tell her about taking us back to the hospital!" Jennifer yelled back.

Carly smiled as she placed her hands on their shoulders. "Alright you two…enough. Let me run in and freshen up and then we will go see your Daddy."

Chris stuck his tongue out at his sister, which she returned without hesitation. Carly laughed as she motioned the children to follow her.

Michael watched them as she went into the house. "Damn!" *That's alright I can wait until you are alone. Carly you better be prepared for what you have coming.* Michael threw the car in gear and spun away from the house. Now that he knew where she was staying it would be easier to get to her.

Hearing the squeal of tires Carly stepped back to the window and glanced out, but all she saw was a cloud of white smoke. An uneasy feeling crept up her spin and she absentmindedly ran her hands over her arms. She forced herself to move away from the window and headed for the bathroom to get ready, but the uneasiness persisted as she turned each spigot and watched the water spray from the shower head.

The piercing sound of the phone jarred Jimmy from his deep sleep – one he desperately needed. Groaning, he reached to pull the woman who made the need for such sleep to him, only to discover he was alone. He sat up thinking he had been dreaming when he saw one of her earrings lying on the floor. His lips merged into a smile as he remembered the earlier events. The sound of the phone ringing again brought him out of his thoughts. "Hello."

"Jimmy!"

"Jillian?" Jimmy swung his legs off the bed. "Is it Rick?"

"He's awake Jimmy and he's off the ventilator!"

"I'm on my way. Does Carly know?"

"I thought she was with you."

"She was until a little while ago."

"Well, I'm sure she is on her way home. The kids will tell her when she gets there."

"I'll give her a call anyway."

"Good."

"Tell that partner of mine I will see him in a little while."

"I will."

"Bye."

"Bye."

Jimmy hung up the phone just to pick it back up. Chris answered the phone after the second ring. "Hello."

"Chris, it's Uncle Jimmy."

"Uncle Jimmy! Daddy's awake! He told mom to tell me he would be at my hero day!"

"So I heard. Chris is Carly home?"

"She's in the shower as soon as she is ready we will go see Dad."

"Tell Carly I will come get you all and we can go together."

"Ok. Bye Uncle Jimmy." Chris hung up before Jimmy could say anything else.

Jimmy laughed as he hurried into the bathroom. It was turning out to be a really good day despite how it began. A sudden feeling of dread coursed through him. Dismissing it, he jumped in the shower. An hour later he was on his way to pick up Carly and the kids. He smiled liking the sound of Carly and the kids. *Who knows Gates, you just could handle being married.* With that thought, he pulled into the driveway of his partners home and watched Chris, Jennifer and Carly walk toward him. The smile that Carly gave him sent his heart racing. *Yup, maybe marriage wouldn't be so bad.*

Jimmy pushed open the door to Rick's hospital room allowing Chris and Jennifer to enter first. They ran to their father's bed both talking at the same time. Rick gave his children a small smile and tried to pay attention to what they were saying, but the medicine they gave him was making it difficult. His throat hurt from the airway tube they had taken out and it made his voice sound raspy.

Jillian put her hands on Chris and Jennifer's shoulders. "Easy kids…Daddy is still very sick so we have to be careful when we are around him. Alright?"

Chris and Jen nodded their heads. "Can I ask Dad about hero day at school?" Chris whispered.

Rick reached out and took his son's hand. "I wouldn't miss it, Chris."

Chris gave his father a big smile. "I told everyone you wouldn't."

"You bet I wouldn't." Rick turned his attention to Jennifer. "I'm glad I'm your hero, Jen bug."

"Dad!" Jen said as she stomped her foot.

"Oh, yea...forgot."

Jimmy stood back watching the scene in front of him and reached out to put his arm around Carly's waist drawing her next to him. When she placed her arm around his in return he smiled at her, giving her waist a squeeze. Rick glanced up to see the way Jimmy smiled at Carly. "Guess you don't need my advice now, huh Junior."

Surprised at Rick's statement he went to stand by his bed. "You heard what I said?"

"Yea, just like I heard Chris and Jen." Rick glanced at Carly and smiled.

"Don't let him get too happy, I wouldn't know how to handle the change."

"I won't, I promise." Carly teased.

"Ha. Ha. Very funny."

Rick gave Jimmy a small smile then closed his eyes. Jimmy instinctively placed his hand on Rick's chest then sighed. *He's resting.*

Carly saw the fear cross Jimmy's face and placed her hand on his back. He gave her a slight smile then moved so Jillian could sit by Rick. "I think we should let Jillian and the kids spend some quiet time alone with Rick. Want to take a walk with me?"

Slipping her hand around his arm she smiled. "I would love too." Carly glanced over at

Jillian. "That is unless you want us to take the kids so you can be alone with Rick?"

Jillian smiled. "No, you two go on. In fact I will take the children home myself." When they started to protest she raised her hand to quiet them.

"I want to, my kids need to know I feel comfortable leaving their dad alone. It will give them some kind of reassurance that he is going to be alright. You two go get some dinner, see a movie, relax."

"I don't know Jillian. I wouldn't feel right about…" Jimmy began.

"Jimmy Gates, if you don't do as I ask right this minute I will bar you from this room all together!"

Jimmy knew Jillian wouldn't do such a thing, but he nodded his head. "Very well…"

Squeezing Carly's hand, he said, "Come on, we better get before she calls security on us."

Carly gave Jillian a hug. "Call, if you need us."

"I will."

Carly nodded then took Jimmy's hand in hers. "Guess we better get out of here."

Jimmy nodded waved goodbye to the kids, gave Rick one more look over to assure himself he would be alright while he was gone, then led Carly out the door coming face to face with Sandy. Carly defenses rose as well as her instinct to protect Jimmy kicked in. Someone else would say she was guarding her territory, but there was something about the woman standing in front of her that she didn't like or trust.

"Jimmy…I heard Rick was awake." Sandy stated.

"He is, but Jillian and the kids are in there with him. I thought they could use some family time together." Jimmy replied coldly.

"Well, I wouldn't want to intrude then. "Sandy flipped her hair back away from her shoulder and stepped closer to him. "I have an idea…why don't we go back to your place and we can pick up from where we left off earlier." She gave Carly a heated glance. "You know, before we were interrupted."

Carly stepped between Jimmy and Sandy, letting her know in no uncertain terms whom Jimmy would be going home with.

"I'm afraid the only person here Jimmy will be going home with is me."

Sandy's eyes flared with hatred, but her voice sounded sickly sweet. "Really? I had the impression from the way you took off before that you didn't have anything to say to him."

Carly stepped closer. "We have worked things out."

Jimmy could only stare in surprise and amusement at how Carly defended her territory. He stepped back and leaned an elbow on the wall resting his head against his fist. *This could get interesting. Come on, Carly, you can take her.* He was male enough to love watching two women fight over him.

Sandy's eyes narrowed. "I see and exactly how did you work things out?"

Carly stepped closer to Sandy. "That is none of your business."

"I think it is."

The smile Carly gave Sandy was far from a friendly one. "You gave up the right to know what Jimmy does and whom he does it with when you made him chose between you and his job."

Jimmy straightened. *How did you know about that?*

"How dare you?!" Sandy snarled.

"I dare because I care about Jimmy. I would never ask him to choose between me and the job he loves."

Sandy's fist clenched and unclenched. "Really?"

"Really."

Sandy started to take another step toward her, but stopped. "Lets see how long you stick to that belief when you are watching him lying in a room like Rick is fighting for his life." Sandy leaned closer. "You won't last an hour when that happens and when you take off, I will be the one to pick up the pieces."

Carly's shoulders straightened. "That's where you are wrong. You see I know what it is like to watch someone suffer and I am a lot stronger than I look. The day that I let you any where near Jimmy again is the day they bury me."

Sandy's smile sent chills through Carly. "Not like that can't be arranged."

Jimmy moved to stand by Carly. "That's enough Sandy, I won't stand here and let you threaten Carly."

Sandy stared at him in surprise. "I wasn't threatening anyone, Jimmy. I was simply stating a fact. No one knows from day to day what could happen."

Jimmy's cool demeanor changed to anger. "I'm warning you, if anything happens to Carly…ever…I will see you are punished."

Sandy gave him a sweet smile. "My, My, aren't you protective." She gave Carly a disgusted look. "She must really be good in the sack."

"Enough!" Jimmy yelled.

Carly placed her hand on his arm. "It's ok Jimmy." Turning her attention at Sandy again, she stated. "If you will excuse us, we have plans to keep."

Carly tugged on Jimmy's arm getting him to walk away.

"Just remember…I know him very well. Isn't that right Jimmy?" Sandy smirked.

Jimmy stopped only to have Carly pull on his arm. When he glanced down, she gave her head a shake. Jimmy knew it was best to walk away, but something told him that Sandy's threat was just that…a threat. He wrapped his arm around Carly's waist and held her against him as they waited for the elevator doors to open. As he gazed at the top of her heard, he wasn't sure which emotion was running the hardest… pride at seeing Carly stand up for herself or anger because Sandy had threatened her. They stepped into the elevator and Jimmy turned to face the doors seeing Sandy staring at them. His arm tightened around Carly's waist. This isn't over, not by a long shot. The doors closed and Jimmy never saw the look of hatred that crossed Sandy's face. "You will pay, I swear Carly you will pay."

Jimmy drove back to his apartment in silence. His mind kept replaying Sandy's words. He glanced over at Carly; her hair blew back from her face from the open window as she stared somberly out it. He reached over taking her hand and she turned to face him. gave him a small smile then returned her attention to the passing view.

Carly's mind played over her words to Sandy. *I know what it is to watch someone suffer. Why did I say that?* The face of her younger brother appeared before her. "Tommy."

"Did you say something?"

Carly jerked her head toward Jimmy. "What?"

"I thought you said something."

Carly looked back out the window as Jimmy's apartment building came into view. "It was nothing."

Jimmy saw the sadness that crossed her face. "Carly…"

"Jimmy, please…"

"Ok." He said with a nod.

Carly smiled her thanks as she opened the door to step out of the car. Feeling Jimmy's hand on her arm she stopped to look at him. "Don't worry about Sandy's threat. I won't let anything happen to you."

She gave him a smile. "I know you won't, but I'm not worried about what Sandy said." At his raised eyebrow, she smiled again. "Really, I'm not."

Jimmy gave her a slight smile then opened the door to get out. He met Carly at the front of his Land Rover, took her hand in his and they walked into his apartment building. Neither seeing the gun trained on them.

Jillian sat watching her husband sleep as the kids sat quietly beside her reading a book they thought their dad would like to hear. She listened to the sound of their voices as they took turns reading to Rick. Jillian knew she should take the kids home, but she couldn't bring herself to leave. Maybe, it was the reassurance he was really getting better she needed, but something told her it was more than that.

"Jimmy, watch out!"

The kids stopped reading and stared at their father in surprise. Jillian jumped to her feet and sat on the side of the bed all at one time. She hugged Rick to her and whispered into his ear. "It's alright, Rick. It was a dream."

Rick leaned back against his pillow seeing the fear on his kids face. "I'm sorry guys, Daddy just had a bad dream." He rasped out.

Chris and Jennifer looked up to their mother for conformation. When she gave them the nod they were looking for they settled back in their chairs, but didn't start reading again.

Rick turned his attention to Jillian. "Call Jimmy for me."

"Rick... he is probably out with Carly somewhere."

"Please Jillian, I need to talk to him." There was a pleading in her husband's voice she hadn't heard since Jimmy had been hit by that car. "Ok Rick, if that will make you feel better.'

"It will."

Jillian reached for the phone by Rick's bed and dialed Jimmy's number. A couple of rings later there was an answer on the other end.

"Hello."

"Jimmy?"

"Jillian, what's wrong? Is it Rick?"

"Rick's fine, he just wanted to talk to you for a minute."

"Sure."

"Jimmy?"

"Yea, Rick. Are you alright?"

"I was going to ask you that?"

"I'm fine, why?"

"Just a feeling I had. Is Carly alright?"

"She's fine, she's standing here next to me."

"May I talk to her?"

"Sure, hold on a minute ok." Jimmy reached the phone out to Carly. "Rick wants to talk to you."

She took the receiver. "Hello."

"Carly, watch out for Jimmy, ok." Rick said.

"Of course."

"You have him watch out for you too, ok."

Uneasiness filled her with his words, but she agreed. Silence so followed then she heard Jillian's voice.

"He's gone back to sleep."

"Is everything alright, Jillian?"

"I think he had a bad dream about Jimmy. He will be fine now that he heard his voice."

"Jillian, do you want me to come back to the hospital and take the kids back to the house?"

"No, don't be silly. You and Jimmy spend some time together. I will take the children home in awhile."

"You sure."

"Yes, now you and Jimmy relax. Rick is going to be fine."

"Alright, if you're sure?"

"I am. Would you put Jimmy back on the phone please?"

"Call if you need us."

"I will."

Carly handed the phone back to Jimmy. "Jillian wants to talk to you."

"Jillian?"

"Jimmy, take care of each other and be careful, ok."

"We will."

"Good. I will let you go. Tell Carly not to worry, ok. If I know her, she is biting her lower lip about now."

Jimmy glanced over at Carly and smiled. "You would win that bet."

Jillian laughed and said a final goodbye then hung up the phone.

Carly watched Jimmy as he slowly hung up. She could see the concern on his face. "Is Rick really alright?"

Jimmy straightened and went to stand in front of her. He ran his thumb over her bottom lip and then kissed it tenderly. "You really have to stop biting your lip, you know."

"What?" Carly had become distracted by his kiss. Shaking her head then giving him a shove. "Don't change the subject."

"I didn't think I did."

"Well, my biting my lower lip has nothing to do with Rick."

Jimmy raised his eyebrow. "Really, then why were you biting your lip."

"It's a habit. I can't help it." She stated as she moved away from him.

"Sure you can. You can stop any habit, if you want to enough."

"Really?" It was Carly turn to raise an eyebrow.

"Sure."

"Why don't you take your own advice?"

"What are you talking about? I don't bite my lower lip."

"No, but you flip your nails."

Excuse me? When have I ever done that?"

"When you were at the hospital waiting on news about Rick."

"I did no such thing."

"You did too. You did it so much so that I finally couldn't take it anymore and I held your hand."

Jimmy's eyes rounded. "I thought you were holding my hand because you were trying to be there for me."

"Well, that too, but…"

Jimmy held up his hand. "Never mind, you don't have to explain."

"Jimmy…"

"Maybe I had better take you home."

Carly's eyes teared up. "I don't have a home, remember."

Jimmy started to correct her, but stopped. "I'm sorry Carly. I didn't mean for this to turn into a fight."

"Didn't you?"

"No, I…well it's…you see when Rick…"

Carly walked to stand in front of him, placed her finger on his lips. "That's another habit you have...never knowing when you'd better stop talking." She reached up, kissed him as she wrapped her arms around his neck. Jimmy hesitated before giving into her kiss then he swung her off her feet and carried her to the sofa. Where he promptly sat her down and pulled away. The surprise, disappointment on her face was almost his undoing, but they had a few more things they needed to clear up before they could be distracted.

"I need to have you answer a couple of questions."

"Now?"

"Now."

If the expression on Jimmy's face hadn't been enough to convince her he was serious, the fact that he walked to the other side of the room sure did.

"Ok, what questions do you need answers to?"

Jimmy stared at the picture of his parents wondering if he would ever find the kind of love they had. He had thought he had with Sandy, but that turned out to be the worst mistake he could make. Now Carly was in his life and he was finding out that she was keeping things from him. Things that she shouldn't even know yet.

"Jimmy?"

Jimmy jumped at the sound of her voice so close beside him. He needed distance, so he walked away to stand near the sofa.

Carly took a step toward him.

"Don't. Please don't come near me right now."

"Jimmy I…"

"How did you know what Sandy asked me to do?" He asked as he stared out the bay window. When there was silence, he slowly turned to face her.

Carly took a step back from the betrayal she saw in his eyes.

His voice was low, but firm when he repeated his question. "How did you know what Sandy asked me to do?"

Carly swallowed and then straightened her shoulders. "Jillian told me."

"That's what I thought."

"She only said something because she didn't want to see you hurt again."

"Yea, I know." He mumbled.

"Jillian, thought I would hurt you."

"That doesn't even make sense."

"Yes, it does, you have to understand her reasons."

"What reason could she have of telling you something that I should have?" When Carly didn't answer, he answered his own question. "It's a woman thing, I know."

"You couldn't be any more wrong."

"Then why? You tell me why she told you about me and Sandy."

"Be fair Jimmy, you knew she told me about Sandy."

"Yea, but you didn't tell me she told you how it ended."

"No, and for that I am sorry. She really did have a good reason for telling me."

"Yea, I know…she didn't want to see me hurt."

"She knew I was about to walk away."

Jimmy spun to face her. "What?"

"That's right. When you were hurt after rescuing Sandy, I wasn't sure I could deal with the job you had. Jillian saw that when we first met. I guess she decided it was better if she told me than watch you get hurt for the same reason all over again. It was her way of protecting you."

"You were going to walk away?" Pain etched his voice.

"I thought about it."

"Why didn't you?"

"I didn't want to hurt you either and…"

"So you stayed out of pity."

"No! I would never do that."

"You just said…"

"I said I didn't want to hurt you and that's true, but I didn't want to hurt me either. It was our first date Jimmy, but even then I knew you were special. I wanted a chance to see where we would go, if we could make it together."

"You hated what I do for a living though."

"I didn't hate it and I don't hate it. To be honest I did think about asking you to find another job, but after what Jillian told me, I knew I couldn't."

"Because you knew that Sandy had already asked me."

"Because I didn't want you to choose your job over me and I knew you would."

"Same thing."

"No, Jimmy it isn't –well not in the way you think."

"How's that?"

"Sandy was only thinking about what she wanted, not what you wanted or needed."

"You were?"

"Yes. I didn't know you well, but I learned how important your job is to you. I saw how hard you tried to save that boy." Carly walked to stand beside him. "I know the kind of man you are and that this is the job that you have to do. I didn't walk away because I knew I would be the one I hurt."

Jimmy looked at her uncertainly. "I don't know Carly."

"That's ok too. I should have told you I knew. I was just afraid that you would use it as a reason to push me away."

How could she know me so well? He raised his hand to touch her check. "I probably would have."

Carly took a deep breath and slowly let it out. "And now? Will you push me away because you know?"

Jimmy pulled her into his arms and a second later heard the shattering of glass; Carly slumped against him. "Carly?"

"Jimmy?"

"Carly, are you alright?"

"I think so." Carly went to stand when a slicing pain went through her side. Looking down she found her side drenched in blood and she glanced up at Jimmy in confusion, seeing the horror cross his face as her eyes closed.

"Carly! Oh, God…Carly talk to me." Jimmy eased her to the floor grabbing the closest thing he could find, the pillow he used earlier. He covered her wound giving as much pressure as he could to stop the bleeding. He looked at the phone on the table knowing he had to keep the pressure going, but needing to get to the phone. Making the only choice he could he kissed her forehead. "Hang on Carly. I'll be right back, I promise."

Jimmy climbed to his feet and grabbed the phone dialing dispatches number. When he had that completed, he hung up and called Regional as he ran to get his emergency bag from his closet then returned the pressure to Carly's side.

"Come on, answer the phone." Jimmy demanded while he took Carly's vitals.

"Regional nurses station."

"Regional, this is Jimmy Gates. I have a woman age twenty-six, height five – five, weight One hundred and fifteen pounds. She has a gun shot wound just below her right breast, entrance from the side. There is no exit wound."

"What are her vitals Jimmy?" Dr. Barrett asked.

"B/P…90/40, pulse 30, respiration 26."

"Jimmy can you start an IV?"

"Negative Doc, I don't have the equipment. A rescue squad as been called."

"10-4 Jimmy. Have you got a pressure bandage on the wound?"

"Yes, well, I'm using a pillow."

"A pillow? Where are you?"

"I'm at home Doc. The victim is Carly."

Kris jerked his head up from his notes to look at Daisy.

"Carly?"

"Yes, doc."

"Ok, Jimmy just keep the pressure on the wound until help gets there. I'll stay on the line with you."

"Thanks."

Jimmy laid the phone down beside him and moved so he could see Carly's face.

"Carly, help is on the way so you hold on ok. Just hold on."

Brown listened to Jimmy as he talked, questions ran through his head. He covered the mouth piece. "Daisy make sure treatment room one is ready for a gun shot victim."

"Ok, Kris."

"Daisy, you may want to get Jillian down here too." At her questioning look, he said. "It's Carly."

"How did Carly get shot?"

"I don't know, but I'm sure we will find out once she is brought in."

Daisy nodded and went to get Jerry then get things set up in the treatment room.

Jimmy's voice brought Kris's attention back to the phone. "They're here Doc."

"Ok Jimmy, get her in here as soon as you get her stable."

"10-4 Doc."

The B-shift from station 15 rushed into Jimmy's apartment or so Jimmy thought. "Jimmy, how is she doing?"

"She's losing a lot of blood, but her vitals are holding at "B/P...90/40, pulse 30, respiration 26."

"Ok, we'll take over from here."

Jimmy nodded finding it hard to step back, but he knew he couldn't do anything more for her until they got her stable. He stared at the single hole that was in the window and felt his body start to shake.

"Jimmy, what happened?"

"I really couldn't tell you."

Dywire saw the way Jimmy's face paled and stood up to steady him.

"Why don't you sit down?"

"I'm fine...worry about Carly."

"Davis is taking good care of her. I'd like to take a look at you."

"Don't be ridiculous, I'm fine."

"Maybe, but I would still like to make sure for myself."

"Paul, I said..."

"Jimmy do as Dywire suggests."

Jimmy glanced up to see Captain Stone standing in front of him. "Cap? Why are you working?"

Harry looked at him in surprise. "For the same reason I showed up this morning with you, it's my shift."

Jimmy frowned. "That was yesterday, Cap."

"No, Jimmy I am afraid we are still on the same day."

"What? No, way." When he saw the concern on Chip's, Max's and Mike's face he knew it was true. In one day, Rick had been hurt, Carly and he had made love, Rick had woken up, Sandy had shown up and Carly had been shot! *Could it have happened all in one day?* If that was true then he was ready for this day to be over.

Jimmy covered his face and dropped to the couch. "Please let this nightmare of a day be over soon."

Chip watched Jimmy as he sat with his hands over his face then turned his attention to Carly as they lifted her to the gurney. 'I'd better call Karen as soon as I can.'

Jimmy heard Carly moan and moved to her side. "Carly? I'm right here."

Carly opened her eyes. "Don't leave me."

"I won't I promise."

Carly closed her eyes again drifting into sweet darkness once again.

"I'm going with you." He told Dywire.

"Sure, Jimmy."

They started wheeling Carly out the door as Vince arrived. "Jimmy, I'm going to need you to stay so I can ask you some questions."

"Vince, if you have any questions to ask me then you do it at the hospital. I'm not leaving her side."

He waited a moment before he nodded and Jimmy ran to catch up with Carly. Vince stepped into the apartment and walked over to where Captain Stone and the others stood. He shook his head. "Why would anyone want to shoot her?"

"I don't know, Vince. I know a certain paramedic that would like to know the answer to that himself."

They all turned to stare at the hole in the window knowing Jimmy Gates wouldn't stop until he found out the reason why.

11

Jimmy stared out the window in Kris Brown's office. It had been two hours since they had brought Carly in and the sun was beginning to set. As he watched the red, orange, yellow colors appear in the distance he felt a sense of relief. The day was almost over and tomorrow would soon be there. Well, he hoped it would anyway. He rubbed the back of his neck as he turned from the window. He smiled at Jillian curled up on the couch with two kids lying beside her. He really should wake her and demand that she go home. He glanced at his watch giving another sigh. *Why haven't I heard something? They should have finished the surgery by now.* Walking quietly across the room so he wouldn't wake Jillian, he opened the door to Barrett's office, stepped out, looked around then stepped back in and closed the door.

Walking back to the window he stared out it once again. His mind flashed back to another time when he was waiting for news about someone. He had stood outside the operating room impatiently with Rick beside him. Jimmy squeezed his eyes shut. *How I wish he could be here now.*

"Jimmy?"

Hearing Rick's voice, he spun around. "What are you doing out of bed?"

"I thought you could use a friend."

Jimmy gave Rick a smile. "I appreciate what you are trying to do, but you really need to be in bed. You are recovering yourself, remember?"

"Yea, but I also know that if our places were reversed you wouldn't listen to reason either."

That crooked grin Rick had come to know over the past six years appeared. "You're right, I wouldn't."

"Besides I gave Daisy here my word that at the first sign of fatigue I would go back."

Jimmy had been so surprised to see Rick, he hadn't noticed Daisy was the nurse behind him. "Daisy…Why did…"

"I knew it would be worse on him, if he didn't come, that's why."

Jimmy nodded. "Thanks Rick."

"You're Welcome."

There was silence for a moment as Rick looked around the room. He smiled at the site in front of him. "Where's Karen? I thought she would be here."

"Oh." Jimmy rubbed the back of his neck again as he faced the window. "She is flying in from Nevada, she was visiting her family. That's what Chip told me anyway."

"I see." Rick watched Jimmy stare out the window. "How long have you stood there?"

Jimmy turned to face him then turned back. "I don't know…I guess since they took Carly to surgery."

"Have you heard anything?

"Nah and I'm starting to worry."

"Jimmy…"

The door opened and Jimmy spun around once again. "Karen."

"How could you let this happen to her? She trusted you."

The breath rushed out of Jimmy from the surprise of her attack. "I would have taken that bullet myself."

"Well, you didn't. Carly is the one fighting for her life isn't she. I can't believe that I even thought she should give you a chance. Look what it has done."

Rick watched Jimmy pale at her words, but before he could say anything, someone else did.

"That's enough Karen. Jimmy is not to blame for any of this." Chip stated.

Karen turned hurt and angry eyes to the person standing behind her. "Chip, don't you defend him! I can blame him, because she was with him when that bullet went through his window. How do you know it wasn't for him?"

Karen faced Jimmy tears filling her eyes. "You should be there not Carly!"

"Karen, that's enough!" Chip demanded.

Jimmy could only stare; slowly he walked toward her, stopping when he was standing next to her. "I wish I was." He said lowly then walked past Chip and down the hall.

Chip stood staring at Karen. He hadn't known when he had been so angry before. "You were out of line Karen." Karen started to speak. "Don't." Chip looked at Rick and Jillian who had woken by Karen's words. He gave Karen one last look. "I'll go check on Jimmy."

"I will Chip." Rick stated.

"No, I will." Karen stated lowly. She looked up at Chip. "I need to apologize. You were right, I was out of line."

Chip gave Karen a small smile, but didn't say anything. Karen walked by him and took his hand. "Try and understand why I reacted like I did."

"I understand Karen, but it still doesn't make it right."

"I know." She started to walk away when he tightened his hold on her hand. "Jimmy went toward the operating room."

Karen nodded again, but was stopped once more. Chip leaned in, giving her a kiss on the check and a smile.

She gave him a grateful smile and then went to find Jimmy. It didn't take her long and when she did he was talking to Dr. Barrett. Jimmy dropped into a chair covering his face.

Kris sat next to Jimmy. "It will be awhile before you can see her, so why don't you go home and get some rest."

"I can't Doc. I promised her I wouldn't leave her and I won't."

"You aren't going to do her any good if you become ill yourself. When was the last time you had any rest?"

Jimmy's mind flashed back to that afternoon when he had fallen asleep with his arms wrapped around Carly. "It feels like its been forever." Jimmy said when he thought of that moment.

"Then go home and get some rest." Kris suggested.

"I told you I wasn't leaving her."

"You also said that it feels like it's been forever since you slept."

"No, I didn't...I'm sorry Doc, I was talking about something else."

"Jimmy your body can only take so much and after the day you have had, I would assume you are running on empty."

"He's right Jimmy, you should go home." Karen stated gently.

"Karen I know how you…"

"I should never have said what I did. I was scared."

Jimmy glanced down at his hands, rubbing them together. "I know how you feel."

Karen sat down on the other side of him, reached down taking his hands in hers. "I know that you would trade places with her." She placed her hand under his chin when he refused to look at him.

Jimmy jerked his head, stood and walked away. "Karen, I appreciate what you are trying to do, but I would rather be alone right now."

"Ok, then I won't bother you, but I am sorry."

"I know."

Kris looked at them both wondering what had transpired between them. He was about to ask when the door to the operating room opened and they wheeled Carly out.

Jimmy stood perfectly still as he pushed memories and feelings away to a place he called his hurt zone. As they passed him, he took Carly's hand bring them to a halt. "I'm still here, Carly." He kissed her forehead before they wheeled her down the hall.

Jimmy never saw the tears that ran down Karen's face, nor the look on Barrett's. And neither of them noticed the small group that had formed behind them. Daisy touched Rick's shoulder and looked at Jillian whom was holding Rick's hand as he watched his friend struggle with his emotions. "Lets get you back to bed, ok."

Rick nodded. "If Jimmy needs me…"

Jillian kissed his cheek. "We will take you to him."

The small group then headed for the elevator knowing it was going to be a long night.

Jimmy leaned on the railing of the front deck looking out at his surroundings. There was a corral straight out in front of him and just to the right was a stable. The lawn in front of the house was manicured and a dark green. The driveway to his left, ran from two feet of the house, curved a bit and continued to the main road.

He shoved away from the railing to walk down the steps, turned and looked back at the one-story, three bedrooms, ranch style house. The porch was seven feet wide and ran the length of the house; one of the first things that attracted him to the place.

Having already been inside, Jimmy knew an entryway meet you as you walked through the door, to the right laid the kitchen, laundry room, back door leading to the back deck- the same size as the front. To the left of the entryway, lay the living room, a hall way led from it to the three bedrooms and the main bathroom. The master bedroom was at the end of the hall, a large master bath with walk in closet was to the right of the room.

The door of the house opened , snapping him out of his thoughts. "Nice place Junior. Are you really buying it?" Rick asked in disbelief.

Jimmy gave his friend a crooked smile. "Already did."

Rick raised his eyebrow in surprise, bring a burst of laughter from his friend.

"Don't look so surprised." Jimmy took the steps two at a time and stopped beside his friend. "This time partner I'm not selling the place to you, no matter how many times you say you save my life."

"It was a thought."

"That's all it was."

The smiles they shared were ones of shared memories. Some really great memories like the part about the house, others…well not so great. Rick's recent injury, Carly's shooting. Granted a month had passed since the incidents and they were both doing great, but they still weighed heavily on him, especially Carly's shooting.

Jimmy shoved his hands into his pockets and sighed.

"Have you told Carly about the house?"

Startled by the question, it took Jimmy a moment to bring his thoughts back to the present. When he finally did, he simply stated. "Not yet."

A guard fell over Jimmy's face, one Rick knew all too well.

"Jillian tells me that Karen and Carly really like the apartment you found for them."

Jimmy gave a half smile, and nodded. "That's good."

"Carly told Jillian that you haven't been around a lot since they moved in."

"Guess not." Jimmy shifted his feet. Another sign of things weighing on his mind.

"Any particular reason why?"

"Not really, busy I guess."

Rick regarded his friend as he scanned the scenery around him.

"Want to tell me why you have decided to buy your own place?"

A shrug of shoulders was his answer followed a moment later in a restrained voice.

"Thought it was about time I made some changes, that's all."

"Do those changes include Carly?"

Rick knew he was pushing Jimmy's patience, but he also knew that if he didn't his friend would crawl deep inside himself. So, Rick pushed some more.

"I thought you liked the apartment."

"I did…do, but I wanted something different, is there anything wrong with that?"

The frustration in Jimmy's voice should his tolerance was waning.

"No, not if you are making the changes for the right reason."

"Rick, all I want is a place of my own, that's it, nothing more."

Rick threw up his hand. "Fine, I just wanted to make sure you knew what you were getting yourself into, that's all."

"Well, I do."

"Fine, I'll drop the subject."

"Good."

"When are you planning to tell Carly?"

His annoyance showed in his expression. "I thought you said you would drop the subject."

"I did."

"No you didn't, you just changed tactics."

"Jimmy…"

"Rick…look, I will tell Carly after I finish closing the deal."

"Fine, I was just asking."

"Yea, right, you were just asking."

"I was."

"Ah ha, we both know Jillian put you up to asking me these questions."

"Maybe she is worried about you."

"I'm fine, ok."

Deciding he should back off a bit, rick agreed. "Ok."

Relief coursed through Jimmy. He knew what Rick intensions were, but he was no where ready to give in on his decision, maybe he never would be. His chest contracted from the pain and once again he pushed it to that place he called his, "Hurt Zone."

"Lets' get something to eat, I'm starved."

"Sure." Rick watched his friend walk down the steps and shook his head. *Jimmy, you are making a big mistake.*

Once Rick joined him in the car, he turned the car around, giving it another quick glance knowing Carly would never see the place. When he sat by Carly's bedside he made a promise to himself, if she pulled through, he would make sure she was never hurt again.

Karen was right, it was his fault Carly was shot. Why he couldn't say, but somewhere deep inside, he knew it for what it was, the true. The truth of the matter was, he wasn't angered or hurt by her words that day, he was grateful for them.

Carly sat staring out the bay window of her and Karen's apartment. You would think being in the heart of the city held some excitement, but all she found herself doing was holding her breath at the site of every car that passed by.

"How long do you intend to stare out that window? Karen asked.

"I hoped Jimmy would stop by today."

"I know what you hoped. Jimmy Gates hasn't stepped foot in this apartment since the day he helped us move in."

"He's been working, trying to make up some hours for the time I was recovering."

"So he says."

Carly faced Karen crossing her arms. "Jimmy wouldn't lie to me."

Karen raised her eyebrow. "You really have it bad, if you believe that."

"Do you think Chip lies to you?" When Karen didn't respond, Carly stated. "I didn't think so."

"Chip isn't trying to think of ways to stay away from me."

"Jimmy isn't either! I know Jimmy and I know he would never lie to me."

"Ok, I'm sorry, I should never have said it."

"That's right you shouldn't have." Defense of the man she loved making her sapphire eyes turn darker.

Karen knew there were no since arguing and headed for the kitchen.

"Has Chip said how Jimmy is doing?" Carly asked.

"All Chip ever says is that Gates is a nut." When Carly spun around Karen threw up her hand. "Chip's words not mine."

Carly nodded as she turned to stare back out the window.

"I have to agree with Chip, Gates is a nut." Karen mumbled.

Carly heard her, but chose to ignore her words. Finally, letting out a sigh of defeat Carly came to her feet. Her every intention to walk away when she saw a Land Rover pull into a parking spot just below the window.

Carly's heart felt as if it was going to burst, she was nervous and excited all at once and it took everything inside her to not run and meet him. Then she heard the knock on the door and she started to laugh at herself. Now she found she couldn't move, her legs turned to jelly and she dropped into the chair closest to her.

Karen came out of the kitchen seeing the flush on Carly's cheeks, the rapid breathing she was desperately trying to control. She took a couple of deep breaths herself to calm her angry nerves, walked to the door and opened it.

"Hello, Jimmy, long time no see."

Jimmy had the grace to blush. "Is Carly home?"

"Yea, come on in."

Jimmy stepped in spotting Carly sitting in a chair by the bay window. For the first time in weeks, he smiled and his heart skipped a beat at her beauty. He hadn't lied to her when he said he was working. He had pulled every shift he could until the Cap had asked him- no - ordered him to take a day off.

"Hello Carly." *Man, this is going to be hard.*

"Hello Jimmy."

Karen hesitated a few moments then spoke. "I have to meet Chip for dinner; will you be here for awhile Jimmy?"

"I'm not sure."

"Well, I guess I will see you later." Karen turned her attention to Carly. "I guess you can stop staring out the window now.”

Carly blushed as Jimmy raised his eyebrow. Karen left them alone, hoping things would be different between them when she got home. Jimmy waited until he heard the door close behind him before he pulled a chair in front of Carly.

"How have you been?"

"Alright, I've missed you."

"Yea, well, I've been working a lot." Jimmy said rubbing the back of his neck.

Carly watched him knowing that was a sign of him trying to ease tension, she also noticed the way the muscle of his jaw kept jerking. The fear of what he was about to say completely filled her. *Don't Jimmy, please don't.*

Jimmy stood and walk where Carly had just been standing a moment ago. "Carly, I've been thinking…deciding…wondering if…"

"Jimmy, I've been doing some thinking myself. I'm not sure how to say this, but…maybe we should see other people for awhile."

Jimmy turned around expecting to find her in tears, but instead found her staring at him with clear eyes. "I was going to say that."

Carly gave a small laugh. "Guess we have been around each other to long if we can read each others mind."

"Guess so." Jimmy moved back to sit in the chair. "I never intended to hurt you Carly."

"I know."

"I told you when we first met that I wasn't ready for any kind of commitment."

"I remember and if you remember I told you the same thing."

Jimmy nodded. "Then we are in agreement."

"Yes."

Jimmy stood finding it the hardest thing he had to do next was to walk out the door. "I'll see you around."

Carly found her legs and stood. "Sure."

Jimmy hugged her to him. "I am sorry."

"Me too."

Jimmy forced himself to let her go, spun on his heels and walked out the door never looking back. Once out the door, he leaned against it taking long shaky breaths. Carly stood where she was unable to move, every muscle in her body jerked with her fighting to keep the tears away until she was sure he was gone. When her body couldn't take the strain any longer, she fell to her knees and cried. There was only one other time in her life that she had felt that much pain. Jimmy walked to his car, got in and gripped the steering wheel until his fingers turned white. After several minutes, he put the car in gear and drove to his new home.

12

Carly spent the next month dealing with the pain of not having Jimmy in her life. All things considered - her life had gotten back to normal. Michael seemed to have taken an interest in someone else so the threat from him seemed to be gone. The police Detective assigned to her case didn't have any clues as to who did the shooting and put the case on the back burner. She could now walk out her front door without having to wonder who was waiting for her or so she told herself. She went to work every day, but usually spent her nights alone in the apartment. She smiled at how often Karen stayed over at Chip's. When she did stay at the apartment she talked about the things her and Chip did when they were together, even trying to get her to join them for dinner, usually Carly's declined. The times she did accept, she always felt like a third wheel.

It wasn't Chip or Karen's fault, it was just she always felt apart from everything and every one. The last time she went with them to dinner, she listened to Chip talk about the last shift he worked and in the process she learned that Jimmy was once again working extra shifts.

"I don't understand why? He has that beautiful ranch he could be enjoying." Chip stated.

"Jimmy's moved?" Carly asked before she could stop herself.

Chip smiled at her. "Yea, he bought this three bedroom ranch style house, with a stable and corral and so much land! It's beautiful. I helped him move his stuff. It's really nice."

"I'm glad he's found something he likes." Carly replied trying to hide the hurt of him moving on while she stayed trapped in a life she felt no part of.

"I guess he likes it, he's hardly there. It's like moving didn't change anything." Chip said shaking his head.

"What do you mean…changes things?" Carly's concern for Jimmy overrode any pain talking about him brought up.

"Well, it's like when he was at the apartment he wouldn't stay there. He worked extra shifts so he wouldn't have to."

"I thought he worked those shifts to make up for hours he lost." Carly stated.

"That's what he told everyone, but I know Gates and there was more to it than that."

"Chip, why do you think that?"

"That's simple; he blames himself for you being shot."

"Chip!" Karen exclaimed.

"What? It's the truth."

Carly was confused. "Why would he blame himself?"

Karen lowered her head. "Because I told him it was his fault."

"You did what?"

"Carly, you have to understand, I was worried about you."

"I can't believe you… How could you?" The tears Carly had managed to battle fell. "I need to go home."

"Carly, wait please." Karen begged. "I apologized to him so many times."

"I'm sure you did and I'm also sure he told you it was ok, right."

"Yes."

"Well, it might have been ok with Jimmy, but it's not ok with me." Carly stood. "I can't believe you could hurt him like that."

"I was upset. I know it's not an excuse, but it's all I have."

Though she knew Karen was in the wrong she gave her a small smile. "I understand I really do."

"Then don't go."

"I need some time to think. I'll see you when you get home, ok."

"Let us take you." Karen pleaded.

"No, you both stay and finish dinner. I think I'll walk for awhile."

"Carly…"

"I'll be alright." Carly gave her friend a hug, said goodnight to Chip and walked away.

That had been two nights ago. When Karen had gotten home she had pretended to be asleep. In truth, she had barely slept that night or the next night. Her mind kept playing over the scene from the last time Jimmy had seen her, the night her heart felt like it shattered. "I know why you did it Gates." She stated to the empty room. Once again she found herself crying into her pillow.

Jimmy walked into Station 110's Apparatus Bay wondering if maybe he should have taken Rick's suggestion and taken the day off. He had worked everyday for the last month. Rick had told him he was crazy, for working so much, but the thought of going back to an empty house didn't suit him; he knew as long as he worked he could keep his feelings in check. There wasn't a day that didn't go by he didn't miss Carly, but for her safety things were better the way they were.

"Hi Jimmy, you get drafted?" Chad Mullins asked with a smile.

Jimmy gave him a crooked grin as he reached out to shake his hand. "Nope, I requested to work."

"Really? Didn't you do the same over at one sixteen's on your last day off?"

"Yea."

Chad stepped back, crossing his arms. "I've heard you have been working a lot this last month."

"So."

"Any particular reason why?"

"No. Why all the questions?"

"I was just wondering why you would suddenly need so much over time."

Jimmy shoved his hands in his pocket; spread his feet apart slightly as the muscle in his jaw started jerking. "Chad, I don't see why my working over time is anyone's business, but just so the record is clear, I want to buy some horses for my ranch. That takes money, to get that money I need to work."

Chad uncrossed his arms. "Sorry, it's just I've never known you to work this much."

"Well, maybe you don't know me as well as you thought you did."

Chad decided to drop the subject. There was something else going on, but knew Jimmy would never tell him. "Sorry Jimmy." Chad stated as he started to walk away.

"Chad wait…I'm sorry. I didn't mean to go off on you like that. I guess working so much is taking a toll on my mood."

"Really, I never noticed any change myself."

"Ha…Ha…very funny."

Chad slapped him on the back. "How about a cup of coffee."

"Love a cup."

"Come on and you can tell me about this ranch of yours."

"Nothing much to tell. I really haven't been there much since I bought the place."

"I would think you would want to spend all your free time there."

Jimmy raised his eyebrow. "What free time, I've been working all month, remember."

"Oh, yea. So you can buy some horses."

"Yea."

Chad handed Jimmy a cup of coffee just as the Klaxons sounded.

They arrived on the scene moments later. It had been a two-car collision. The driver in one car didn't make it so Jimmy ran to help the couple in the other car. The man behind the wheel held his wife in his arms as he tried to stop the bleeding on her leg.

"Are you hurt anywhere besides the cut on your head?" Jimmy asked.

"No, I don't think so. It's my wife…I can't stop the bleeding on her leg."

"Ok, let me take a look. Can you move?"

"Yes."

"Ok, I need you to slide out so I can get to your wife, alright." The man hesitated. "Look that is the only way I can help your wife. You want me to help her, right."

The man nodded and then did as Jimmy asked. Quickly moving into position, he worked to stabilize the woman and then moved her to the ground so he could get to her injury. The man stood over him asking if his wife was going to be alright. "She's going to be fine. Her vitals are stable and she will be in good hands when she gets to Regional."

"Is she's going to be alright?" Joe Howard asked again.

"She will be fine." Jimmy picked up the Bi-phone. Regional this is County 110, how do you read me?"

The sound of Jimmy Gates's voice coming over the link caused Daisy to raise her eyebrow as she glanced up at Kris Barrett. "He has worked every day this month."

"I know...I'm starting to worry about him."

"I know what you mean." Daisy agreed.

"Regional, this is County 110, how do you read me?"

Kris walked to the link. "We read you loud and clear 110."

"Regional, we have a woman injured in an automobile collision, age approximately 27, weight 120, height 5' 5. She has a deep laceration to the upper part of her left thigh. There is tenderness in her upper mid section and she could have a possible concussion."

"Is the patient conscious,110?"

"Negative. Her vitals are as follows..." Jimmy waited for Chad to give him the vitals. "Vitals are...B/P...100/60...Pulse 120...Respiration...26 and shallow."

"10-4 110...Start IV with Ringers, keep pressure on her leg and transport as soon as possible."

"10-4 Regional."

Jimmy hung up the phone and helped Chad establish the IV then moved Jerry's wife to the gurney and then to the ambulance. Jerry rode in the back with his wife so Jimmy could attend to his injuries. They were three minutes from Regional when Mrs. Howard took a turn for the worst.

Jimmy grabbed the Bi-phone. "Regional, patient has gone into respiratory arrest. I'm starting CPR."

"10-4, 110." Daisy replied back.

They pulled into Regional with Jimmy giving her CPR never stopping until Dr. Evans and Dr. Barrett took over.

A few minutes later Jimmy walked out the door seeing Jerry standing outside the door with Chad.

"My wife, how is she."

Jimmy glanced back at the door. "I'm sorry Mr. Howard." Jimmy watched as the truth of what he was saying sunk in.

"You said she would be ok."

"At the time, I thought she would be. I am sorry."

"Sorry! You're sorry!"

"Look Mr. Howard…"

"No, I don't believe you. She isn't dead, she can't be."

Jimmy wanted nothing more than to tell him what he needed to be true. Having come so close to losing Carly, he understood Joe Howard's' anger. It wasn't fair that Jerry lost his wife. "I wish she were…but…"

Jerry turned white then closed his eyes. Jimmy and Chad caught him before he hit the floor. They put him in treatment room three and stayed with him until Barrett could check him over.

The ride back to the station was done in silence. Jimmy couldn't get the look of devastation on Joe Howard's face out of his mind. *It isn't fair, it just isn't fair.*

The rest of the day was spent going on a run every hour or so, by the time his shift back at Station 15 started he was exhausted and not sure he was ready for another day like the one he had just finished.

Rick walked into the dorm in the station finding Jimmy changing his uniform. "How'd it go yesterday?"

"Fine. Nothing special." Joe Howard's wife face flashed in his mind. *Nothing I want to talk about anyway.*

Noticing his expression change Rick became concerned.

"Something wrong Jimmy?"

Rick knew him too well - since trying to lie wouldn't work he told him half the truth. "Just tired, I guess I should have taken your advice yesterday."

"When do you ever take my advice Junior?" Rick teased as he leaned against his locker.

Jimmy gave him a scoff/laugh. "Yea."

"You working tomorrow also?"

Jimmy shoved his shirt into his pants. "No, I think I will take a break."

"Good. You are starting to look a little rough around the edges."

Jimmy sent him a crooked grin. "Nothing new in that, is there?"

"No, but you are looking a little rougher than usual."

He started to reply when the Klaxons sounded, but had to settle by giving Rick a smirk as they ran for the squad. Climbing in the cab Jimmy grabbed his helmet, shook his hair back, slipped his helmet on, adjusted the strap while he ran his hand along the brim of the helmet. He took the paper from Rick as the voice over the intercom repeated their destination.

"Squad 15, woman hurt. One fifteen Crestview Apartments. Time out …8: 05."

Jimmy's heart felt as if it came to a complete stop.

"That's Carly's and Karen's apartment."

Rick gave his partner a quick glance, threw the gearshift into drive and hit the gas. It was all he could do not to speed more than he had to. Still that five minute drive seemed interminably long.

Jimmy barely let the squad come to a stop when he threw open the door and jumped out. He ran to the compartment doors to get the equipment and slung the doors open as he sidestepped to pull out the drug box and then reached for the Bi-phone while Rick grabbed the oxygen tank. His heart felt like it was going to burst out of his chest as he and Rick raced to the building. Thoughts of Carly lying on the floor with blood pouring from her side filled his mind. *Please god, let her be alive.* Jimmy took a deep breath as he went through the door. "Carly, are you alright?" The last thing he expected to see was her walk out of a bedroom. He stumbled with relief then the knowledge that if Carly wasn't the one injured it had to be Karen hit him.

Carly cried with relief at seeing Jimmy. "It's Karen, Jimmy. Help her, please help her."

"Where is she Carly? Is she in the bedroom?"

The tears Carly had tried to hide from Karen fell. "You have to help her."

Jimmy grabbed Carly's shoulders, giving her a slight shake. "Carly, is she in the bedroom?"

"Yes…on the floor."

Jimmy let go of Carly, picked up his gear and ran for Karen's room with Rick right behind him. They found her lying face down at the foot of the bed. Jimmy kneeled on one side of her as Rick kneeled on the other. Rick touched her neck. "She has a pulse, but its weak."

Jimmy felt her limbs. "Rick, it feels like she has a fracture of her upper right arm, her legs seem to be ok."

"Jimmy lets see if we can roll her over."

"Ok."

Jimmy reached up and touched her shoulder causing a cry to escape from Karen.

"Sorry, Karen, Rick and I need to turn you over, ok."

"Carly…"

"Carly's right here. Now I want you to let us do all the work ok. You just lie still ok."

"Carly…"

Rick and Jimmy eased Karen onto her back.

"Carly's fine." Rick told her.

Jimmy glanced up at Rick almost sick from the condition of Karen's face. "Rick…"

Rick nodded as he leaned in closer to Karen. "Karen, can you tell me where you are hurting?"

Karen licked her swollen lips. "My shoulder, my stomach, my arm."

"Karen I'm going to touch your stomach, you tell me where it hurts."

"No, please…it hurts all over."

Rick looked up as Jimmy finished taking her vitals.

Jimmy gave Karen a gentle smile. "Karen, we have to see how bad you are hurt. To do that Rick needs to touch you."

"It hurts so much."

He squeezed Karen's hand. "I know it does, I promise he will be as gentle as he can be, Ok."

Karen took a shaky breath. "Ok…Jimmy…"

"Yes."

Tears spilled from Karen's eyes. "I didn't tell him…"

Jimmy glanced up at Rick. "Tell who, what?"

"I didn't tell him where Carly was. He kept hitting me, but I wouldn't tell."

Jimmy heard the gasp from behind him, but didn't turn around. "Who hit you?"

"A man in a mask." Karen stated as she started to shake.

"She's going into shock." Jimmy stated as he grabbed a blanket from the bed.

Rick grabbed the Bi-phone. "Regional, this is County 15."

"Go ahead 15." Daisy's voice replied over the link.

"Regional, we have a woman, age 26, 5'4, weight approximately 120, she appears to have a dislocated shoulder, fracture in her upper right arm, severe bruising and tenderness in her abdomen. She also has cuts and bruising on her face. Vitals are…"

Daisy looked around just as Mike Masters walked by. "Mike, it's 15."

Jimmy gave Rick the vitals.

"B/P…90/60, Pulse…60, Respiration…26 and shallow." Rick repeated.

"10-4 15, start IV solution with Ringers." Mike replied.

"IV solution with Ringers, 10-4 Regional."

"Has the ambulance arrived, 15?"

Rick looked up as the attendants came through the door. "That's affirmative Regional."

"Transport as soon as possible."

"10-4 Regional."

Rick hung up and stood to allow the ambulance attendants in. He stepped back next to Carly, putting his arm around her waist. "She's going to be alright."

"This is my fault." She turned her face into Rick's shoulder.

"You can't blame yourself."

Carly stared up at him with shame and self hatred in her eyes. "Who else is there?"

Rick turned his attention back to Karen. "The man that did this."

Jimmy listened to the quiet conversation behind him. His heart told him to turn to Carly and take her into his arms, but he knew his job was taking care of Karen and that was what he would do. "I'll ride in with her Rick." Jimmy looked at Carly. "You can ride with us, if you want."

"Yes, I have to be there for her." Carly whispered.

Jimmy gave Carly an understanding smile. "I know. Ride up front with the driver, ok." Carly nodded then stepped aside as they wheeled Karen out.

The ride to the hospital took less then ten minutes, but as Carly sat in the front seat of the ambulance she felt as if it had taken a lifetime. *This is my fault.* The Paramedics of station 15 waited outside the examination room until they knew something definite.

"We're going to have to tell Chip." Jimmy stated.

"I know, I just wish we didn't."

"Yea."

They looked at each other and then left the room. They had let Carly wait in the nurse's lounge so that was their next stop. Jimmy returned to the lounge and found her staring out the window. "Carly…"

Carly spun around at the sound of her name. "How is she?"

Jimmy walked over to stand in front of her. "Karen is stable. She does have some internal bleeding that Barrett is going to have to go in to stop, but he's confident that she will be alright."

Carly fell against him sending him back a couple of steps in surprise. Hesitating, he slowly wrapped his arms around her and kissed the top of her head.

"That's ok. Let it out." Jimmy let her cry against his shoulder as he ran his hand slowly up and down her back.

Carly controlled her tears and raised her head. "Who's going to tell Chip?"

"Rick and I will when we get back to the station."

"Will you…" Carly hung her head…"Will you tell him, I'm sorry."

"You have nothing to be sorry about. This wasn't your fault."

Carly raised her head. "We all know that isn't true, Jimmy. We all heard what she said. If she had told him where I was he wouldn't have hurt her."

"We don't know that. Whoever this man is more than likely intended to hurt her even if she had."

"It was me he was after. It's because of me." Carly turned to stare out the window.

Jimmy knew how she was feeling all to well.

"Carly, we have to go, but I'll be back as soon as I can, ok."

Carly only nodded her head, never turning to look at him. When the sound of the lounge door shut, Carly's shoulders started to shake as she said a silent prayer. *Please God, don't let Karen pay for whatever it is I have done.*

Rick backed the squad into the station bringing it to a stop then glanced over at Jimmy. "I think we better talk to the Cap first."

"Yea." Jimmy opened the door of the squad and got out.

Rick soon followed as they went to find Captain Stone. They found him in his office.

Captain Stone looked up from the paperwork on his desk.

"You two look like someone beat your dog. What's up?"

Jimmy gave Rick a glance as Rick took a deep breath.

"Cap, the call we just came from was Carly's and Karen's apartment."

Captain Stone sat up straight in his chair. "Is Carly alright Jimmy?"

"She's fine Cap. Physically that is."

"You saying it was Karen?"

"Yes, Cap. Someone beat her."

Harry stood leaning on the desk. "What?"

"From what we can find out the person wanted to know where Carly was. Karen wouldn't tell him." Jimmy explained.

"Have you told Chip?"

Jimmy shook his head. "We wanted you to know first. Cap, I know where Chip will want to be. Do you think…"

"Say no more Jimmy; I'll have him a replacement over here within the hour."

"Thanks Cap." Jimmy said as he pushed away from the wall. He looked over at Rick. "Guess we better go get this over with."

"That isn't going to be easy."

"Yea, I know."

They left the Captain's office and Harry got on the phone to headquarters.

Chip was sitting on his bunk reading when they found him.

"Is Carly alright?"

Jimmy sat down next to Chip not being able to speak at first.

"Yea, Carly is ok."

"Whew, that's a relief when I first heard the address I thought for sure something serious happened."

"Chip…" Rick started.

"I'll tell him, Rick."

Rick nodded and watched as Jimmy fought for the words. "Chip…"

Chip moved to face Jimmy. "You said Carly is alright."

"She is…"

"Then why so serious."

"Chip…the rescue was about Karen."

"Karen?"

"Someone attacked her in the apartment."

"Gates, I don't think this joke is very funny."

"It's not a joke Chip." Rick said lowly.

Chip came to his feet. "Why would anyone want to hurt Karen?"

When neither answered, he became angry, "Why would anyone want to hurt Karen?"

Jimmy slowly came to his feet. "He wanted to know where Carly was, Karen wouldn't tell him."

"You're telling me…Karen was hurt because of Carly."

"Chip, you can't blame Carly."

"Why not? If Karen had moved in with me like we planned then she would be safe."

They looked at each other in surprise. Rick returned his attention to Chip. "You and Karen were going to move in with each other?"

"We talked about it, but Karen wanted to stay with Carly for awhile then you…" He turned to face Jimmy. "Decided to end things with Carly. Karen said she couldn't leave Carly alone."

Jimmy felt a wave a guilt. "I'm sorry Chip."

"Gates, don't tell me you're sorry, tell Karen." Chip threw the book he had been holding on his bed and brushed by Rick.

He watched Chip leave then looked back at Jimmy. "He's upset Jimmy."

"I know, I would be too."

They both knew where he was heading and it was just a matter of minutes before Chip was back in the dorm changing clothes.

Chip sat by Karen's side once she was allowed visitors and stared at her hand while he waited for a response…any kind of response from her. When she squeezed his , he wasn't quite sure he felt it. His head jerked up and he saw her the small smile she gave him through her bruised and swollen lips.

"Hi there handsome."

"Hi yourself."

Tears fell down Karen's cheeks. "I'm glad you're here."

"I wouldn't be anywhere else." Chip stated then stood to place a tender kiss on her lips.

Carly closed the door silently. "I'm so sorry Karen. Please forgive me."

She turned to leave running straight into a wall of flesh. When she looked up she found herself looking into Jimmy's deep brown eyes. He wrapped his arms around her wishing he could stop the guilt she felt, knowing from experience no words could.

13

Carly compared the waves that crashed against the rocks where she sat to her churned emotions. Her best friend and roommate was being released from the hospital that day and there she sat. She knew she should be there with Karen, but she also knew Chip would take care of her. Raising her head, she took a deep breath of the ocean's breeze and slowly let it out. She shoved her hair away from her face once again. The wind was high that afternoon as the sun shined down on her. When had her life changed from a peaceful and what some might consider dull, to a life of fear and pain. Her hair slapped her in the face again and she pushed it away as before.

Carly thought of Jimmy and her heart filled with something she called neither pain nor unhappiness and for a brief moment, she didn't think she could breathe. The feeling consumed her and she closed her eyes. How she missed the feel of his arms around her, the comfort she had found in them. Her eyes flew open and this time when her hair slapped her in the face from the force of the wind she didn't push it back. "I miss the feeling of belonging." She said to the sea.

Promise me, you won't let Mathew be the reason you hide from love. The sound of her brother's last words radiated through her head. Again, her heart felt like it would burst and the pain that came with it seemed unending. "Oh, Tommy, I tried. I really tried."

Promise me.

"Oh, Tommy, how I wish you were here. You always knew what I should do even as kids." Carly whispered. "I may have been the oldest, but there were times I felt it was the other way around."

She always came to this spot when she wanted to talk to her brother. People would think she was crazy if they knew, but talking to him always made her feel better so even after his death she continued talking to him. The waves crashed at her feet as in answer to her and she gave them a tender smile. "You are still with me, aren't you?" The waves lapped again and her smile widen. "I thought so. It's been a year Tommy. A year today that I watched you take your last breath." Tears fell as she closed her eyes. "Why Tommy? Why did you have to die? I don't know if I will understand…you who had so much to live…you who gave so much, not only to me, but to all that knew you."

The memory of Jimmy finishing the race for her flashed through her mind causing her to smile again. "You would have liked him Tommy." She said through tears. Carly let out a small sigh. "I miss him Tommy. I miss the way we would curl up on his couch and talk. He always made me feel it was ok to tell him about you. Then there were the times we would watch a movie on TV. He never said anything when I chose a sappy movie." Jimmy had never said that to her, but she did hear him one day tell Rick. Carly never became angry or hurt by his words because he did it for her.

Her eyes rose to look out at the horizon. "It's one of the reasons I love him so much." Letting out another sigh she looked down the beach seeing a couple walking with their arms around each other. "Jimmy and I used to do that." She shook her head. "When did I become so pathetic Tommy? I used to be a strong independent woman, with a mind of my own. Now all I ever seem to do is look back and wish for something that can't be." She slapped her legs with her hands. "Well, no more. I will no longer be scared of my own shadow or cry over a man that has made it clear he doesn't want me!"

The memory of Jillian calling her right after Jimmy walked out of her life flashed through her mind.

"The man is miserable without you. You should see him outside with Rick. He looks as if his world has come to an end."

"Jillian, I want to believe you, but he was the one that wanted to break things off."

"Yes, I know, but you know why, don't you?"

"Yes, because he's not ready for a commitment."

"I'm sure he's afraid things will end like they did with Sandy."

Carly sighed. "If Sandy is the reason then we didn't stand a chance anyway."

"Carly, if you…"

"No Jillian, I am not begging him. Jimmy made his decision, now we both have to live with it."

Carly stood shaking away the memory. She knew the real reason why Jimmy had come to her apartment that day, but knowing didn't make it hurt any less.

She looked back out at the horizon. "I better get going. I'll talk to you again soon, thanks for listening." She could almost heard him say…"Anytime sis." For the first time in weeks Carly really smiled.

"I thought you might be here."

Carly jumped at the sound of Jimmy's voice. "How long have you been there?"

Jimmy heard the anger in her voice and gave her a small smile. "Just long enough to hear you tell Tommy goodbye."

Carly brushed past Jimmy feeling her arm hit his and her heart skipped a beat in her chest. *Keep going Carly, you keep going.* "Did you need something?"

Yea, you. "Thought you could use a friend today."

Carly stopped in her tracks. *Friend! He dares says Friend!* "Thank you Jimmy, but I'm doing fine as you can see."

"Are you?"

Carly swung around to face him. "Yes, I am."

Jimmy watched the way her shoulders straightened knowing that was her way of defending herself, but he could see the pain in her eyes. "I know how hard today is for you."

Carly felt her resolve start to slip. *Oh no you don't Gates!* "Do you? How many siblings have you had to bury?" As soon as the words were out she regretted them.

"None, but I have had to bury people I love."

Carly expected Jimmy to walk away, but he stayed where he was. The silence that followed was almost deafening. "Jimmy, I'm sorry. I shouldn't have said…"

"It's alright. I guess I deserved that."

Carly dropped her head. "No you didn't."

She felt his hands on her shoulders and let herself be taken into his embrace. She wrapped her arms around him. *Oh, how I have missed this.*

"Carly, did you really think it was a good idea to come here alone considering what has been happening?" Jimmy asked against her head.

She let her shoulders drop in defeat. He only came because he feels guilty. "I didn't really think about anything except Tommy." She moved out of his arms missing the feeling of belonging all over again. "I appreciate you worrying about me, but I am no longer your concern."

Jimmy grabbed her hand as she turned to leave. "I will always worry about you Carly."

She pulled her hand from his. "I don't want your concern."

"Carly wait."

"No, Jimmy. I don't think I have any more waiting in me."

"I was hoping we could talk."

She turned away from him. "We don't have anything to talk about. You made your decision that day you came to the apartment to tell me we couldn't see each other any longer."

"You wanted that too."

"Yea, I said I did, didn't I?"

Jimmy grabbed her arms and made her face him. "If you didn't mean that, why did you say you felt the same way?"

Carly lifted her face so she could look into his eyes. "So it would be easier on you."

Jimmy could only stare at her. Walking away was the hardest thing he had ever done, but knowing she wanted it too had made it easier. He pulled her into his arms wrapping her tightly against him. "I'm so sorry. I was only trying…"

"To keep me safe, I know."

"How did you know?"

"Chip."

"Chip? How would Chip know?"

"I guess he knows you better than you think."

"Why does that thought frighten me?"

Carly laughed against his chest.

Jimmy smiled. "I've missed this."

Carly's arms tightened around him. "So have I."

"How about I take you home?"

Carly moved away. "I'll be ok going back to the apartment by myself."

"Who said anything about the apartment?"

Carly looked up at him in surprised. "Where else would I go?"

"Home, with me. That is if you want to."

Carly felt as if her world shifted and things were as they should be. "If it's what I want…" Deciding words wouldn't be enough she stepped up against him and placed her lips on his. The kiss she received back told her, he had missed her as much as she did him.

Carly broke the kiss. "Lets go home."

"Your wish is my command."

"Well, in that case…"

Jimmy grabbed her and swung her off her feet. "Not one word young lady, not one word."

Laughing, she buried her head in his shoulder. "As you wish." She stated as she kissed his neck.

Jimmy groaned knowing it would be a long drive back to the house.

They both new that this new beginning didn't wipe out the past and the path ahead of them wouldn't be easy. They both had issues from previous relationships that wanted to rear their ugly heads and trip them up, but they knew with a lot of hard work they would make their relationship a success. It was something they planned to put their whole heart and soul into to make sure it happened.

The lights from the Apparatus Bay and the streetlights shined out on the street as Rick backed the squad into the station. It had been a long and exhausting day. Rick switched the ignition off as he glanced at Jimmy. "I'm beat."

Jimmy stretched. "Yea, I know what you mean. I'm looking forward to a quiet day at home tomorrow."

"You sure have lost your desire to work over time. Any special reason?" Rick teased.

Jimmy gave Rick a frown. "I have no idea what you are talking about."

Rick leaned on the hood of the squad. "Well, it seems this last month you have changed."

"Changed...how's that?" Jimmy asked furrowing his brow.

"Well, your mood seems to have improved. I was just wondering if maybe the fact Carly is staying with you has anything to do with it."

"I don't know what you mean, my mood is the same as always."

"Yea, impossible."

"Ha...Ha... Very funny."

"Come on partner lets go get some rest." Rick laughed.

"I'm right behind you."

They had only taken a couple of steps when the Klaxons sounded once again. Jimmy dropped his head giving it a shake. "Man, this is going to be a long night."

"Yea, tell me about it." Rick sighed.

"Station 15...Brush fire. Topanga Canyon three miles in. Time out 9:20."

Rick waited for Captain Stone to hand him the slip of paper he would need. " A Brush fire is definitely going make it a long night."

"Not to mention a long day tomorrow." Jimmy sighed.

"Yea." Rick stated as he put the squad in gear and pulled out of the station.

Three days later the team of Station 15 was close to exhaustion. They took there breaks when needed, ate when they could and slept in shifts.

Jimmy swallowed the last of the coffee in his cup, glanced at Rick as he stretched. "Man, I could sleep for a year."

"Yea, me too. Jillian must be worried."

"She knows you will call when you can."

"I know, still I wish I could let her know I'm ok."

Jimmy nodded as he glared out at the flames that seemed to be everywhere. "Yea, I feel the same about Carly. I wonder what she's doing right now."

Michael and Sandy sat in the car watching for Carly to come out of the doctor's office after her yearly checkup. Sandy glanced over at Michael, whom she had become friends with after her break up with Jimmy. Nothing else had developed between them making her wonder why. He was handsome enough and with his blonde hair and blue eyes any woman would be tempted. Her thoughts turned to Jimmy and his dark hair and eyes. It seemed that for now she would only want one man. There was just one problem someone else stood in her way, but that was to change very soon. A deliberate smile came to her face as she turned her attention back to the building. "She sure is taking her own sweet time."

"I hope nothing serious is wrong?" Michael stated staring at the building.

"You really have it bad for this girl."

"You saying you don't feel the same about Gates?"

"Point taken, walking away from Jimmy was the worst mistake I made."

"I don't get it. What is so great about that guy?"

"Careful your jealousy is showing."

Michael gave Sandy a heated gaze. "Look your job is to get Gates to fall back in love with you, not comment on how I feel."

"Don't use that tone with me Michael. I know what I'm supposed to do. It makes things difficult when they are living together."

"You had a month when they were broken up, why didn't you do something then?"

"I could ask you the same question." Sandy said.

"She wouldn't take my calls so I decided to just wait."

"So, now you know my reason." Sandy looked back at the building and sighed. "So here we sit waiting and watching for what exactly?"

"For the opportunity to get her alone."

Sandy smiled. "Now I like that thought."

Michael shot her a glance. "We are not going to hurt her, is that clear."

"Easy boy, I was just thinking out loud."

"I mean it Sandy, Carly is not to be harmed. I just want a chance to talk to her."

"Talk to her, huh?"

"Yes."

"Exactly what is it you plan to say to her?"

"What I've always told her, that I love her and we belong together."

"Ok, what if she doesn't want to listen? What then?"

"She will listen. I don't care how long it takes."

"I see, so we are waiting for her to come out of that building so you can kidnap her?"

Michael gave her another look and started to answer when he saw Carly emerge from the building.

"There she is."

Sandy followed Carly with her eyes as she crossed to her car.

"Something's going on with her."

"What do you mean?"

Sandy pointed. "Well, look at how distracted she is." A smile spread across her face. "Maybe she was told some bad news and our problem will be solved."

"That's not funny."

"Yea, I know, I couldn't get that lucky."

"Shut up Sandy, I mean it."

Sandy laughed. "Lighten up, I'm just kidding, besides anything happens to her and Jimmy would never get over it. The more I think about your idea the better I like it. This could work for both of us."

'**Squad 15**…fireman down …Old Topanga Rd."

Jimmy and Rick jumped in the squad and they were soon on the way to the location. Every rescue was important to them, but it seemed that when it involved a fellow firefighter it hit closer to home. They arrived in a few minutes of the call and found themselves staring into the worst part of the fire. They saw Captain Stone working with Mike and Max trying to free someone pinned under a tree.

"Chip!" They responded at the same moment and they ran to help free him. When they approached, they could see one of Chip's legs was pinned. Captain Stone yelled over the roar of the fire. "We've almost got him free. He's in a lot of pain."

Rick nodded. "I'll get the Bi-Phone and drug box."

Jimmy nodded and then joined in to free the down fireman. By the time Rick returned they had him safely out from under the tree and where they thought it would be safe to work on him.

Jimmy examined Chip's leg causing him to groan in pain. "Sorry Pal."

"It's ok. Can you give me something for this pain?"

"Rick will be here soon and then we will take care of you, ok."

"Ok. I'm glad it's you and Rick."

"Wouldn't have it any other way."

Chip gave him a smile as Jimmy moved his hand along his leg again.

"Sorry, Chip it appears you have a couple of broken places in your leg. We are going to have to splint it."

"Ok, whatever you say."

Jimmy grinned. "Now I know you are in pain."

Chip smiled. "Yea, well don't get to use to this power Gates."

Jimmy gave him a scoff/laugh. "Wouldn't dream of it, Keller."

Rick came back a few minutes later and they soon had Chip ready to transport. They had him on a stretcher when they heard the Captain yell. Jimmy looked up watching in horror as another tree started to fall and Rick was in it's path. "Rick, watch out!" He jumped to his feet running toward his partner, reaching him as the tree fell toward him. He gave Rick a hard shove sending him out of the path of the tree. Rickfell to the ground, rolled and came to his feet all in one movement then watched in horror as the burning tree came crashing down on Jimmy.

"Jimmy!"

Making sure Chip was taken to the ambulance Captain Stone called for help. The tree was quickly extinguished and Rick raced to his partner's side.

"Jimmy, can you hear me?" Rick didn't expect an answer, but he hoped he would receive one. When it didn't come, he found Jimmy's arm and felt for a pulse and dropped his head in relief. "He has a pulse, but it's weak! Lets get him out of here!"

Rick stepped back and let Mike and Max once again work to get one of their fellow workers out from under a tree. *Please God, let him be alright.* Ten minutes later Jimmy was on his way to the hospital with Rick right beside him.

14

"Jimmy? Jimmy, open your eyes, ok." Carly asked again as she held his hand. It had been three days since she found out Jimmy had been hurt. She had been on her way back to her car – in shock – when the nurse from Dr. Patterson's office came running out the door of the building calling her name.

"Miss Gibson, you have an emergency message from a Jillian DeLaney."

If Jillian said it was an emergency then it had to be about Jimmy. Carly's heart felt like it came to a stop one moment then the next it was pounding against her chest as she reached out to take the note. Her hand shook and she squeezed her hand around the note, held it to her heart, thanked the nurse, turned and started walking to the car. The nurse stared at her in surprise. "Aren't you going to read the note?"

Carly opened the door to her car, not looking back as she spoke. "I don't have too." She got in her car, backed out of the parking space, never seeing the three people that observed her.

Tears filled her eyes as she forced herself to look at the man she loved lying so still. *How could this be happening, now when I need him the most?* A sudden wave of nauseous hit her and she threw her hand over her mouth running for the bathroom. A few minutes later she rinsed her mouth out and splashed water on her face. Her stomach growled from hunger, but the thought of food only sent her into another bout of nausea. Finally, Carly made her way out of the bathroom with a cold wet cloth to soothe her red cheeks.

"There you are; I was beginning to wonder if you were ever going to come out."

Carly jumped at the sound of Karen's concerned voice. She must have paled because Karen took a step toward her. "I guess going three days without eating is starting to catch up with me."

"You still haven't eaten?"

"Can't keep anything down. I think I'm coming down with something."

"Why don't you let Dr. Barrett take a look at you?"

"No!"

"Why not?" Karen asked in suspicion.

"He would make me go home and I'm not leaving Jimmy." Carly sighed in relief when she saw Karen look over in Jimmy's direction. *Good she believed me.*

Carly hadn't lied, she just wasn't ready to tell anyone the truth. If they knew what Dr. Patterson had told her they wouldn't stop until she was at home resting?

Carly walked to Jimmy's bedside. "Home isn't home without you."

Karen understood all to well what Carly was feeling. She had just come from visiting Chip; grateful even more now that he was only recovering from a broken leg.

Karen walked over to stand beside her friend, placing a hand on her shoulder. "Carly, Jimmy wouldn't want you to make yourself sick because of him."

Carly laughed. "If you only knew."

"Knew what?"

"Nothing."

" What aren't you telling me? What did the doctor tell you when you saw him?"

Carly sat in the chair she had been using. "I really can't think about myself right now, all I care about is Jimmy waking up."

The sound of the door opening had them both pivoting around.

"I'm glad you're here, maybe you can talk some sense into her." Karen stated when Jillian and Rick walked in the room.

"Why? What's going on?" Jillian asked.

"She hasn't eaten nor slept since she has been here, do you know that?"

Jillian sighed. "I had hoped my talk to her yesterday would have helped."

"Well, it doesn't appear to have. I'm telling you, she is going to drop on her face if something isn't done soon."

"Stop it!" Carly yelled as she jumped to her feet. "Stop talking about me as if I'm not here! I know how you all feel, but I'm not going to leave him…I can't. If I leave then he might…" Carly sank to the chair dropping her head on the side of the bed as she clung to Jimmy's hand.

Jillian took a step toward her only to be stopped when by Rick's hand. "Let me talk to her."

Rick stooped down next to Carly resting his arm on the back of the chair.

"Carly, lets go for a walk ok."

"I don't want to leave him."

"I know you don't. We won't go far, I promise."

Carly raised her head. "What if something happens and I'm not here?"

"Jillian and Karen will be here. One of them will come get us."

She turned a tear stained face to Rick. "I can't lose him. I just can't."

"I know." Rick felt his heart skip a beat as he looked at his partner. "Jimmy is tougher than any of us know. He won't give up without a fight."

Carly stared at the man she had come to love more than anything then nodded. "Ok, I will go for a walk, but not very far."

"Agreed."

Jillian watched her husband with pride. *You always have that way about you, my love.*

They left the room and stopped just outside of the door so Carly could lean against him. He could see how tired she was, but it was the trembling of her body that worried him.

"Carly, lets get you something to eat."

"I couldn't Rick. I can't keep anything down."

"Have you tried?"

Carly let her eyes drop to the floor. She thought about lying to him, but just then her stomach made a grumbling noise.

Rick smiled. "Well, I guess that answered my question."

Carly blushed, started to say something when she felt a slicing pain go through her. When it finally passed it became more like pressure in the bottom of her stomach.

"You alright?"

"Yea, I just need to lie down for a bit."

"Ok, but I want you to try and eat also."

All Carly wanted to do was curl up in a ball and make this feeling go away. It hurt to walk so she found herself leaning heavily on Rick.

Noticing how pale Carly had become, Rick became concerned and in the next minute she slumped against him. He swung her off her feet and hurried to the elevator. Once to the emergency room he almost ran to an examination room. He saw Daisy at the nurses station. "Daisy, Carly needs help."

The head nurse hurried to the phone and had Dr. Barrett paged then followed Rick into examination room two.

Carly woke to the sound of rain hitting glass. Slowly, she opened her eyes letting her gaze fall on the window. *It looks like tears.*

"How are you feeling?"

Carly jumped at the sound of the masculine voice. *No, it couldn't be?* Slowly she turned to confront the person she had hoped she would never see again. "Mathew?"

Mathew Winston sat on the side of the empty bed beside her. "Yes, sweetheart. Surprised to see me?"

"I wouldn't say that exactly." Carly looked away from him and stared at the raindrops that ran down the glass of her window. It seemed to her those represented the tears she couldn't shed, no matter how much she wanted to.

Mathew watched the way her face contracted in pain, but decided to ignore the look.

"You knew I was here?" He thought he had been so careful.

"Hoped you would stay out of my life more like it." Carly replied still staring at the window.

Mathew clenched his fist. *How dare she? I'll take care of that high and mighty attitude soon enough.* He forced a smile to his face. "Now sweetheart, is that anyway to talk to the man you are going to marry?"

Carly's head jerked around to face him. "Of course not."

"That's better."

"It is the way I would talk to you though." Sarcasm dripped from her voice when she spoke.

Mathew jumped to his six feet height, his blue eyes flashed with anger and the muscles in his cheeks jerked. Carly controlled the fear that rushed through her. "What? You planning on beating me again, Mathew. Well, go ahead and try. I will scream so loud that they will hear me in Montana. You wouldn't want that, would you?"

"I should have killed you that night."

"You almost did, if I remember."

The smile he gave her sent chills through her body. "I doubt baby brother will come to your rescue this time."

"Get out Mathew!"

"What? Did I touch a sore subject?"

"I said get out!" Carly sat up forgetting about the IV attached to her arm. She gasped in pain as the needle dug further into her arm.

Mathew smiled, walked to stand beside her putting pressure on her arm.

Carly bit her lip and cried out. "How did you find me?"

"It wasn't easy, your family made it hard for me to do. It wasn't until after your brother died that I was able to track you down."

"I don't understand why you even bothered. You told me enough how much you hated me and wished you had never met me."

Mathew leaned closer to her and whispered. "You know why?" The anger in his eyes caused Carly to pull away. "You just had to tell Linda what I was capable of doing, didn't you?"

"I couldn't you hurt like her like you did me."

"I would never have hurt her. I loved her and because you couldn't keep your nose out of my business, she left me."

"I'm glad! You aren't capable of loving anyone."

The needle in her arm pushed farther into her making her cry out. The statisfaction she saw in Mathew's face angered her. Taking a deep breath, she raised her other hand and swung. The sound of her palm connecting to his face was loud and clear.

"Why you…"

"Go ahead, do it! You almost succeeded before, who knows maybe you will this time!"

Mathew glared at her with so much anger she wondered if maybe she pushed him too far.

He leaned in to an inch of her face and snarled. "They never discovered who killed your brother. Who knows, maybe I'll get lucky again and the same will happen with you."

Carly's eyes blurred from the tears. "You… you were behind it all."

An ugly sneer crossed his face. "I always heard, what goes around comes around."

The tears fell like the rain outside. "You killed Tommy because I told Linda what kind of man you really are."

"Think what you want, but I admit to nothing."

He didn't have to his message was clear. He intended to kill her.

Mathew stepped away, releasing the pressure on her arm. His hazel eyes darkened almost to the point of blackness. He ran his hand through the waves of his light brown hair as he sat back on the empty bed. "So, here I what you are going to do. You are going to check yourself out of this hospital and we are going to get married. Then we both will disappear where no one can find us."

Denial sprung to her lips, but she never got to voice it. "I see you may have to be persuaded. Lets put it simply, if you fell to do exactly as I say, Jimmy Gates won't be waking up at all. Do I make myself clear?"

Carly could only stare at the man she once thought she loved. How could she have been so wrong about him? What could have happened to him to turn him into the man he had become?

"Do we have an understanding?"

To tell him no would be insane. He already admitted to the killing of her brother, so she knew he would have no problem killing Jimmy.

"Answer me!"

Carly jumped from the anger in his voice. She had no choice, she had to do as he said.

"Hey you, are you awake?"

Relief rushed through her hearing Jillian's voice, but Mathew's expression told her she better remain quite. Carly was relieved, yet at the same time was afraid for her friend.

"Is she awake Jillian?" Rick asked from behind his wife.

Carly felt tears of relief when she heard Rick's voice. Mathew wouldn't try anything as long as Rick was there.

"I'm…awake." Carly stated.

The glare Mathew gave her told her she would pay for her attempt at bravery.

Jillian smiled at her friend, but noticed the flush on her face and the one on the man that stood next to the other bed.

"I'm sorry, did we interrupt?"

"As a matter of fact…." Mathew began.

"You didn't." Carly chimed in. She gave Mathew a heated look then glanced at Jillian and Rick. "Mathew was just leaving."

Jillian glanced between the two of them. Something wasn't right. She saw the blood that ran from Carly's arm and the red marks around it. Jillian reached back for Rick's hand, glanced in Carly's direction , hoping she would know she understood. Rick and Jillian both knew about Mathew so it was no surprise to Carly when they made sure one was on each side of her.

"What happened to your arm? Jillian asked.

Carly glanced at Mathew for a moment. "I moved my arm and I guess I shouldn't have."

Rick sized IV over. "We better get Barrett in here to look at this."

"Rick, I'm sure I'm fine."

"Maybe so, but I'm not willing to take the chance. Jimmy would never forgive me."

The mention of Jimmy's name made Carly look up at Mathew again.

Rick noticed her reaction and squeezed her hand. He gave Mathew a small smile. "Why don't we let these two talk while we go get the doctor?"

Mathew nodded, but once out the door he made his excuses and quickly left. He stepped onto the elevator and waited for them to close. *Damn! Why did they have to come in?* He had her were he wanted, just a few more seconds and she would have given in and he could have made the rest of her life miserable. The need to make her pay for interfering in his life was overwhelming. Now what was he supposed to do? Mathew knew himself well enough to know he wouldn't do anything to Carly as long as she had people around to support her. His strength showed when people were vulnerable. The doors to the elevator opened and he stepped out. A slow smiled eased across his face. "I will have to find another way to make her pay." And as he walked out of the hospital entrance an idea started to form.

Carly slumped back against the pillows letting out a sigh. She looked at the door knowing that Jillian and Rick's appearance had only postponed Mathew's plans. What had just occurred wasn't forgotten by anyone, but for now it was put on the backburner. The question now…Would Mathew try again or let her alone?

Carly tried to give her a brave front.

"I'm fine, considering everything that just happened." Goosebumps spread across her skin when she thought about the hatred in Mathew's eyes.

Trying to detour her thoughts Jillian turned the conversation to the reason of Carly's hospital stay. Granted it wasn't a much better topic.

"I'm sorry about the baby."

Tears filled Carly's eyes. "Me too."

"I know it's hard to believe right now, but things will get better. Once you and Jimmy are back on your feet, you can try again."

"That's just it Jillian, we weren't trying. Finding out I was pregnant was a surprise to me, we had been so careful. When I was on the way to the car, I kept trying to think of ways to tell him." She lowered her eyes. "I guess it doesn't matter now."

"Have you decided not to tell Jimmy about the miscarriage?"

"What good would it do?"

Jillian shrugged her shoulders. "None I guess."

Carly lifted her eyes to stare at her friend. "But, you think I should anyway."

"It's not my decision to make."

"No, but I would like to know what you think anyway. If it were you, would you tell Rick?"

Jillian thought back to when she and Rick were first married. "I did."

Carly blushed in embarrassment. "I'm sorry Jillian. I wasn't thinking."

"Don't be, it was a long time ago."

"I thought Rick knew you were pregnant when you miscarried."

"No, I told him after I miscarried. What I didn't know was he had already figured it out."

"Really, How?"

"I'm not really sure, he just told me he knew and that he couldn't have been happier."

Carly was silent for a moment. "Tell me what to do Jillian."

Jillian took her friend's hand. "I'm afraid this is something only you can decide."

The door to the room opened and Dr. Barrett walked in with Rick.

"Let's see what kind of damage was done here." Kris stated as he looked at her arm. "We will take ex-rays to be sure, but I believe nothing broke off."

"I'm sorry, Dr. Barrett. I just forgot about the IV when I moved my arm."

"Well, that was part of it, but from the look of the marks on your arm and the amount of blood coming from the wound, I would say you had a little help."

Carly glanced at Rick then lowered her eyes. A few moments later, she looked back up at Dr. Barrett to see an understanding smile on his face.

"I have some good news for you. Jimmy's starting to wake up."

Carly sat up wincing from the pain in her arm. "I want to see him."

"Alright, but after we have this attended too. Agreed?"

"Agreed."

Twenty minutes later Carly was sitting in a wheelchair beside Jimmy's bed. The threat Mathew made repeated in her mind. Maybe she should leave, it would keep him safe. *Maybe, Maybe not? How can you trust anything that man says except the harm he would inflect. What would keep him from killing him as he did Tommy? Nothing!*

Carly held Jimmy's hand and ran her fingers over the back of it. There were a strength and a gentleness in his hands that she had never know from a man. Granted she had only been with one before and there were no gentleness in those hands.

"Hi, beautiful."

Her head snapped up and tears filled her eyes. "Hi, handsome. Welcome back."

As groggy as Jimmy was, he could see the sadness in her eyes. He didn't have to guess at what she was going to tell him. Jimmy pulled his hand out of hers leaving Carly to stare at him in surprise. "You don't have to say anything; I can see it in your eyes."

"You do?"

"Let me save you from having to say it. You're leaving because you can't handle being involved with a fireman."

"Jimmy…"

"It's alright, I know the drill."

"You might know the drill, but evidently you don't know me."

Jimmy stared at her. "What, you saying you aren't leaving me?"

Carly pushed herself out of the wheelchair and sat down beside him. Jimmy noticed the chair, hospital gown and robe she wore for the first time. "Why are you in a wheelchair?"

"We can talk about that later, right now I just want to concentrate on you and this." Carly leaned toward him, placed her lips on his, after a few moments she broke the kiss. "Does that convince you that I'm not going anywhere?"

Jimmy raised his hand to touch her face. "It's a start." He grinned.

Carly gave him a smile in return. "What else do I need to do to convince you?"

"You could marry me?"

Carly's heart caught in her chest then took flight. "Before I answer you there is something I need to tell you first. If you still feel the same after hearing what I have to say, ask me again and I will give you an answer."

Jimmy hadn't intended to propose that way, but once he had, he was glad he did. "Ok."

Carly took a deep breath then told him about Mathew and all he had done to her and why she had been afraid to trust her heart in the beginning. When she was finished, she waited for him take in all she had told him. When she thought he had processed it all she continued, "He came to my room today."

"What? Are you ok?" He asked as he tried to sit up, regretting the action immediately.

"I'm fine, please don't get upset."

"What did he say to you? I can tell he upset you?"

She recounted the earlier events and waited for his reaction. Part of her expected him to tell her leave. He must have known what she was thinking, because he took her hand and said, He will never hurt you or anyone you care about again. We will find away to have him answer for the things he did to you and your brother."

Relief flooded her expression and she leaned in to kiss him.

"I love you."

"That's a good thing because I love you too."

Jimmy tried to push himself up more in the bed, but the effort and pain were too much for him to handle.

He decided he was better off staying just where he was.

"You still haven't told me why you are in a wheelchair and in this hospital gown?"

Carly's eyes dropped to his hands and started biting her lower lip.

"Ok, now I know something is wrong."

"What?" Carly asked distracted.

Jimmy touched her bottom lip with his index finger. "You are biting your lip again."

"Oh, Sorry."

"Tell me why you are in the hospital."

Carly studied him for a moment finally coming to the decision that he had a right to know. She took a deep breath and told him about the miscarriage then waited for his reaction.

Jimmy sucked in his breath feeling a mixture of blaming himself and anger. How much sadness was this woman supposed to endure because of him?

"I'm sorry Carly. It's my fault you lost the baby."

"How can you say that?"

"If you hadn't been worrying about me then you would still be pregnant."

"We don't know that."

"How can you be so forgiving?"

"There is nothing to be forgiven." She touched his face lovingly. "I want you to forgive me."

"What for?"

"For not being able to carry our baby."

Jimmy shook his head. "It wasn't your fault, it was mine."

Carly placed her finger over his lips silencing him. "Why don't we just agree that it wasn't either of our faults."

"Ok."

"I mean it Jimmy. I won't blame myself, if you don't blame yourself."

Jimmy was silent for a moment. "Alright."

Carly smiled then stood. "I better let you get some rest."

"Where are you going?"

"Back to my room. I guess I'm more tired then I thought."

"You haven't answered my question."

"What question was that?"

"Will you marry me?"

Carly stood perfectly still then leaned down to an inch of his mouth. "I would be honored." She then kissed him so he would know how much his asking meant to her.

"We will have other children, I promise."

"I can't think of anything else I would love more." She kissed his cheek. "Now you rest and so will I."

Jimmy nodded then watched as she sat back down in the wheelchair and left the room.

They knew that neither would forget the child they lost, but they also knew if they were blessed with any others they would be cherished and loved more because of the loss.

15

Jimmy hurt all over and he closed his eyes. Suddenly he remembered why he was in the hospital.

"Rick?" *What happened to Rick? I have to know he's alright.*

Throwing his legs off the side of his bed, he stood. In the next second, he found himself on the floor. Stunned, he laid on the floor unsure of what happened. He tried to pull himself up and realized he couldn't move his legs.

"Dear God, no." Jimmy whispered. What kind of husband would he be to Carly if he couldn't walk? What about his job? He would have to give it up?

"Hey, junior what do you think you are doing?"

Jimmy looked up to see his best friend and partner rushing to his side and for a moment he forgot about his legs. "You're, alright."

"I'm fine, thanks to you." Rick placed his arms under Jimmy's. "Come on, lets get you back in the bed."

"I can't feel my legs, Rick."

Rick froze for a moment then tried to make his voice sound as calm as he could. "It's probably just from the lack of use, lean on me."

Jimmy knew the chances of what Rick said was slim to none, but refrained from saying anything as he let Rick help him back into bed.

"I'm going to go get Barrett, you stay in that bed."

"I have no choice."

"Jimmy…"

"I know it's just from the lack of use."

"Right."

Rick let the door shut behind him and then leaned against it. *Please God, No.* He forced his legs to move and hurried to get Barrett.

Two days later and still no change in Jimmy's condition and the realization he may never walk again began to set in.

"Carly stop it!" She froze in mid-sentence. "You know I may never be on my feet again, so stop acting as if I will."

"We don't know that."

"Well, I do! My life as I know it is over."

"Jimmy, you can't give up. We have to believe…"

"If I can't do what I love then who am I?"

Carly walked to stand by the side of his bed. She picked up his hand holding it against her chest. "You are the man I love and together we can do anything."

Jimmy allowed himself a smile. "I used to think so, now…"

"No, doubts, you will get better."

"Things don't happen just because we want them to."

"No, they happen because we work to make them happen."

"I don't know…"

"Well, I do. It may take time, but we can make things happen. We can get married…"

Jimmy jerked his hand away. "I can't marry you like this Carly. It wouldn't be fair."

"Fair to whom, Jimmy… me or you?

"You, of course."

"I don't think so. I think you are feeling sorry for yourself."

"What if I am?"

I just never thought you would. You're stronger than that; a lot stronger."

"I'm not sure about anything any more."

Carly touched his hand. "Are you wishing that you hadn't pushed Rick out of the way?"

"No."

"Have you stopped loving me?"

"No."

"Why are you giving up?"

"I'm just facing reality."

"No, you're not, if you were you would fight to get back to work, you would fight to keep me."

"Am I losing you?"

Carly took a deep breath and slowly let it out. "I'm going to do something for you – something for us both."

"What's that?"

"I'm going to release you from our engagement."

Jimmy started to protest, but decided it might be for the best. "Thank you."

Carly nodded fighting back the tears. "I will be around if you decide you need me, but I won't watch you become half the man you are."

"I'm already half that man."

"No, you're not-not where it counts…here." She placed her hand on the center of his chest.

"I'm sorry." He whispered.

"Me too, Jimmy, me too." Carly leaned down to place a tender kiss on his lips. "I love you, remember that alright."

Jimmy felt as if his world was collapsing when she pulled away from him and started walking to the door. "Carly… don't go."

Carly's hand froze on the handle, her head dropped slightly as she turned to face him.

Jimmy intended to let her walk out of his life, but when he thought of life without her couldn't do it. "Please stay… I can't do this without you."

Carly walked back to stand by his side. "Together?"

"Together."

She bent to give him a kiss when she saw his foot move. "Do that again."

"Do what again?"

"Your foot, move your foot again."

"Carly, you know I can't."

"I just saw you do it, now move your foot!"

Jimmy decided he would give into her request even though she had been seeing things. He looked down at the foot of the bed then stared in surprise as he saw the covers move. "I don't believe it!"

"Again!" Carly said excitedly.

This time he moved his leg. He let out a laugh and reached out to hold Carly's hand. He tried the other leg and watched as it moved as well.

Carly hugged him. "I'm going to get Dr. Barrett or Dr. Evans."

She ran from the room and down the hall spotting Dr. Masters.

"Dr, Masters, its Jimmy! He can move his legs!"

Mike Masters looked up at Carly seeing the tears running down her face.

"Calm down, you said he can move his legs?"

"Yes, would you check him out?"

"Sure, go find Dr. Barrett and tell him, ok."

Carly nodded and ran for the elevator. Her heart felt as if it were going to bust from excitement. *He's going to walk again; he's going to walk again!*

A few minutes later not only were Dr. Barrett in Jimmy's room, but so were Daisy and Dr. Jerry Evans. Since she had to wait outside while they looked him over Carly decided it was the perfect time to call Rick.

"I'm telling you Jillian, that man is impossible!" Carly yelled between clenched teeth. "I am doing my best to be patient, but if he..."

"Ok, try and calm down."

Carly spun around to face her friend. "Calm down! I can't believe you just said that to me."

"I'm sorry, but it's hard to understand what exactly Jimmy has done when you yell."

Carly took a deep breath and slowly exhaled.

"That's better, now tell me what has he done that has gotten you so upset."

Carly slumped onto the couch next to her friend. "He is just so stubborn. I keep telling him to slow down, don't work so hard, but does he listen to me. No, of course he doesn't!" She yelled once again jumping to her feet.

"So when is he planning on going back to work?"

Carly froze in her tracks. "How did you know?"

Jillian stood and walked to stand next to her friend as she put her arm around her shoulders. "I know the signs."

Tears filled Carly's eyes. "I just love him so much. Why can't he see that?"

"Oh, sweetheart, he knows you do, but you know what his job means to him."

"Yes, sometimes I think he loves it more than me."

"I hope you haven't said that to him."

Carly gave Jillian a teary look causing her to groan out loud. "Oh, my, I bet that went over well."

"He stormed out of the house, jumped on one of the horses - bare back - and took off. That was early this morning."

"I'm sure he will be back soon."

"I just don't want him to be hurt again. I can't stand the thought of losing him."

"You could, if you try and make him choose between you and his job."

"I know - I told myself I would never do that, but..."

"I understand believe me. I have my days too when all I want to do is tell Rick to quit."

"You do?"

"Of course I do. All the wives have at some point and time, the difference is if you love him enough to let him be who he is."

Carly walked to the front Bay window in her and Jimmy's home. "I wouldn't want him to be less than who he is, but that doesn't make it easier."

"No, it doesn't."

Jimmy rode Sheba until her black coat was covered in sweet. "Whoa, girl." When Sheba came to a stop, he slid off her back holding onto the mane. He ran his hand down her neck. "Easy girl, I'm sorry, I should never have treated you this way." Sheba jerked her head up and down as if in agreement. Jimmy gave a small laugh. "Come on girl we will walk the rest of the way."

Slowly he led her to the stream he knew was just about half a mile up the road. Once there he allowed Sheba to drink first then took a handkerchief from his back pocket and dipped it in the water. Gently he slid the handkerchief over the horse's back. He did it over and over until he knew Sheba was cooled down. Only then did he allow himself to drink from the stream and let his mind run over that mornings' events.

"I can't believe you!" Carly Exclaimed.

"What?" Jimmy asked.

"You just told Captain Stone you would be back to work on Monday."

"Yea, so? "You aren't ready to go back."

"Why not? I have Dr. Barrett's release saying I can return to work."

"You have to give yourself more time."

"Why?"

"Jimmy, you haven't been out of the hospital that long."

"It's been two weeks, that's long enough."

Carly turned away from him covering her face. "Why do you have to be so stubborn? Why do you push yourself when you know you aren't ready."

"Carly, I am ready. I have to get back to work. I'm going stir crazy sitting around."

"Then do something else."

Jimmy felt an old familiar feeling come over him. "I love what I do, I thought you understood that."

"I do, but sometimes I think you love it more than you do me."

'There it is.' Jimmy stood staring at her for a moment then he spun on his heels and headed out the door. He could hear Carly calling after him, but he didn't care. Getting away was the only thing he could think of so he grabbed Sheba by the mane swung up on her back never looking back.

Jimmy stared at his reflection in the water wishing Rick was around so he could talk to him.

"Hi, junior."

Jimmy jumped to his feet. "Rick, how did you know..."

"Carly called Jillian."

"I guess she would have."

"Jimmy, Carly's..."

"Moving out? I was wondering how long it would take for her to realize she hated my job."

"Jimmy..."

"I mean it happened with Sandy, right? What made me think Carly would be any different?"

"Jimmy..."

"That's ok, I learned to live without Sandy, I can do it again."

"Jimmy..."

"I just thought she was different, ya know."

"If you..." Rick shook his head and started walking away.

"I should have my head examined...Where you going?"

"I thought I'd take a walk while you finished talking to yourself."

"Ha, Ha, very funny."

Rick gave him a smile. "Are you finished?"

He gave him a crooked grin. "Yea, I'm done."

"Good, now let me do the talking."

It was dark before they returned to the ranch and after stabling Sheba, they walked in the house finding Jillian sitting on his couch reading a book.

"She's in the bedroom."

"Thanks."

Jillian caught Jimmy's arm. "She loves you."

"I know. Thanks for staying with her."

Jillian nodded then walked to stand by Rick at the door. The sound of the click of the door shutting made Rick and Jillian smile.

"Is he alright?" Jillian asked, wrapping her arm around Rick's waist.

"Yea, he just needed to cool off. I think they will be alright."

"I'm glad." Jillian kissed Rick on the cheek. "Lets go home, ok?"

They closed the door behind them and walked to their car with their arms around each other.

Jimmy closed the door quietly behind him then walked across the room to sit beside Carly on the bed, before he could say a word she sat up throwing her arms around his neck.

"I'm sorry, I never meant to say what I did." Carly cried into his shoulder.

Jimmy wrapped his arms around her. "I know you didn't, but I'm glad you did."

"Why? Are saying we are...over? She pulled away afraid of his answer.

"No, I could never walk away from you." Jimmy wiped away the tears.

She dropped her head against his shoulder. "I was so afraid that I had ruined everything."

"All you did was tell me how you feel."

She jerked her head up. "I don't feel that way." At his raised eyebrow she blushed and stumbled over her words. "Well not really. I just love you so much, but I love you enough to want you to do what you love. You are a firefighter, I know that and I accept it."

"Do you?"

"Yes, I wouldn't want you to be anyone else, after all it is the man that I fell in love with."

"Do you love me, Carly?"

"Of course I do." Jimmy leaned down to an inch of her mouth causing her to suck in her breath. *It's unfair how he can still take my breath away with just a glance.*

In the next moment he was standing leaving Carly staring in surprise. He saw the disappointment cross her face. "I think I'll take a shower and then get some much needed sleep." Carly watched in a daze as he walked into the bathroom in their room and closed the door.

Jimmy stood at the door of the bathroom trying to control his urge to open the door behind him and finish that kiss he came so close to giving her. *It's unfair the way she can still affect my heart.* Taking a deep breath he pushed away from the door and striped out of his clothes. Stepping into the shower he slid the glass door closed letting the cold water run over his body.

Jimmy stared out the window of the kitchen door at the station. He had been back to work for a week and him and Carly hadn't made love in that length of time either. Granted, he made the decision, he had even moved into the spare bedroom. He knew Carly thought he was punishing her, but in truth he needed the time to himself, time to make sure that things could work out between them. Carly truly amazed him even though she had to wonder what he was doing and why, she never pressured him.

"Jimmy?"

"Morning Rick?"

"You looked like you haven't slept in a week."

. "Guess I haven't." He stated with a scuff/laugh.

"Everything alright with you and Carly?"

"Sure, why do you ask?"

"You've been more than your usual...unusual self this past week."

"Very funny."

"You might as well tell me now because you will anyway."

Jimmy gave him a grimace as he walked away from the door. "There's nothing to tell."

"I know you better than you think."

"I...well...it's just..."

Rick shook his head as he listened to his partner struggle to find the right words. When it seemed Jimmy wasn't going to finish his sentence, he turned to leave only to hear Jimmy start speaking again.

"I know...but...I don't know..."

"When you stop debating with yourself, I'll be in the dorm." Rick stated and turned to walk out of the day room.

Jimmy stood staring at him. "You were the one that asked."

"Yea, and I'm sorry I did." He teased.

Fine. I didn't want to talk about it anyway."

"Ah, ha."

Jimmy opened his mouth to speak when the Klaxons sounded. He stood still for a moment then ran for the squad.

"Station 15 Man down, 5th and main. Time out...2:20."

Captain Stone grabbed the mic. "Station 15, KMG 365"

Rick waited for the slip he knew he would get and then handed it to Jimmy. Whatever had been on Jimmy's mind was now replaced with the rescue that lay before them.

Carly briefly glanced at the pile of paperwork on her desk. She knew they needed her attention, but all she could do was think about Jimmy. The last week had been strange. He acted the same toward her except in one department.

Carly, I need those drafts."

Carly jumped. "I'm sorry Don...what?

"Are you alright?" Don sitting down on the corner of her desk.

Don Watson was Carly's associate and someone she considered a friend. Carly glanced back out the window to hide the tears. "I'm...fine."

"Why don't I believe that? Is it that fireman of yours?" Don saw the slight shudder of her shoulders. "He's gone back to work, hasn't he?"

Carly could only nod.

"Do you love him?"

Carly spun around to face him. "Why does everyone keep asking me that? Of course I do! More than my own life!"

Don stooped down so he could look her in the eye. "Then trust him to know what's best for him."

"That's just it, I'm afraid he will decide that's not me." The tears she tried to hide fell unhindered.

"I seriously doubt that. I have seen the way he looks at you. The man is crazy over heels in love with you."

"I know he loves me, but..."

"What?"

"I may have lost him because I let him know how much his job scares me."

"If Jimmy Gage walks away because you told him how you felt, then he's not the man I think he is."

"Then you don't think I've ruined everything?"

Don gave her a small smile. "No, if things are different now, it's only because Jimmy needs time."

"I have tried to do that, at least I hope I have."

"Then he will come around. Everyone needs space Carly, even people in love."

I know...it's just so hard sometimes."

"Yes, I know." Don stood giving her another smile. "So, what about those drafts?"

Carly nodded her head and shifted the papers on her desk around until she found what she wanted. When she handed them to Don she didn't let go causing him to look at her. "Thank you Don."

"That's what I'm here for." He's blue eyes twinkled as he gave her a wink.

"You are the best."

"Yea, if that's the truth then why are you head over heels in love with a fireman instead of me?" He teased.

Carly laughed as he hoped and he tweaked her nose with his finger. "Talk to you later kid."

"Ok, big brother."

Don laughed and shook his head. "Now why do I get that with all the girls?"

"Just lucky I guess." Carly teased.

He laughed again then turned to walk out of the room.

After her talk, Carly was able to get some very much needed work done. The sound of someone knocking on her door made her look up and she realized it was five o'clock. "Come In?"

The door opened and Carly jumped to her feet. "Michael?"

"Don't be afraid."

She saw the letter opener on her desk and grabbed it.

"I'm not going to hurt you. I just came to tell you good bye."

"Why should I believe you?"

"I understand why you don't, but it's the truth. I have put in for a transfer."

"Why?"

"I finally realized that you will never love me."

"Really? You came to that decision just like that." Carly snapped her fingers to emphasis the point.

"No, not just like that. I watched the way you cared for Gates while he was in the hospital."

"You did?"

"Yes, I was hoping that seeing how dangerous his job could be, you would decided like Sandy did to walk away, but you didn't."

"So you're leaving...just like that."

Michael gave her a small smile. "I don't blame you for not trusting me. I haven't given you much of a reason too, have I?"

"Michael, what is it you want?"

"I just wanted to wish you the best. I hope Gates can be the man you need."

"He is."

Michael nodded his head. "Then I guess there's nothing more to say."

Carly's instincts to her to keep her guard up.

"You really don't trust me, do you?

"Should I?"

"No, I guess not. Be happy, I really want that for you."

Carly didn't answer, she just stood holding the knife in front of her.

Michael nodded, turned, opened the door and walked out of her life.

"Well, did she believe you?"

"Yes, I thinks she did."

Sandy gave a whoop of laughter. "This is going to be easier then taking candy from a baby."

Michael gave Sandy a look of concern. "I told you, no harm is to come to Carly."

"Oh, I promise; I won't lay a figure on her."

There was something about the way Sandy had emphasized the word "I" that made him uneasy. "I mean it Sandy."

"I know, I promise."

Michael nodded, but there was something Sandy was holding back and he didn't like it. He didn't like it one bit.

16

Rick turned off the ignition, slightly shifted. "Alright, I'm waiting."

Jimmy gave Rick a confused look. "Waiting for what?"

"For you to tell me what's wrong?"

"Oh that." Jimmy opened the cab door and got out. "Nothing's really wrong…I…just need to figure out a few things."

Rick closed the door on his side of the squad and leaned on the hood. "About."

He shifted on his feet. "It's nothing."

"Are you still bothered by what Carly said last week?"

"Maybe…yea, I guess I am." He answered, running his hand through his hair as he spoke.

Rick walked to stand beside his friend.

"I thought you worked things out?"

"We did, sort of."

"What do you mean sort of?"

"I moved into the spare room."

"I'm sorry. I really thought Carly would come around."

"Oh, she said she didn't mean what she said."

"You don't believe her."

"Yea, I know she's sorry she said something."

"But…?"

"I also know she meant what she said."

"Jimmy…"

"Look Rick, I just need some time, that's all."

"Ok, then what?"

"What do you mean?"

"After you had the time you need, what are you going to do?"

Jimmy let out a sigh. "I don't know; that's my problem."

Rick was silent for a moment. "Well, think about what it is you really want before you make any decisions."

"I know what I want."

"What's that?" The expression on Jimmy's face told him all he needed to know.

"Then don't let what you have slip away."

"I'm not sure how to fix things."

"I think you do, in fact I would bet you have already started to formulate some kind of plan."

"Maybe…" Jimmy grinned.

"So what's the problem?"

"I might need some help to carry it out."

"What are we waiting for?"

The two men grinned at each other and headed into the dorm area.

Carly walked to her car looking behind her every few minutes. How she hated feeling scared again. *Why can't he leave me alone?* She put the key into her lock, opened the door, something was placed over her mouth. She clawed at the hand that held her to no avail and slowly slipped into unconsciousness.

The darkness started to ease as she heard her name being called. Her head pounded as if someone was beating a drum.

"That's it, come on wake up."

"Daisy…?"

"Yea, it's me."

"What happened?"

"You don't remember?"

"I remember opening my car door…" Carly jerked up, grabbing her head.

"Easy."

"You are one lucky girl."

"Someone put something over my mouth. It smelled so strange."

"Chloroform."

"Why?"

"Guess that would have to be something you told us."

" I don't have a clue. Why would the person just leave me?"

"They didn't, a Don Watson stopped them. He was the one that brought you here."

"Jimmy! You didn't call Jimmy, did you?"

"Not yet, we wanted to examine you first."

"Don't call him."

"Excuse me?"

"He would only worry and want to be here."

"I should hope so."

"Daisy, please, promise me you won't call him."

"I promise, but I don't understand why you don't want him to know."

"He has only been back to work for a week, I don't want him to miss any more."

"He might get a little suspicious when you aren't home in the morning."

"No, he won't. I'll be there when get gets home."

"You are being admitted for observation."

"I'm fine." Daisy raised her eyebrow. "Well, except for this headache. Please Daisy, Jimmy has been through so much, don't make him worry about me too."

"He will do that anyway when you tell him."

"I'm not going to tell him and I don't want anyone else to either."

"I can't promise you that."

"Yes, you can."

"Carly…"

She pushed herself up and waited for the nauseating pain to ease. "It's what I want Daisy."

"We will see what Dr. Barrett says, ok."

"Dr. Barrett can't tell Jimmy anything unless I say so."

"Are you going to hold him to that?"

"Yes, I am. I will tell Jimmy when I feel its right not before."

"Ok, what about the person that did this? You just going to pretend he isn't out there?"

"I have for months now, so what's the difference?"

Daisy was running out of arguments. "Fine, if this is how you want it."

"It is."

"I will tell Dr. Barrett what you have decided." Daisy stated as she walked to the door.

"Thank you."

"Don't thank me; you just make sure Jimmy Gates knows that I tried to talk you out of it."

"I will." Carly smiled.

"Oh, your friend is still here. I will send him in, alright."

"Thanks Daisy."

"Yea, uh huh." Daisy stated walking out the door shaking her head.

In twenty minutes Carly was sitting in Don's car on her way back home.

Don glanced over at her noticing how pale she looked. "I really think you should have stayed."

"Please Don, I really don't feel up to this anymore."

"That's why you should have stayed." Carly shot him a glance which only made him smile. "Tell me Miss Gibson, does that look work on Jimmy?"

"No."

"I didn't think so."

"Oh hush up."

Don muffled another laugh.

Around a half hour later they pulled into the drive. His intention was to see her safely into the house and tucked into bed then he would leave. Don stretched as he stood from Carly's couch. He had every intention of leaving after he made sure she had fallen asleep, but he felt uneasy leaving her alone. What if the man tried again? So he grabbed a blanket and pillow he found in the next room and crashed on her couch. Picking up the pillow and blanket he took it back to where they belong.

As he put the things away, he noticed the articles lying around the room, cologne on the dresser…Old Spice. "Well, now I know why Carly felt she had ruined things." He whispered. Sitting the bottle down, he walked back into the living room. What happened between them was none of his business. Deciding to check on her one more time Don walked to open her bedroom door. He found her still sleeping hugging the pillow beside her. *Gates, I hope you know what you are doing?*

Quietly he closed the door and walked back into the living room. He had just reached the front door when he heard the sound of a vehicle coming to a stop. This could get messy if Gates is a hothead. Taking a deep breath he opened the door and walked out onto the deck.

Jimmy had everything worked out, thanks to Rick and the Cap. Now if Rick came through on his end everything would be great. Jimmy stopped his Land Rover in front of the house and opened the door to get out when he saw the front door open. He smiled knowing Carly's first question would be how did his shift go? The smile left his face when he saw a man walk out the door, only then did he notice the car he parked next too.

Don saw the surprise that crossed Jimmy's face to be quickly replaced with fear. Holding up his hand, he said, "Mr. Gates, I'm Don Watson. I'm a friend of Carly's."

"I see." Jimmy said as he took the steps two at a time.

"I know what you must be thinking…"

"Do you?" The muscle in Jimmy's jaw flexed. "I doubt that."

"I just wanted to make sure Carly was safe after what happened last night."

Jimmy felt his heart fall to his stomach.

"I'm sorry; I thought Carly had told you." Don stated seeing surprise cross Jimmy's face.

"Told me what?"

"She said she had taken care of everything. If I had known then I would never have brought her home."

"Mister, I don't know what you're talking about, but if Carly's been hurt…"

"Someone tried to kidnap her last night."

Jimmy's knees must have buckled, because Don reached out and grabbed his arm. "You alright?"

"Where's Carly?"

"In bed, sleeping. I just checked on her." Jimmy's eyebrow rose. "That's all I did, Gates."

Jimmy shoved past him and almost ran into the house. He opened the door to their room finding Carly just has Don had said, asleep. He sat down beside her and swept her hair lightly back away from her face. Jimmy's voice broke as he whispered against her check just before he gave her a light kiss. "I love you."

After a few seconds he stood and turned to leave the room and saw Don watching him from the door. "I want you to tell me what happened last night."

Jimmy led him into the kitchen where he made a pot of coffee. It wasn't that he wanted a cup so much; he just needed to be busy. When he was finished, he faced Don. "Ok, what happened?"

Once both men were seated, Don told him of the events that occurred the day before.

"Why didn't she tell me?"

"I guess she didn't want you to worry. I know she would do anything to keep you from worrying about her."

"I know Carly tries to take everything on herself, but she should have told me."

"Maybe she felt she couldn't."

Jimmy jerked his head up from looking at the coffee cup he held between his hands. "There isn't anything Carly couldn't tell me."

"Even though you sleep in separate rooms?"

Jimmy shoved his chair back causing Don to do the same. "Now before you start yelling, let me explain. I noticed your things in the other room when I put the blanket and pillow away I used."

Jimmy slowly sat back down. "I see."

Don ran his hand through his hair. "What happens between you and Carly is none of my business, but I do care about her. I think of her like I do my own sister." At Jimmy's raised eyebrow he smiled. "Well, I do now anyway. Carly loves you; there is no one else for her."

"I know she loves me."

"But, your job scares her."

"She told you."

"Yes, but only because I caught her staring out the window trying to believe she hadn't ruined things between you."

Jimmy glanced down at his coffee.

Don leaned against the table. "If you let this fear get between what you both have, you will regret it for the rest of your life."

"I know that and I had made my mind up not to let it, but now…"

"If I know Carly at all, she will tell you."

"Yea; when our grandchildren are grown."

Don laughed knowing Jimmy was probably right. "Maybe." He looked down at his watch. "I better make myself scarce. The last thing I want is to get her dander up."

"Don't I know it?" Jimmy teased.

They pushed away from the table and Jimmy reached out his hand. "Thank you for being there when she needed someone. I don't know what I would do if anything ever happened to her."

"I'm glad I could help." Don stated taking Jimmy's outstretched hand.

"Do you have any idea, who could want to kidnap Carly?"

"I have an idea."

"Then I hope you can get to him before there is another attempt."

"You can count on it."

They shook hands again before Jimmy escorted him to the front door.

Carly woke to the sound of the shower running. Unsure what time it was, she glanced around the room for a clock. "Ten O'clock!" Carly exclaimed. "I can't believe I slept that late." She stated as she threw the covers back jumping to her feet. She dropped back to the bed when her legs refused to hold her. *Why can't I stand? I should be over the Chloroform, shouldn't I?* With her head still pounding she tried standing again, this time she remained on her feet. The sound of the water running stopped and Carly felt her heart jump into her throat. It was all she could do not to run from the room. "It's only Jimmy, stop being so paranoid." Even with that knowledge she still jumped when the door opened.

Jimmy walked into the room wrapping a towel around his waist, stopping when he saw Carly watching him. Her tongue darted out to wet her lips and then she started biting her lower lip. He finished wrapping the towel around him as he walked past her. "Something wrong, you look a little nervous."

"No…no…nothings wrong, I just didn't expect you to be using the bathroom."

Jimmy turned slightly, glanced at her, then turned back as he combed out his hair. "Is there a problem with me using it?"

"No, it's just…"

Jimmy stopped in his movement to watch her in the mirror. *She looks pale.* "It's just what?"

Carly lowered her eyes. "You haven't been…"

Jimmy turned to face her. "I haven't been…"

"Using it."

He faced the mirror again. "Guess, I decided I should change that."

Carly's eyes jerked back up to meet his in the mirror. "Does that mean…you are moving back in here?"

"That depends."

Carly's heart thumped in her chest. "On what?"

Jimmy lowered the comb, placed his hands flat on the dresser leaning toward the mirror. "If you tell me what happened yesterday."

Carly paled. "I don't know what you mean?"

Jimmy let his shoulders give in defeat. "I guess I'll be using the other bathroom from now on." He picked up his comb, turned to face her, "When you decide to tell me the truth, I'll be here."

Carly watched him pick up the clothes he had laid across the chair in the room. He took a step toward the door. "Wait." Jimmy froze in his movements. "How did you find out?"

Jimmy turned slowly toward her. "Does it matter? The fact is I know, but I want to hear you tell me."

Tears filled her eyes. "There really isn't much to tell."

" Sorry, wrong answer." Jimmy took another step.

"Jimmy, please…don't go."

He faced her once again.

"I was only trying to keep you from worrying."

"Carly."

Carly nodded her head as she reached out to grab the foot post. "Michael came by to see me yesterday."

"He did what?"

"Nothing happened, he wanted to tell me goodbye."

"I'm sure."

"I didn't believe him either until he walked out the door."

"You believed him?"

"I wanted to. I wanted all the threats to be over, for the fear to be gone." Sitting down on the bed she covered her face. How her head still hurt, she took a deep breath and continued. "I left my office around five thirty because I wanted to make sure he had left. Even then I kept looking over my shoulder." She crossed her arms to stop the cold that seemed to fill her. "I had put my key into the lock of my door when someone grabbed me from behind and put a cloth over my mouth." She looked up at Jimmy. "I tried to pull the hand away, I even tried screaming, it only made the smell worse. The next thing I remember was waking up with Daisy calling my name."

"Why didn't she call me?"

"I made her promise not to and I told Dr. Barrett he couldn't say anything to you either."

Jimmy stood from where he sat on the arm of the chair. "He should have told me anyway."

"He couldn't, because I told him not to."

"That shouldn't make a difference we're…"

"We're what Jimmy?" Carly stood angry that he had found out and angry at herself for wanting what would never be. "It's not like we are married, is it? You have no right to know anything, if I don't want you to."

"I have no right? What about the fact that I love you? Doesn't that give me a right to know?"

Carly used the words Jimmy had asked her a week ago. "Do you love me?"

The pain he saw cross Carly's face tore him apart. In two long strides he was beside her, he pulled her into his arms. "Yes, I love you. My life would be incomplete without you."

Carly wrapped her arms around his waist feeling his skin under them. She laid her head on his chest loving how it felt against her cheek as she inhaled the scent of his soap. *How I missed this.*

"I'm sorry, Jimmy."

"No, I'm sorry. I wanted to protect myself from your leaving so I tried to leave first."

"I never want to leave you." Carly lifted her head so she could look into his eyes. "When whoever had me last night, all I wanted was you."

Jimmy placed his hand on the back of her head and held her to him. "I'm so sorry, I wasn't there."

"You were; you were what kept me fighting."

"If anything had happened to you…"

"Nothing happened."

"Nothing will either. I called the detective and he is on his way over. I plan to make sure that Michael never comes near you again."

Carly raised her head to say something, but instead broke out of Jimmy's arms and ran for the bathroom. A few minutes later she felt the cold cloth against her forehead and signed from the coolness. Then she began to shiver, yet her body felt on fire. Jimmy lifted Carly into his arms and carried her back to their bed. Once she was settled he quickly dressed then rushed her to Regional General Hospital. By the time she was in the examination room her fever had spiked to one hundred and five.

17

"Did everything go as planned?"

"I couldn't have planned it better; even had a little bonus." Mathew stated.

"Really? What? Did she die right there?" Sandy's eyes gleamed with hope.

'No, a friend of hers came just in time to think he was saving her."

"Jimmy?"

"No, someone she works with I believe."

"Why, do you consider that a bonus? What if he gets her help before anything can get in her system?"

"You don't have to worry about that, she tried screaming so she got a really good dose of both the Chloroform and the virus."

The smile on Sandy's face made Mathew wonder what kind of person he was dealing with. He laughed to himself. *The same kind you are.*

"I wish I knew what was going on. Do you think if I showed up at the hospital that someone would get suspicious?" Sandy asked in excitement.

"I would give it a day or so."

Sandy's shoulders dropped in disappointment. "I'm not sure I can wait that long."

Mathew dropped his arm around Sandy's shoulders. "Remind me never to cross you."

Sandy laughed. "I'll do that." She dropped the smile. "I'm really not a bad person; if Carly had just left him like I hoped she would none of this would have happened."

"Carly has a way of getting in the way that's for sure." He glanced down at Sandy. "Did I ever thank you for tracking me down? If you hadn't then I would have never known where to find her."

"I think you hate her more than I do."

Anger flashed through Mathew's eyes. "Maybe."

"What did she do?"

"She stuck her nose where it didn't belong."

Sandy heard the underlying threat and dropped the subject. "You didn't say anything to Michael about what we were planning, did you?"

"No."

"Good because if he ever found out I was behind hurting Carly…" Sandy felt a shiver go through her.

Mathew studied her. "You think he would hurt you?"

"I know he would, He loves her for some unknown reason. He made me promise not to lay a hand on her."

"You kept your promise."

"Thanks to you." Sandy moved closer to him. "How can I repay you?"

Mathew leaned down and whispered. "I'll think of something."

Sandy smiled. "I bet you will."

"Jimmy?"

"Karen." Jimmy answered matter of fact voice.

"Yea, I know you didn't expect me."

Jimmy leaned back against the chair. 'It doesn't surprise me."

Karen watched him run his hand over his face. "Have you gotten any rest at all?"

"I drift off now and then when I'm next to her."

"Look, I'm here so why don't you go home and rest."

Jimmy shook his head as he gave a small stretch. "I wouldn't be able to rest."

"You aren't doing Carly any good by wearing yourself out."

"Karen I appreciate your concern, but I'm not leaving her."

"Ok, so you won't leave, but how about taking a break and getting something to eat."

"I'm not hungry." He stood up and started to pace. "What I don't understand is why they haven't said anything. It's been two days, they should know by now."

"They will tell you when they know something."

"That's not good enough!" Jimmy shook his head. "I'm sorry Karen, I'm just…it's the not knowing."

"Yea, I know."

Jimmy stopped his pacing and sat back down and placed his arm around her shoulders. "She'll be ok."

Karen nodded against his shoulder fighting back the tears, after a few minutes she raised her head. Jimmy looked at her in surprise. "I wouldn't want Chip to get the wrong idea." She teased.

"Yea, he would too." He teased. "Speaking of Chip, how was your trip?"

Karen gave Jimmy a small smile. "It was nice."

"Nice, huh? Well, I guess that's saying a lot considering you went away for two days with Chip."

"I resent that pal."

Jimmy smiled at Chip as he joined them. "What else is new, pal?"

"Now is that anyway to treat a newly married man?" Chip asked as he dropped his arm around Karen's shoulder.

"A What?"

The surprise on Jimmy's face sent Chip into a laughing spell. "Easy there." He looked at Karen. "Think we might need to call Barrett or Evans to give him shock treatment."

Jimmy looked from one to the other then pointed his finger at them. "You're serious, you got married."

Karen held out her left hand displaying the wedding band.

Jimmy shook his head in disbelief. "I never thought anyone could get this guy to say I do."

Chip grinned. "What can I say I know a good thing when I see it."

Jimmy reached out his hand. "Well then congratulations."

Chip took the outstretched hand. "Thanks Jimmy."

"Chip Keller married. The guys will never believe it, what am I saying? I don't believe it."

"Well, believe it Jimmy my boy."

The door to Carly's room opened ending any comment he was about to make and he moved without a word.

"Her fever broke." Kris Barrett stated lowly.

"Thank God." Karen stated.

Chip placed his arm around her giving her the support she needed.

Jimmy hadn't said a word he had however noticed the look on Barrett's face. "She's not out of the woods, is she?"

Kris folded his stethoscope. "I'm afraid not Jimmy. The virus attacked her vital organs so they are weak."

"I see. Doc, what kind of virus is it?"

"It's close to a virus that we dealt with a few years ago, but there is something different."

"What?"

"That's where we are stumped."

"You mean you don't know."

"Exactly."

Jimmy ran his hand through his hair.

"We have every reason to believe Carly will survive." Jerry Evans stated. "If her organs start to improve in the next twenty four hours then the out look is good."

"If they don't?" Karen asked.

"She will…she has to. May I go in?"

"Of course." Kris answered.

Jimmy opened the door to Carly's room, slowly walked over to her bed and picked up her hand. "Don't you leave me, do you hear."

"I hear." Carly whispered.

Jimmy's eyes jerked up to meet Carly's. "Hi."

"Hi." Carly frowned. "You need a shave."

Jimmy gave a low laugh. "I'm sure I do."

"What am I doing here? We were at home."

Jimmy sat down on the side of her bed and held her hand against his chest. "You have been very sick."

"I was wondering why I felt so bad."

Jimmy shook his head and smiled. "You are impossible."

"Yea, but you love me anyway."

"You can bet my life on that."

"That's ok, I don't bet, I'll just take your word for it."

Jimmy cleared the lump from his throat as he kissed the back of her hand. "Now you are starting to sound like me…joking when you feel like crap."

Carly gave him a weak smile. "I know of worse things."

"I love you."

"I love you too."

Jimmy watched as Carly closed her eyes then leaned down and kissed her cheek. "You sleep, ok.

Carly nodded and drifted off, while Jimmy sat by her side for another night.

Rick worked under the hood of the squad while his Jimmy worked underneath the squad. "How is Carly doing?"

Jimmy grunted as he tightened the bolt he was working on. "She's doing great; in fact, we have a date on Saturday."

Rick stopped in his movement, furrowed his brow. "Excuse me, did you say, you and Carly have a date Saturday?"

"Yea."

Rick leaned on the motor as he looked down to watch his friend. "May I ask, why?"

"Why - what?"

"Why a date?"

"Why not?"

Rick gave Jimmy a strange look and shrugged his shoulders. "Why not?"

"I just thought after all Carly has been through." Jimmy grimaced as he strain to tighten another bolt. "That she should have sometime to relax, you know take her mind off everything."

"And you think a date will do that?"

"I hope so."

"Where are you taking her?"

"To the Amusement Park."

This time when Rick stopped, he backed away from the squad. "The Amusement Park?"

Jimmy pushed out from under the squad and stood, placing his hands on his side. "Yea, what's wrong with that?"

"Nothing, nothing at all, except it sounds like something you would love not Carly."

"Ha… ha... For your information Mr. smarty pants, it was Carly's idea." Jimmy grinned at Rick's surprise expression. "That's right, her idea. It turns out she loves that place."

Rick shook his head. "Just when I thought Carly was the mature one."

"Very funny."

The Klaxon sounded before Rick could make a comment and both he and Jimmy quickly moved the tools out of the way. Jimmy shoved the cart he had been lying on back toward the back of the squad while Rick quickly shut the hood.

"Squad 15, woman shot. 219 Crestview Apartments. Time out. 6: 29 pm."

Rick grabbed the mic writing down the address as he spoke. "Squad 15, KMG 365." He through opened the door to the squad and handed Jimmy the paper.

Jimmy ran through the door first coming to a complete stop. He stared at the woman lying on the floor with blood pouring from her stomach. "Sandy?" The next moment he was by her side taking her pulse as he looked up at the man pressed against the wall. "How did this happen?" Once again Jimmy found him self staring in surprise. The surprise turned to anger. "What did you do?"

Michael shook his head. "It was an accident...we were fighting for the gun."

Jimmy quickly looked around spying the gun that now was underneath the table.

"Sandy, can you hear me? It's Jimmy."

It was a moment before he saw her eyes flutter and he let out a sigh of relief. "Don't worry about anything; we will get you to the hospital."

Rick opened the Bi-Phone. "Regional, this is Squad 15." He waited a moment as he waited for Jimmy to take Sandy's vitals.

"Regional, this is squad 15."

Daisy's voice came back to him. "Go ahead 15."

"We have a woman shot, age 27, stand by for B/P."

Jimmy raised his head with the stethoscope ear pieces in his ears. "B/P... 90/50; respiration...36, Pulse...130."

"Regional...B/P...90/50, respiration...36, Pulse...130."

"15...start IV with ringers. Keep an eye on the B/P and transport as soon as possible." Dr. Evans replied.

"10-4, Regional, IV with Ringers."

Jimmy ripped open the IV bag and started the IV. Rick looked up at Michael seeing how pale he was for the first time. "Are you alright? Have you been hurt?"

Michael shook his head and licked his lips. "Is she going to be alright?"

Jimmy jerked his head in Michael's direction. "It's a little late to be worrying about that, don't you think?"

"It's not what you think. I was trying to stop her."

"Well, I guess you have done that, haven't you."

"Jimmy." Rick said lowly.

"Sandy, you hang in there, ok."

Sandy opened her eyes as tears slid from them.

Jimmy wiped them away with his finger. "You will be alright. I want you to believe that, ok."

Sandy gave a slight nod and Jimmy moved to stand up. She grabbed his arm. "I'm sorry Jimmy."

"I know." He smiled at her tenderly.

The tears fell down her cheek faster. "You don't understand. I wanted her dead."

Fear froze Jimmy's movement. "Who?" Jimmy asked even though he knew the answer.

"Carly." Sandy closed her eyes briefly then opened them again. She licked her dry lips and took several breaths before she spoke again. "Michael was trying to stop me." She licked her lips again. "We fought for the gun and it went off."

Jimmy wanted to ask her why, but knew time was of the essence. "Don't talk; there will be time for that later."

Sandy shook her head. "No, have to say this now."

"Sandy, you can tell me everything later."

"NO!"

Rick was even surprised by her determination. "Sandy, we need to get you to the hospital."

"I loved him Rick, you know I did."

Rick touched her shoulder. "Yea, I know. Now relax and we will have you at the hospital in no time."

"Tell him I only wanted him back, he'll believe you if you tell him."

"I'll tell him."

"If she had only walked away then I wouldn't have hurt her."

"What?" Jimmy responded.

"I am the reason Carly got so ill. I stole the virus and gave it to Mathew. He never intended to kidnap her. It was set up to look that way so no-one would realize what was happening."

Jimmy sat back on his heels in disbelief.

Sandy reached her hand out to touch his arm. "I'm sorry Jimmy."

Jimmy sucked in his breath and released it "I know. Now just rest, ok and let us get you to the hospital."

Sandy nodded her head, closed her eyes and let her hand drop from his arm.

Jimmy grabbed her wrist giving a sigh of relief. "She alive."

"Let's get her out of her."

They lifted her onto the gurney then into the ambulance. "I'll ride in with her, ok."

"Sure Jimmy."

Jimmy jumped into the back of the ambulance. Rick shut the doors and stepped back. He watched the ambulance pull away before he hurried to the squad. Vince had arrived so he knew Michael had a lot of explaining to do.

Carly walked out of the examination room facing Dr. Barrett. "So, may I go back to work?"

"I see no reason why not."

"Good, I was beginning to go stir crazy just sitting around the house."

"You mean Jimmy hasn't been hovering?" Kris teased.

"Well, he's tried, but I haven't let him."

Kris raised his eyebrow. "Really?"

Carly laughed. "Ok, I haven't let him very much."

"That's what I thought."

Just then Jimmy came around the corner standing on the side of the gurney doing CPR. "Breathe! Don't you die on me Sandy, breathe!" Carly stepped back in horror as she watched Jimmy working on the woman who had done nothing but make their life a living nightmare. A sense of pride came over her as she watched him work to keep Sandy alive and once again she was reminded of why she loved him so much.

They rushed the gurney into the examination room she had just left, leaving the door open. Carly knew she should leave, but she couldn't move. Her feet seemed to be stuck to the floor and her eyes transfixed on the man working so hard to save Sandy's life. She watched as he pushed again and again on her chest, listening as he begged her to live. Suddenly he stopped and stepped back then she heard – Clear – and watched Sandy's body jump causing her to jump. Jimmy began compressions again. He stepped back and she heard – Clear – only for him to begin again. The touch of a hand on her shoulder caused her to jump. "Rick..." Carly sighed placing a hand on her chest.

"You alright?"

"I'm fine." Carly stated as she turned her attention back to the people in the room.

Rick started to suggest that maybe Carly should wait in the nurses lounge when Jimmy stepped back and wiped his head just before he lowered it. The sound of Carly's gasp made him glance in her direction.

"Carly..."

Carly stepped toward the door as she watched them pull the sheet over Sandy's face. Jimmy wasn't sure what surprised him most, the fact that Carly had witnessed Sandy's death or the compassion he saw on her face. Slowly he walked out to stop in front of her, he looked up at Rick. "We couldn't save her." He looked at Carly. "I wish you hadn't seen that."

Carly looked at the blood on Jimmy's hands and she reached out and touched them.

"I am." She lifted her gaze to his face. "It just proved to me I was right."

"About what?" Jimmy tried to hide the uncertainty in his voice.

"Of what kind of man you are and why I love you so much."

Jimmy let out a sigh as he turned to look at Sandy lying so still.

"You should go say goodbye." Carly suggested.

Jimmy jerked his eyes back to look at her. She gave him an understanding smile. "You shared a part of your life with her, it's only right that you were there with her when her life ended. I'm sure she was comforted by the fact you were."

Jimmy was at a lose for words.

. "Go on." She insisted.

Jimmy walked slowly back to the room not realizing Carly had walked behind him until he turned to shut the door. Carly gave him another smile, reached for the door and slowly closed it.

Rick walked up to stand beside her, placed an arm around her shoulders, hugging her to him. "You are a very special woman."

Carly shook her head. "No, I'm not. I'm just a woman that loves that man with all her heart."

Rick squeezed her shoulders again. "Come on, we'll wait for him in the cafeteria."

18

Carly sat staring at the cup of coffee she held in her hands as she waited on Jimmy. Ten minutes later he sat down beside her and took her hand in his. "Are you alright?"

Carly lifted her head and tried to smile. Her heart broke seeing the sadness in his eyes. She should hate Sandy, but she couldn't. As she looked at Jimmy, she wondered, if she might have reacted the same way that Sandy had. Carly gave her head a slight shake – No, she couldn't, but when she looked at Jimmy, she knew he was hurting and she wanted to ease that hurt. "I'm fine."

"You sure?"

"Yes."

"I know it wasn't easy to hear that someone I knew was trying to kill you."

Carly placed her other hand over his giving it a slight squeeze. "No, it wasn't, but it wasn't just someone you knew, Mathew was part of it also."

"I'm sure the police have him by now."

"I hope so. What about Michael? What will happen to him?"

"Probably nothing, he was trying to stop her when the gun discharged."

Carly nodded her head as she pushed back her chair to stand. She gave Rick a small smile then looked back at Jimmy. "I guess you better get back to the station."

Jimmy stood and moved beside her. "We can stay awhile longer. I really don't want to leave you alone right now."

"I'll be alright, besides the danger is over, we can all relax."

"Maybe you could call Jillian?" He directed his question to Rick.

"Sure."

"There's no need to do that. I'm fine, I'm just worried about you."

"There's nothing to be worried about." Jimmy replied.

"You sure?"

"Yes."

"If that's true, why haven't you washed Sandy's blood from your hands?"

Jimmy stared down at his hands then started to rub them. "I forgot it was on them."

Carly covered his hands with hers too still them. "It's ok Jimmy. You can grieve."

Jimmy blinked several times and took a deep breath. "I better get this off my hands before we have another run. I'll be right back."

"He's going to need a friend." Carly stated.

"Yea, I know. He'll talk to us when he needs too, just give him some time." Rick placed his arm around her shoulders, making her wonder when he had moved. "He'll be ok."

"I know I just love him so much."

"Jimmy knows that and it'll be because of that love he will be his old self before too long."

"I hope so Rick, I really hope so." She said then rested her head on his shoulder while they waited for Johnny to return.

Carly woke to a bright and sunny day. She let her hand slide to Jimmy's side of the bed knowing he wouldn't be there. He had worked the last couple of days instead of taking his day off. As she stretched she wondered if he would call to tell her he was working once again. Slipping out of bed she headed for the shower. He would call soon enough she guessed, no sense worrying though that was exactly what she would do.

Once Carly was finished with her shower, she dressed in a light blue T-shirt and a pair of blue jeans. She dried her hair and she placed a hair band over it pulling it back away from her face letting the rest fall over her shoulders. Reaching for her make-up she debated about putting it on, but decided she would. When she was finished in the bedroom she walked down the hall toward the kitchen stopping in her tracks.

"Jimmy, you startled me."

"I'm sorry; I thought you heard me come in."

"I guess the hairdryer must have covered the sound."

"Guess so."

Carly noticed the cup sitting on the table. "Did you make enough for two?"

Jimmy looked up from his paper. "Excuse me?"

Carly pointed at the cup. "Coffee, did you make enough for two?"

"Oh, yea, sure there's enough." He returned his attention back to the paper giving it a snap.

Carly stood still for a moment then mumbled, "Thank You." as she walked into the kitchen to pour herself a cup. She had just poured her a cup when she felt arms wrap around her. She screamed sending the cup flying and the coffee spilling over her hand.

"Are you alright?" Jimmy asked as he spun her around. He pulled her over to the sink and ran cold water over her hand. "I'm sorry, sweetheart. I shouldn't have came up behind you like that."

"It's alright."

Jimmy knew she wasn't alright from the way she trembled in his arms. "I know you are still nervous about having someone walk up behind you. I just thought..."

"Since Sandy died I would be ok."

"Yea, stupid I know."

Carly turned to face him and when she did her body moved against him causing him to catch his breath. *Maybe I can help him after all.* "As long as I know you are alright, I will be just fine." Carly moved closer. Jimmy caught his breath - Carly smiled - Jimmy returned the smile.

Carly whispered against his cheek. "Don't you need to rest?"

"That wasn't exactly what I had in mind."

"What did you have in mind?" She asked brushing her lips across his cheek.

"Anyone home? Jimmy we're here."

Jimmy groaned as Carly stared at him in surprise. Clearing his throat, he stepped back .

"Yea, Rick; we're in the kitchen."

The sound of Chris and Jennifer running toward the kitchen made Jimmy decide he better take a shower. He knew what kind of shower it would be too. Carly caught the glint in his eyes and let out a small giggle.

"Go ahead and laugh. I will have the last one." He gave her a quick kiss just as the kids came in.

"Yuck!" Chris stated.

"I think it' nice." Jennifer said.

"You would, you're a girl."

"Ok, you two. I'll be back in a few minutes. Put something on that hand while I'm gone."

"Yea sure."

"Jimmy, you're not ready?" Rick asked when he walked into the kitchen.

"Don't rush me, don't rush me."

Carly slapped her hand across her mouth to keep back the laughter bringing the red mark to Rick's attention.

"What happened?"

"Oh, I spilled coffee on my hand."

"Let me take a look."

"My husband the paramedic." Jillian stated as she too came into the kitchen. "Why don't you go talk to Jimmy while he gets ready and I'll take care of Carly."

"Bossy isn't she?" Jimmy teased.

"She has her moments."

"I heard that."

Rick kissed her check. "I wouldn't have it any other way."

"Suck up." Jimmy stated

"You better believe it."

Carly and Jillian giggled as the men left the kitchen and the kids headed out the back door to play with Husky- Jimmy's Alaskan Husky.

Jillian took Carly's hand. "Now let me look at that. Where's your burn cream?"

"In the top drawer on the right."

While the women talked in the kitchen, the men talked in the other room.

"So, how did Carly spill the coffee on her hand?"

Jimmy stopped putting the shaving cream on his face. "I came up behind her."

"I guess she's still jittery."

"Yea, it will probably take her awhile to get past everything."

"Carly's strong, she'll be ok."

"Yea, I know she is...still..."

"You worry about her."

"Yea."

"Just shows how much she means to you."

"I guess."

"I bet if I would talk to Carly, she would tell me she worries about you."

"Probably."

"Can't say I blame her."

Jimmy turned to face him. "What do you mean?"

"I'm worried about you too."

"I'm fine, Rick."

"So you keep telling me."

"It's the truth."

"Ok, I'll take your word on it."

"Thank You."

Rick sat on the bed for a few minutes then walked to lean against the bathroom door.

You sure Carly won't mind us coming along. This was supposed to be a date for the two of you."

"I'm sure. Carly loves you all."

"I know, but it seems to me that..."

"What?"

"You are finding reasons not to be alone with her."

"Don't be ridiculous Rick."

"Am I?"

Of course you are." Jimmy splashed water over his face then reached for a towel. After drying his face he found a change of clothes and quickly changed into them.

"Ok, I'm ready, lets get started."

The rest of the day was spent with kids laughing and the adults smiling. Rick and Jimmy even joined the kids on a ride called "The Spider." Of course, it did take some convincing for them to do it. Jimmy talked Carly into riding the Roller Coaster with him. She spent the whole ride with her face buried in his chest and his arms wrapped tightly around her. It was her favorite ride. By the end of the day everyone was happy and exhausted. The kids fell asleep on their parents lap in the back seat of Jimmy's Land Rover, so when they pulled the car into the driveway Carly suggested that they spend the night and after a little convincing Jillian and Rick agreed.

They put the kids in one of the spare rooms and settled them down for the night. Carly had made a fresh pot of coffee while Jimmy made a few sandwiches. The rest of the night was spent with the four friends talking. When Carly and Jimmy finally said goodnight to Rick and Jillian it was close to one in the morning. They stopped in front of the other spare room said a quick goodnight and parted.

Carly snuggled against Jimmy when they finally settled in bed. "I love you." She whispered against his chest and fell soundly asleep. Jimmy kissed her head. "I love you too, more than you will ever know." He felt the smile she gave him wondering if she was still awake until he heard the soft steady rhythm of her breathing. Tightening his hold on her, he too fell asleep.

The sound of Jimmy's whistling drifted into the kitchen where Max, Mike, Chip, Captain Stone and Rick all sat drinking their morning coffee.

"Someone's in a good mood." Chip stated as he sipped his coffee.

"Yea, it's been awhile." Max replied.

Rick sat down his cup and placing his arms around it as he leaned in to speak. "It's been hard on Jimmy these past few months."

"Yea, we know Rick, we know." Chip said.

Rick started to reply when Jimmy made his appearance. "Morning; beautiful day isn't it?" Everyone stared at him up surprise, including Rick. "What, a guy can't be happy?"

Chip drank from his cup again. "Sure Gates, but were not used to it being you, that's all."

"Shut up Chip."

Chip grinned satisfied and pushed his chair back. "I think I'll go check the hoses."

Rick shook his head. "Chip should be a washing Machine."

"Why do you say that?" Harry asked.

"He's an agitator."

A burst of laughter spurted out from everyone.

"I heard that."

They all laughed again just as the Klaxon sounded.

"Squad 15, heart attack...210 Westwood Dr. Cross Street...Clavier. Time out...8:10 am.

"Squad 15, KMG 365." Captain Stone stated into the mic.

Rick glanced over at his partner just before they pulled out. He had seen the apprehension that had crossed his face when the Klaxon rung.

The squad pulled up in front of the house as a woman came running to the curb.

"Please help him." She cried as she grabbed Jimmy's arms.

Jimmy placed a hand on her shoulder. "Is it your husband?"

"Yes, he's in so much pain."

"Ok ma'am, we will do all we can."

Jimmy stepped to the squad throwing the compartment doors open and doing a side step as he slid back to get the drug box and oxygen out as Rick grabbed the defibrillator and EKG machine. They ran behind the woman into the house seeing a man stretched out on the couch.

"Sir, how bad is the pain?" Jimmy asked as he rushed to his side.

"It's bad." The man said as he clutched at his chest.

Jimmy eased down beside him. "Sir, we are going to do all we can to ease that pain, alright."

The man nodded as Jimmy looked up at his wife. "What's his name?"

"Dave."

"Well Dave, what we are going to do is hook you up so the hospital can see what we see, ok."

"Sure."

As soon as Jimmy had Dave's shirt open Rick placed the tabs for the EKG on his chest while Jimmy took his B/P. "Dave, have you had any heart problems before."

"Yes, about a year ago I suffered a light heart attack."

"Ok, how long were you hospitalized?"

"About a week."

"Lite huh?" Jimmy whispered. He touched the man's upper stomach to get his respiration. "Rick his respiration is 16"

"Ok."

Rick opened the Bi-phone. "Regional, squad 15."

"Dr Master's voice came back at him. "Go ahead 15."

"Regional we have a male approximate age 47, complaining of a heavy chest pain radiating down his left arm. We are going to send you a strip, Vitals are...B/P 160/102, Pulse... 86, respiration 16. He's in considerable pain.

"10-4. Start Iv with D5WTKO and administer 5Mg MS."

10-4 Regional." Rick hung up the phone and started helping Jimmy with the IV and MS.

Jimmy got on the Bi-Phone. "Regional, IV is in, MS is in."

"10-4, 15."

Jimmy looked at the screen. "He's gone into V-Tack Rick! Regional Patient is in V-Tack."

"Administer 100 MG Lidocaine IV push, then start a Lidocaine drip."

"10-4 Regional." This time Jimmy went to help Rick and while they were administering the Lidocaine, Dave went into Cardiac arrest. They grabbed him off the couch while Mike Masters told them to defibrillate which they did twice. "Nothing." Jimmy stated as he grabbed the Bi-phone. "Regional we have defibrillated twice with no results."

"10-4 15 insert an Esophageal airway and defibrillate."

"10-4 Regional." Rick pressed the button on the paddles once again and glanced at the monitor almost holding his breath. When he saw the regular rhythm he sighed in relief. Jimmy dropped his head in relief. "We got him back." He looked up at Dave's wife in tears. "We will do everything we can."

" Thank you."

Jimmy nodded then turned his attention back to his work. Five minutes later they were at Regional and Dave was getting the care he needed. When Jimmy walked out the door Dave's wife grabbed his arm and hugged him. "Thank you." When she pulled away she did the same to Rick. They told her she was welcome then headed for the squad.

Once in Jimmy turned to face Rick. "I wasn't sure we could save him."

"Yea, I know."

"It's good to feel good about what we do again."

Rick watched his friend closely. "So you were apprehensive about the run."

"Yea, I knew it wouldn't be Carly because she is with Jillian and Karen, but there was a part of me...well...you know."

"Yea, I know." Rick started the squad. "You sure were happy this morning any particular reason why?"

Jimmy grinned that grin that so many women fell for. "Any reason I shouldn't be?"

Rick shrugged. "No, just this morning you were a little more so."

"Let me ask you something?"

"Ok."

"Weren't you happy on the day you decided to ask Jillian to marry you?"

"You're going to ask Carly to marry you?"

"Yup."

"You're sure this is what you want to do?"

Jimmy stared at him in surprise. "I thought you would be happy I was finally settling down."

"I am I just want to make sure you really want this."

"I have wanted this for months, but something always seemed to happen and now..."

"You feel things are right."

"I guess so."

Rick drove in silence for a moment. "When do you plan to ask her?"

Jimmy grinned as he rubbed his hands together. "I'm so glad you asked that question."

"Tell me again, why you love this?" Jillian gasped out as she tried to keep up with her friend.

Carly smiled. "It's energizes me."

Karen placed her hand on her chest trying to catch her breath as well. "I guess I am more out of shape then I thought."

"Ok, I get it you both want to take a break, right?"

Karen and Jillian looked at each other then back at Carly. "No, of course not." They spoke at the same moment.

Carly laughed and slowed her pace. "Ok, lets walk for awhile. It's not good just to come to a quick stop."

Karen sighed with relief. "Sounds good to me."

"Yea, me too." Jillian chimed in. They walked for a few minutes without speaking. Carly was just enjoying being out with her friends not having to worry if someone was watching. Mathew had been picked up and was waiting trial. She wasn't looking forward to testifying, but at least her life could get back to normal. Glancing over at Karen and Jillian she watched the reflection of the sun bounce off their wedding rings. "What's being married to Chip like?"

"Great, he's still very romantic."

"It has only been a couple of months." Jillian teased.

"Yea, I know, but it's still nice the way he waits on me."

"Enjoy it while you can."

Karen tilted her head. "You mean Rick doesn't do things for you?"

"Sure he does, but sometimes he needs a little reminder, just like any man."

"Yea, it seems lately Jimmy comes in and picks up the paper and I don't see his face again until he's ready to eat."

The three laughed as they came to a turn in the track. Jillian saw a huge shade tree and sighed. "Lets take a break."

"Yea, you may be use to this but, us old married women aren't." Karen teased.

Carly knew she shouldn't be bothered by Karen's words, but she was, still she smiled and nodded her head unable to speak.

"You alright Carly. You seem a little sad." Jillian asked.

"No, I'm fine." She leaned against the tree closing her eyes when she opened them she discovered she was alone. Karen and Jillian were almost running around the next bend. "I thought you said you were tired!"

Carly started to follow them when she caught a glimpse of a red rescue truck coming to a stop. She was suddenly reminded of another time she watched one like it pull up. The number 15 stood out plain on the door and Carly knew that whoever it was they were getting the best team in the department. The door of the squad opened slowly and a moment later Jimmy stepped out.

Carly caught her breath as she watched him start to walk toward her. Her tongue darted out to wet her suddenly dry lips. *Control yourself girl, he's here to help someone in trouble.* Suddenly it struck her that he was indeed coming toward her, quickly she looked around and realized that she was standing in the exact spot when she first saw him. The quick grin that flashed across his face told her it was no accident that she was.

Jimmy stopped in front of Carly. He ran his hand through his hair and then slowly dropped to one knee, reached in his pocket and pulled out a small velvet box asking as he opened it. "Carly Gibson, will you do me the honor of becoming my wife?"

Carly's gaze went from Jimmy to the ring and then back to Jimmy. Tears filled her eyes. "Yes, yes I would love to be your wife."

Jimmy slipped the ring on her finger then stood. "I love you so much and I couldn't find a more perfect spot to ask you then where we first met." He pulled her into his arms. "I fell in love with you that day."

Carly tightened her arms around his neck. "I know how you feel."

Jimmy's brow lifted. "You fell in love with you then also?"

"No silly, I fell in love with you that day." Carly laughed as she moved closer to him.

"Oh, well, that's better. I would hate to think I had asked you to marry yourself."

"Gates, will you shut up and kiss me."

"If you insist."

"I do."

"Save that for the vows." He teased.

"Well, I'll just say it again, ok."

"Ok." Jimmy tightened his arms around her and brought his mouth close to hers. "No, second thoughts."

"None."

Jimmy let his lips touch hers wondering if he would ever get tired of feeling them. He was just about to deepen the kiss when the sound of the Klaxon from the squad reached him. He broke the kiss. "Gotta run, we will celebrate tomorrow when I get home."

"Count on it." Carly whispered.

He quickly gave her another kiss.

"Jimmy, we got to go!" Rick yelled from the squad.

"I'm on my way!"

Carly watched him run toward the squad loving the view she was seeing. Taking a deep breath she slowly let it out. "You just wait until tomorrow Gates, you just wait." The sound of laughter from behind her made her turn around. Seeing her two friends she placed her hands on her hips. "I don't know how you do this. Can we rest?" She mocked.

Karen and Jillian laughed as they hugged her. "We had to think of something. Now let us see that ring." Jillian stated excitedly.

Carly held out her hand. If Carly were to tell the truth, she couldn't stop looking at it either. Her dream was finally happening, she was marrying the man she loved.

19

Carly stared at her reflection in the long length mirror that had been brought in. The dress she wore was made for a princess, though Carly knew she was far from, but on that day she felt like one. Her hair laid straight down her back in spiral curls, there was a tiara the veil was attached to, the white of the dress bringing out her tan. She took a shaky breath as she ran her hands down the side of her dress. "I wish you were here Tommy."

Jillian placed her hands on Carly's shoulders. "He is."

Carly smiled at her friend in the mirror. "Thank You." The sound of a knock on the door brought their conversation to a close. "Carly?" Jimmy enquired. She spun to face the door in surprise. Normally she wasn't a superstitious person, but after everything that had happened the past few months she wasn't going to take a chance.

Jillian patted Carly's shoulder. "Don't worry I won't let him in."

"Thank you."

Jillian walked to the door eased it open and poked her head out the door. "Jimmy Gates you know you can't come in here."

"Why not? It's not like I haven't seen Carly before."

"Jimmy Gates..."

"I have a surprise for her."

Carly walked to stand behind the door. "What kind of surprise?"

Jimmy heard the swish from Carly's dress and his heart did a flip. "Well I guess you will just have to let me in to find out."

"That's not fair."

"I think it is. You kicked me out of my own home yesterday so the least I should be able to do is give you my surprise personally."

Jillian slipped through the crack of the opening making sure not to tear her dress. When she stepped out Jimmy gave a low whistle. "Maybe I should marry you instead." Jimmy teased as he slipped his arm around Jillian's waist.

"I heard that Gates." Carly said behind the slightly opened door.

"Junior, if I were you I'd take your arm from around my wife." Rick teased.

Jillian gave Jimmy a slight shove. "You are impossible." Turning to give her husband a kiss on the check. "I thought you were keeping an eye on him."

"Can I help it if I turned my back and he was gone?"

"I'm not a child."

A "Hump" came from behind the door as Rick crossed his arms and Jillian gave him a raised eyebrow.

"Well, I'm not."

Rick shook his head and looked at his wife. "Maybe we should renew our vows as well, you look beautiful."

"Thank you kind sir." Rick stepped back, giving Jillian a smile. She wore a spaghetti strapped   blue   silk   gown   that   was   form   fitting. Jillian caught Jimmy just before he slipped through the door. "Oh no you don't." She stated as she stepped in front of him.

"Oh, come on Jillian, just for a moment."

"No sir, now get."

Jimmy dropped his head in defeat. "OK."

"Wait! What about my surprise you said you had?" Carly asked.

"Oh, I almost forgot." He faced Rick.

"I was just coming to tell you they are here."

Carly stamped her foot. "Who's here?"

"A head popped through the door. "We are."

Carly let out a cry. "Mom!"

Nina Gibson smiled at her daughter. "Yes baby, your Dad and I are here."

Tears filled Carly's eyes, the last she had heard they were out of town and wouldn't be able to get back in time. "But, I thought..."

"Do you think I would let my little girl get married without me being able to give her away?" Ed Gibson asked.

"Dad! Oh Dad, you are really here."

Ed wrapped his arms around his daughter. "Yes baby, I'm here." He hugged her for a moment then took a step back. "Now let me look at you."

Carly turned in a circle for them. "What do you think?"

Nina smiled at her. "I think you are the most beautiful bride I have ever seen."

"Thank you Mom." Carly started biting her lower lip. "Have you met Jimmy?"

"Yes and he seems to be a wonderful man and handsome."

"I think so." Carly hugged both her parents. "I can't believe you both are here."

"We wouldn't have missed it, sweetheart. I know your brother would be so proud of you." Ed stated.

"I wish he was here."

"He is."

Carly smiled as she dabbed at her eyes with a tissue. The sound of the music started and Carly felt her heart skip a beat.

"You sure this is what you want? Nina asked.

"Oh, yes mom, I'm very sure."

Jillian and Karen came in the room. "Are you ready?" Karen asked.

Carly nodded unsure if she could speak.

"Lets do it." Jillian said.

Carly looked at her Mom just before she hugged her. "I love you, mom."

Nina kissed her daughter's cheek. "I love you too." She replied before she was escorted outside to her chair by Rick's son Chris. He was dressed in a black suit and tie, trying to look all grown up and serious. After a few minutes Carly nodded her head indicating she was ready. They opened the bedroom door, walked down the hall and waited just inside the patio doors out of sight.

When the first sound of music began Karen made her way out the door. She smiled seeing Chip looking so handsome in his black tux standing next to Rick. Jillian made her way out next and she smiled at Rick who stood next to Jimmy. Rick mouthed, I love you bringing a bigger smile to her face as she took her place next to Karen.

Carly clutched her father's arm and felt a comforting pat making her look up at him.

"You are beautiful."

"Thankyou,Dad.
He gave his daughter a kiss on the cheek. "Jimmy Gates better be good to you."

"He is Dad."

If he had any doubts about Jimmy's feelings for Carly they disappeared the moment Jimmy set eyes on her. The love that crossed his soon to be son- in - law face was evident and at that moment he knew his daughter had made a good choice.

Jimmy stood beside Rick trying not to show how nervous he was, but the glances Rick gave him, told Jimmy he wasn't doing such a great job. In truth, he just wanted to see Carly walk out the door. *Maybe we should have eloped.*

Rick leaned close to him. "If you had eloped Jillian would have killed you."

Jimmy stared at him. "How did you..."

"I know you remember."

Jimmy shook his head. *Sometimes he scares me.*

Rick smiled. *He's so predictable.*

Carly and her father stepped out the door at the sound of the music. Her heart skipped a beat seeing Jimmy standing so tall and handsome. *How did I get so lucky?*

Jimmy sucked in his breath. "She's so beautiful. How did I get so lucky?" He whispered.

Chip leaned toward him. "I've often wondered about that myself, Gates."

Jimmy gave him a scowl. "Oh shut up, Chip."

Rick gave his head a slight shake. *How did I get stuck between these two?*

Chip smiled. 'I'm happy.'

Karen watched the satisfaction that crossed her husband's face. When she caught his eye she gave her head a slight shake. Chip just grinned more knowing he had something else to tease Jimmy Gates about.

Jimmy watched Carly as she slowly walked toward him. It seemed forever for her to reach him. He reached out to shake his soon to be father in law's hand and watched as Ed gave his daughter a kiss on the cheek. He stepped back to wait until he could say, "Her mother and I do."

Jimmy placed Carly's hand in the bend of his arm and faced the minister. He listened as the minister talked about marriage, the ups and downs they would face. He repeated the vows he needed to say to make Carly his wife then slipped a plain good band on her finger. A tear fell when Carly repeated her vows and Jimmy wiped it away with his thumb.

"With the power invested in me I..."

"Wait." Jimmy stated. The minister as did everyone else stared at him in surprise. "There is something I want to say, if that's alright."

"Sure, if you would like to."

Jimmy took both of Carly's hands in his trying to find just the right words. Jimmy stared at her hands for so long that Carly wondered if he was going to speak at all when he finally looked up.

"Carly you came into my life like a whirl wind. I never expected to feel as I do much less wanted too. I was ready to spend my life without knowing what loving someone really meant. When I saw you that first time, trying so hard not to show how much pain you were in, I knew I should run as fast as I could in the opposite direction." The small burst of laughter brought a smile to Jimmy's face. He reached up to touch her face. "You showed me what the power of love can do and I promise you here and now that no matter what we will always have that kind of love."

Carly let the tears fall as Jimmy turned to face the minister. "As I was saying, "I now pronounce you man and wife. Whomever God has joined together, let no man tear apart."

"Just let them try." Jimmy whispered.

Carly smiled, Rick and Chip grinned as they shook their heads.

"You may kiss the bride."

"Gladly." Jimmy wrapped his arms around Carly kissing her. The sound of clapping brought them apart. "We will finish that kiss later, Mrs. Gates."

"Promises, promises."

Jimmy gave her a wink bringing a giggle from Carly.

How long is this reception. Carly wondered.

The moonlight sparkled across the water like diamonds as the breeze slightly blew across the sand, brushing Carly's hair gently away from her face. The events of the day played through Carly's mind bringing a smile to her face. If she closed her eyes, she could still feel Jimmy's arms around her as they danced their first dance as man and wife. The sound of music drifted down around her and she found herself once again standing in the middle of the dance floor that was placed in their back yard. Jimmy stood in front of her with his hand held out. She took his out reached hand, stepped closer to him as he wrapped his left arm around her waist. Carly's eyes misted as she heard the song that Jimmy had chosen for their first dance.

Arms wrapped around her bringing her back to the present. "Could I have this dance?" Carly turned in his arms, wrapped her arms around his neck. "For the rest of my life."

Jimmy smiled bringing his lips to hers as their wedding song played on the stereo. Slowly, he started to move with the music encouraging Carly to follow him and there on the balcony of their hotel room, in the moonlight for the second time in a day Carly felt the tears fall as Jimmy softly sang along with the song. She laid her head on Jimmy's shoulder watching the way the light made her rings on her hand sparkle as they danced.

The smell of Jimmy's cologne filled her senses sending desire to be closer to him through her. She touched her lips to his neck as the song ended. Slowly, she traced it until she reached his chin where she placed her lips against his dimple. The sound of Jimmy's intake of breath told her it was having her desired affect. She smiled against the side of his mouth then proceeded to kiss his other dimples while pressing herself against him.

On her second round of kissing, Jimmy gave a low groan, slightly bent sweeping her off her feet. In one quick move, he stepped through the doors into their room closing the door with his foot. Without taking his eyes from Carly's he walked to the bed, gently lying her down. He stretched out beside her placing his arm around her waist.

"Now it's my turn." He whispered against her throat. Carly licked her lips bringing a crooked smile to his face. True to his words, Jimmy returned the sweet torture she had bestowed on him just moments before.

Carly woke to the sound of Jimmy's breathing and his arm wrapped around her. The sun from the balcony doors shinned through bringing with its warmth. She rose up on one elbow watching him sleep, he had his left arm slung over half his face along with a satisfied smile. She leaned against him placing a kiss on that dimple that could make her heart melt just at the site of it. "I love you." She whispered against his cheek, placing a kiss there then another on his neck.

Jimmy woke to the feel of Carly's lips against his cheek. He didn't breathe much less move afraid he would shatter that moment, Every nerve in his body jerked with the need to pull her to him, but he wanted to see how far she would go. Jimmy didn't have long to wait, she ran her hand down his stomach feeling the scar and her lips soon found their way to it. Jimmy caught her shoulders pulling her on top of him seeing the satisfaction in her eyes. "You knew I was awake." Jimmy said smiling.

"The minute I heard you take that deep breath."

"I will make you pay."

"Promises, Promises."

Epilog

Carly leaned against the fence of the corral watching the horses as they ran. A pair of arms came into view on each side of her as hands gripped the fence. "Now you are my captive."

Carly smiled as she leaned her head back against Jimmy's chest. "Well, I guess I will just have to learn to live with it."

"Really? Well, don't force yourself." Jimmy stepped back letting his arms drop, giving her a smack on her backside.

Carly yelped. "One day Gates."

"Promises, Promises."

Carly tried to look threatening, but knew she hadn't succeeded. Shaking her head she faced the horses again. A feeling of dread filled her knowing that Jimmy would be returning to work the next day. She longed to be back in Hawaii where they took walks on the beach, sat on the balcony watching the waves hit the shore at night. She would miss waking up next to him each morning and not having to think about anything but him.

"Why so sad?" Jimmy asked wrapping his arms around her.

"I'm not sad, just wishing."

"Wishing for what?"

"To be back in Hawaii; I hate that the honeymoon is over."

Jimmy kissed her neck. "Who says the honeymoon is over?"

Carly sighed in contentment. "You know what I mean. You will be going back to work tomorrow and so will I."

"So?"

"I'm just going to miss being with you, that's all."

"You going some where?"

"Jimmy, you know what I mean. Being like we were in Hawaii. Taking walks, going horseback riding, just being together."

Jimmy squeezed her against him, kissing her neck again. "Well, we still have today. Why don't we pack a lunch and go for a horseback ride now? We could find a secluded spot and pretend we were on a deserted island all alone."

"Sounds good, only problem with that is we have to come back."

Jimmy turned Carly to face him. "Tell me the truth, are you missing us being alone or are you worried about me going back to work?"

Carly lowered her head only to have Jimmy place his finger under her chin to force it back up. "I want you looking at me when you answer."

"Both."

Jimmy hugged Carly to him. "Thank you for being honest."

Carly wrapped her arms around his waist. "I know I'm being silly. I can't help it."

"I know, but I thought we had worked through all this?"

"We did."

"So where is all this coming from?"

"I don't know." Carly hugged him then looked up at him. "I'm just being selfish. I have loved having you all to myself. I guess I don't want to let that go." Giving him a kiss on the cheek Carly pulled away from him. "Enough of this; I was promised a horseback ride, so I will go pack the lunch while you saddle the horses."

"Yes, ma'am."

Jimmy watched Carly as she walked away. He knew his job scared her, but he also knew she loved him too much to let that fear come between them.. He reached for Carly's hand. "Ready?"

"Ready.

Jimmy nodded and gave Sheba a nudge with his heel and clicked his tongue. "Lets go girl." Carly did the same and they rode away from the house side by side. Jimmy knew that what they had been through had only made their love stronger, made them stronger not only as a couple, but as individuals. He had finally found the meaning of the Power of Love.

April M. Smith is the author if A Star in the Night and The Measure of a Man - the first of the three part series Station 15 - The Power of Love is the Second of the three. Look for Forever Love, the third and final story of the series.

Made in the USA
Lexington, KY
20 March 2017